# Glass Ornament Christmas

## Cheryl A. Hunter

# Glass Ornament Christmas

Grand Owl Publishing
Cheryl A. Hunter
©2021

Cheryl A. Hunter

© 2021 by Cheryl A. Hunter

Grand Owl Publishing

cherylahunter.com

Artwork by Cheryl A. Hunter

ISBN:  978-1-7328351-8-4

Christmas Is a Time of Joy,
Of Twinkling Lights and Shiny New
Toys,
Of Making Lasting Memories,
For Big and Little Girls and Boys

Cheryl A. Hunter

Chapter 1

Shayla Toselli peddled her bicycle down a shallow hill, rounded the corner, and came to an abrupt stop on the main street of town when she saw a small girl walk up to a carriage and offer posies to the lady inside. The little girl was no more than seven or eight years of age. Her dress did not quite cover her ankles, but that helped to keep it clean when walking along the dusty street. The girl's hair was golden and grew straight past her shoulders. The lady inside the carriage looked out at the girl. She did not smile or acknowledge the child. The woman had a rose colored hat adorned with feathers and a bow perched on top of her head, and her dark tresses curled and flowed down her back. The little girl continued to stare at the carriage door holding up the posies. Finally, the lady's coachman took the flowers and handed the child a coin. The girl's eyes sparkled, and a smile broke out on her face. She bobbed a curtsied and ran off to bring her bounty home. The family would eat well tonight.

Shayla hopped off and pushed her bicycle along as she slowly walked down the street. She supposed she was lucky. Her parents came to Canterbury Corner, a small but bustling town a short train ride from London, when she was just nine years old. They opened a glass factory, and fourteen years later, her family's shop was well known, and their work was sought after by many of the upper class which meant that Shayla never had to sell posies on the street.

The air was crisp, and the sky was bright. This was unusual in late November because it was almost always damp and cloudy at this time of year. It was the perfect day for window shopping even if the shop windows were not overflowing with exotic goods like in London. She and her father, Henry, had recently returned from purchasing glass supplies in that magnificent city. Shayla sighed heavily. She enjoyed the excitement of big city London, and she already missed the hustle and bustle of the city and walking along the crowded streets. There was such a variety of people in London too, street performers, smartly dressed businessmen, and elegant ladies in wide gowns with puffy sleeves on their way to the latest play or musical performance. The shops were full of the latest fashions, including some from Paris, and the food in the markets, Shayla let out an audible sigh as she thought about the pastries and the assortment of fruits that were available.

She looked down the main street of Canterbury Corner. It was a growing city. There were new shops, and the train brought in an assortment of goods. It was not a big city, but Shayla knew she would miss it and her friends if she ever moved away. No matter where life might take her, she would want to return, at least occasionally.

The shops along the street had not yet opened, and few people were out in the town center this early in the morning. She often took a bicycle ride to town before the streets became crowded. She stopped to look at the Christmas window display of the general store. She stepped closer to the window to get a better look. At this time of year, the window showcased a variety of children's toys. There was a small rocking chair with a stuffed bear sitting on it. A ball sat between the rocker's legs, and there was an assortment of small painted tin toys on a shelf above. An elaborately carved music box caught her eye. She imagined the twinkling music it likely played. The window also displayed a variety of China dolls in pretty lace dresses, board games, jacks, and jump ropes.

The next store window featured ladies' clothing. There was a shimmery white wrap draped over a small table. Shayla imagined a lady would wear the elegant wrap when she went shopping or to church. There were several pairs of embroidered dancing slippers next to the table, but Shayla's eyes sparkled when she saw the beautiful lavender gown. She looked at it longingly and sighed. It was similar to the dresses she saw in London, and it was far too fancy for the Christmastide celebrations she usually attended with her family. Oh yes, they all dressed up for church and for dinner, but this was a ball gown and not appropriate for a Christmas family gathering or even the Christmastide festivities in the town. It was, however, perfect for the Duke's Christmastide ball. She let out a sigh. She was not going to the ball this year or any other year. Shayla looked at the dress and imagined the looks on the faces of the young men she knew if she showed up to an event in such a lavish gown. Why they probably would not recognize her.

She looked down at her blue bicycle outfit and laughed to herself. Her clothing was quite plain, and her bloomers were a bit worn she noted. The black boots on her feet were old, but they were her most comfortable pair. Shayla knew all too well that if she mentioned the dress to her father, he would purchase it for her. He spoiled her so. She thought of her Aunt Margaret. If she had that gown, her aunt would insist that Shayla attend at least a few of the seasonal parties she was sure to be invited to this year. Although her family, like many other craftsmen families, was part of the growing middle class allowing them access to other social classes, Shayla had no interest in attending parties in the hopes of marrying up. In fact, she was not very interested in marrying at all. She fancied herself one of the new independent women forging their way in the world. Shayla never had much patience for the fussy, and quite frankly stuffy, rules of behavior of the upper crust of society, but maybe her mother did want her to enter society as her Aunt Margaret told her time and time again.

The memory of her mother was vivid and bittersweet. She closed her eyes and consciously remembered her mother as she did every day, so she would never forget how her mother looked, walked, and smelled. She could smell the spicy scent her mother always wore. Shayla had a bottle of that perfume on her dresser, but she never wore it. Occasionally, she opened the blown glass perfume bottle and breathed in the scent, but she never put it on. The memory made her sad, but she straightened up and continued pushing her bicycle down the street toward the edge of town. It was time to get to work.

As she walked along, several shiny black carriages rolled by kicking up dust as they brought women to the town to shop and brought men in to do business. She heard the train whistle announcing the arrival of the morning train from London as it chugged around the bend toward the station not far from the glass shop. As the festive season approached, more and more people left their fancy city homes and came to quiet Canterbury Corner for the holiday.

It did not take Shayla long to reach the end of the row of shops that made up the town center. There were only a few residential homes between the edge of town and the glass shop, so she hopped up onto her bicycle and peddled away.

Her mood lightened as she approached the shop. The store front sat along the road, and the factory expanded out behind it. It was a sturdy brick building with two large front windows in which Shayla and her father set up displays of their wares. She hopped off her bicycle, stood in front of the windows and assessed the displays. She frowned. The windows needed greens to make them look festive. She decided to make time later in the week to harvest enough greens for garlands. It was still weeks away from Christmastide, but an eye catching display was needed to attract customers to the shop especially since the Christmas Village opened in a few days.

Shayla leaned her bicycle up against the side of the building, untied her umbrella, and took it off the handlebars. Then she unlocked and opened the wooden front door. The tiny bells tinkled overhead. She quickly closed the door, walked further inside, and gave a little shiver. It was cold in the front shop, but that would change soon. The furnaces were likely already up to temperature, and soon the entire shop would be so warm, the front windows would be wet with condensation.

Before going to the workshop, Shayla pulled back the window curtains and leaned in to rearrange several lamps. She then moved a few vases and bowls around on the display to feature her more decorative and expensive pieces. She hoped to attract the attention of the people who rode by in carriages on their way to the town center. The factory needed to be away from homes and other buildings for safety, but it meant people came purposely to the shop instead of just wandering in as they did other shopping. Christmastide usually was a very busy time of year for sales and special commissions. Like the one she was working on for the Duke of Wellshore. She looked up and saw that all but three of the clear glass icicles she made already sold, so she needed to make more today. Yes, the windows needed greens, but for now, she was satisfied with the way they looked, so she walked out the back door toward her small workshop in the middle section of the building.

At the end of the hall, Shayla took off her grey wool coat and hung it on a peg in the hallway. She took off the matching bonnet and gloves and put them on the shelf above the coat hooks, and then, she went into the spacious room off the workshop. This room was called the preparation room, but it doubled as a lunchroom and sometimes a storage room. There was a window on the side wall that let in light, and there was a door to a small private office on the opposite wall. Shayla took pants and a short sleeved, white shirt off the pegs, and then she ducked into the private office to change into them. She pulled on the pants and tied the ankles, so the material did not billow out, and then she pulled on the shirt and tucked it securely into the pants. She stuck her feet into short, worn but sturdy boots then went back into the preparation room and pinned up her long, dark brown hair, and topped it with a grey cap. While she walked into the furnace room, she tied her apron around her waist, and to cover her arms, she pulled on long tight gloves that were missing the fingers.

It was much warmer in the furnace room, so she grabbed a towel to wipe her brow and placed it over the arm of the chair she sometimes used when she worked. The annealing oven had not yet been emptied, so Shayla opened the door and began removing the glass pieces she made yesterday which had cooled overnight.

A young boy came into the room and ran over. "Mornin' Miss Shayla," he said as he moved in front of her. It was his job to empty the oven, but Shayla loved to unload and check the pieces she made the previous day. Still, she smiled at him and moved aside so he could do his job.

"Good morning, Joseph. And how are you this fine day."

"Alright." He was one and ten and had only recently started working in the glass shop. He laid the pieces on the covered work bench for her inspection. "These are very pretty, Miss Shayla."

"Thank you, Joseph." She held up an ornament and smiled. It was perfect. She carefully placed it in a box lined with black velvet. She was nervous, but she felt confident that the Duke would be pleased with the ornaments for his Christmastide Ball guests. As she boxed up another ornament, she hoped he would make the final decision on the designs he preferred today. The Christmastide Ball was in just under a month, and she had a great deal of work to complete in that short time.

She glanced up and saw her uncle Hal. He took off his coat and hung it on a peg next to hers then opened the door to the furnace room. He was a large burly man with thick forearms and calloused hands. He wore a similar outfit to Shayla's, but his almost entirely grey hair was cut short, so he did not need a cap. "Shayla, how are you this morning." He walked up to the work bench and looked over her shoulder at the ornaments. "Beautiful. Your work continues to get more refined and delicate. The Duke will be pleased."

Shayla smiled and nodded to him as she continued to examine yesterday's work. When she finished, she went to the workbench along the opposite side wall and began sketching the designs she wanted to create today. She planned to make delicate flame work holiday flowers and attach them to globe ornaments. Everyone loved flowers, especially in wintertime, she thought to herself. She sketched an ornament with velvet red poinsettias. She stared at the drawing for a moment and frowned. That was too traditional. Delicate white flowers, she decided, with dark red centers and tiny leaves with curling vines. Yes, that says Christmas. She lowered her head and sketched out a few more designs.

Hal watched her sketch, erase, and sketch again as she worked out the designs. He knew better than to disturb his niece when she was designing and then blowing and shaping the glass.

"I am going to use the molds to create shaped ornaments, today," Shayla said to her uncle as she pinned up the designs to a rope hanging near her worktable.

"The Duke wanted all round globes," he replied.

"These are not for him. These are for the window display. I will also make more icicles at the flame today."

Hal and Joseph stood by and watched as Shayla took a blow pipe off the rack and heated it. She then made her first gather and got to work.

Soon the workshop was busy. Hal checked on the workers in the factory and then decided to return to the small workshop. Shayla's father, Henry, came in and hung his coat on a peg. He was of similar build to his brother Hal, but Henry had slightly longer hair. He took a day jacket off the peg and put it on and then tied on a cravat. "The Duke will be here this morning," he said to his brother who stood near the large window and drank coffee while he watched Shayla work.

"The ornaments are boxed and ready," Hal replied.

Henry opened the door just enough to get inside the furnace room. He walked over to the bench, opened a couple of boxes, and peeked inside at the ornaments. He looked over at Shayla and smiled. She was turning a large lump of molten glass in the furnace. Her brow was furrowed as she concentrated on evenly heating the glass. She was so engrossed in her work that she did not see him watching her. She reminded him of her mother, who had also been a glass blower. He missed his wife so much, and he was determined to make certain his daughter was happy and financially secure in her own right. He picked up the velvet lined boxes containing the samples for the Duke's inspection, nodded to Hal, and went out to the front shop to greet customers.

Chapter 2

Adam, the youngest brother of Duke Elliot Preston, the newly minted Duke of Wellshore was recently discharged from military service and residing with his brother while recovering from a leg wound. The coachman opened the large, black lacquered carriage door bearing the Duke's crest in gold. Before exiting the carriage, Adam carefully scanned up and down the busy street. He knew full well that trouble could be anywhere. He saw no sign of danger, so he stepped down. He was happy he decided to leave London, and his mother, and come to the country to help his brother, but there were so many expectations here. He should have stayed at the estate and tended to personal matters instead of agreeing to accompany his brother as he saw to errands in town. The young Duke, who was only six and thirty, always attracted a great deal of attention which was something that Adam fervently sought to avoid.

Elliot only recently inherited the title after their two much older brothers unexpectedly died in a carriage accident earlier in the year. He brushed the lapels of his black wool overcoat. "Come on," Elliot said as he started down the street. "Let us look in the shops before we go to the bank and the glass maker's shop. I wish to select a Christmastide gift for our mother." Elliot walked with his head held high and a smile for everyone, but Adam continuously surveyed the people they passed. He gave two men who lingered on the corner a stern look prompting them to cross the street.

"However did you manage to convince Mother to stay in London and not come to the country early?" Adam asked as he moved his brother along.

Elliot grinned. "She will be here before the start of Christmastide." He looked at his brother. "I thought you needed a break from her constant smothering."

Adam laughed out loud. "Yes. Thank you, dear brother." He bowed with a flourish of his hand.

They walked toward the front door of a shop, but before they entered it, a woman with two daughters and several maids in her wake bustled up to them. "Your Grace," the woman said in a sweet voice as she and her daughters curtsied before him. "It is lovely to see you about today."

Elliot took off his hat and bowed. "Lady McKenna. It is always a pleasure to see you and your lovely daughters." He looked over at his brother and inclined his head.

Adam did the same. "My lady." One of Lady McKenna's daughters smiled shyly up at him and batted her eyes. Adam inhaled deeply to keep calm and nodded to her. He did not want to encourage her, but he could not be rude. His brother needed to be in the good graces of the people and could not afford for his youngest brother to be disrespectful.

Lady McKenna smiled at Adam. "Captain, it is good to see you out and about. How is your injury if I may inquire?"

"I am well on the mend, thank you for your concern, My Lady." Adam bowed his head to her again.

"My daughters are looking forward to His Grace's Christmastide ball, Captain. I hope you are as well." The two girls blushed, and Adam reluctantly smiled at them. He knew every mama within twenty miles was going to parade her daughters in front of him hoping for a match, but he was not interested in marriage right now. One day perhaps, but not now.

"Well, regrettably, we must be on our way." Elliot bowed. "Enjoy your shopping, ladies. It is a fine morning to be out." The three women curtsied again, and Elliot and Adam bowed and continued down the street to a different shop.

They walked less than a block when another lady and her daughter stopped them. When they made their escape, Adam looked at his brother. "Does this happen every time you are on the street?"

Elliot sighed. "Unfortunately, yes. Everyone needs to speak to the Duke and be in his good favor." Elliot smirked. "However, today, we seem to be stopped by more ladies than is normal." He laughed and put his hand on his brother's shoulder. "Word is out that you might be looking for a wife now that your military service has ended." He smiled at the horrified expression on his brother's face. "You are thirty years old and a very eligible bachelor now."

Adam gasped. "I most certainly am not looking for a wife. And if I were, I certainly would not pick a woman who was so obviously looking for a husband."

"Going to hold out for romantic love, are you?"

"I think I will remain a bachelor for some time."

Elliot laughed again. "Well, I feel it is my duty, as your eldest brother, to warn you, Amelia is going to make certain you have a large selection of women to choose from this Christmastide." Adam gasped, and Elliot patted his shoulder and leaned over so no one would overhear him. "She is planning a party and charity event soon, and you are at the top of the guest list, my dear brother."

"Tell her not to go to any trouble on my account."

"You tell her," Elliot laughed, "like that will make any difference. My very lovely wife fancies herself a match maker. And right now, she has her sights set on you."

Adam frowned. "Can you not control your wife? You are a duke for Christ's sake."

Elliot looked at his brother. "When you are married, you too will find that a smart husband allows his wife a great deal of latitude because when she is happy, he is happy."

Adam took a deep breath and narrowed his eyes at his brother. "So, your happiness is more important than mine?"

"Exactly," Elliot replied brightly.

Adam sighed. He needed to stop his sister-in-law, but he knew that would prove difficult. She was a very determined woman.

"And speaking of my beautiful wife, I want to purchase flowers for her." Elliot opened the door to the florist, and they went inside. Adam stood solemnly just inside the shop door while Elliot placed his order.

"I will send my coachman in to pick up the flowers when I am ready to return home," Elliot told the woman behind the counter.

"I will have the bouquet ready, Your Grace."

"Thank you."

Adam looked out the shop window. The coast was clear. If they hurried, they could make it to the next shop without an interruption. He hurried his brother out the door. They were able to get inside and look at the wares in two shops without having to stop and talk with any ladies.

Elliot frowned and was undecided on a gift. "I have time to shop for Mother. Perhaps something will grab my attention next time I am in town," he said to Adam as they left the second shop and continued walking down the street.

Adam was alert as he walked along, but he looked down and tried not to make eye contact whenever he passed a lady regardless of her age. He thought the coast was clear, but he looked up into the smiling face of a clever young woman who stepped out of a shop as he and Elliot passed. He and his brother had to stop to bid the woman good day. Was it his imagination or was the town full of women out shopping today?

The two men looked in a few shop windows, and then up ahead, Adam spotted Lady Justine and her daughter, Clara, walking into the bank where he and Elliot were headed next. His mouth went dry. Although Clara was indeed a beautiful young lady with long, curly, golden hair and a slim figure, she and her mother had cornered Adam just the day before when he left the local pub. Lady Justine insisted that he accompany them as they shopped, and she made it very clear that she considered her daughter an ideal match for Adam. It took him nearly an hour to graciously leave their company.

"Elliot, I will meet you at the glass shop," he whispered as he quickly turned around and headed away from the bank.

"Coward," Elliot said quietly to Adam's retreating back. His brother had fought in many battles and was a hero, yet he could not face a woman and her daughter. He watched as his brother ducked his head, crossed the street, and blended in with a crowd in front of a shop. Elliot took a deep breath and walked to the bank's front door which opened immediately.

"Your Grace," an older man said as he bowed, and Elliot entered the building.

Adam walked away quickly, and fortunately, without Elliot, he was largely ignored.

He stopped to look in a hat shop. The clerk snapped to attention when he recognized Adam. "May I be of assistance, Captain Preston?"

"I am looking for a ladies' hat. Something large and frilly for my mother."

"This way please." The clerk led him to a display of hats. There were several contenders, but Adam decided to purchase a lavish, cinnamon colored, wide brimmed hat that had lace trim and large white flowers. It was perfect for his mother. She adored hats, and this one was sufficiently frilly, and as a bonus, it also had owl feathers decorating the band. The store clerk tucked the hat in a box and tied it up with a ribbon. Pleased that he found such a splendid gift for his mother, he strolled toward the edge of town to the glass shop.

It was a sunny day, so Adam took his time. He passed the last of the shops on Main Street and continued down the road that eventually took a turn and headed toward the railroad tracks. As he approached the red brick glass shop, he heard the low and constant roar of the furnaces, and plumes of smoke poured out of several chimneys and streaked across the clear blue sky. Majority of the building's windows were propped open, and some were wet and dripping with condensation.

Adam's head snapped up when he heard high pitched giggling. Several young women wearing pastel colored dresses were strolling in his direction. Fortunately, they were so engrossed in their conversation that they had not yet noticed him. He kept his head down and turned up his coat collar to blend in with the few people on the street. When he arrived at the front door of the glass shop, he slipped inside the door, closed it quickly, and watched as the young women crossed the street and walked away.

"Good afternoon, Sir, may I help you?" someone asked from behind him. Adam straightened up and turned toward the voice with a smile for the clerk.

Henry recognized the Duke's brother. "Captain Preston, I am sorry, I did not recognize you from the back."

Adam waved his hand at the neatly dressed clerk. "Not to worry, Sir."

"Is something wrong, Captain?" Henry anxiously looked around the shop.

"No. Nothing is wrong. I am just avoiding women."

Henry raised his eyebrows. He walked over to the window and looked out. "If that be the case, I am sorry to inform you, Sir, Lady Justine's carriage is approaching the shop. The lady is coming to pick up an order of goblets for her annual Christmastide party."

Adam looked horror stricken. He scanned the room. "Is there a back door out of here, Sir?"

"Yes. But it is through the workshop. The furnaces are hot and dangerous. Normally, customers are not allowed back there."

"Sir, the furnaces are not as dangerous as Lady Justine and her very lovely daughter." Adam looked around frantically. "Is it through that door?"

Henry nodded, and Adam hurried to the back of the store and through the small door. As he closed it behind him, he heard the bells above the front door tinkle announcing the arrival of the ladies.

Now that he was safe, he relaxed and walked quietly along a darkened hallway to a large room with several tables and benches. There was a small room off to one side, and to the right was a half wall with a large window. He heard the roar of the furnaces on the other side of the wall and felt heat radiating through the glass. Adam walked to the window and watched the activity in the room. A large burly man worked with a glowing lump of hot glass on the end of a pipe. He twisted the pipe then rolled the molten glass on a metal table. He heated the glass again, rolled it, then pressed it on the marble table and started to flatten it with a round paddle. He picked up a round metal object and pressed it into the hot glass further flattening it. He then tapped the pipe and detached the piece. A boy came over and scooped up the flat glass with a metal tool.

"Sir, may I help you? Are you lost?"

Adam turned his head and looked for the person who spoke to him. A tall man came through a door on the far end of the room and approached him. Adam estimated he was probably five and twenty years old. He had a broad chest and strong arms. His long, straight, black hair was gathered together at the back of his head with a thin strip of black leather. He wore a tattered tight white shirt, black pants that were tied at the ankles, boots, and an apron. He pulled off thick gloves as he approached. "The show room is down the hall, Sir."

"Yes, I just came from there. The man up front said I could use the back door through the workshop."

The young man scrutinized Adam for a moment before he recognized him. "If Mr. Toselli sent you back here, it must be alright. Please follow me, Captain." He did not know why Adam was trying to use the back door, but it was not his place to question, so he beckoned Adam forward. He opened the door to the workshop just enough for them to get inside. As soon as the door opened, Adam felt the full heat from the furnaces hit his face. "Be careful, Sir. Stay close to the wall. We will have to wait until the blowers are finished. We cannot let in a cold draft from outside while they work."

Adam nodded. "The windows are open. That is not a draft?"

The man shook his head. "The window provides ventilation, but the door to the outside is large, and it will let in a rush of cold air.

Adam leaned against the wall to wait. He was fascinated by what he saw. He watched as the two blowers worked the glass in and out of the furnace, and he realized the one closest to him was a young woman. She was tall and slender, but there was no mistaking her gender because her curves filled out the men's clothing that she wore. Adam's eyes moved up her body to her glove covered arms and then to her long and delicate fingers poking out of the cut off gloves. She deftly dipped a rod into the opening in the furnace, twirled it, and pulled out a molten lump of glass. She walked to a door in the furnace, and a boy pulled it back. She stuck the glass inside the furnace and began turning the rod. She pulled it out and twirled it in the air. She heated it again, and then she took the glass to a marble table where she rolled it around and around before she returned it to the furnace. She did this several more times. She always kept the pipe moving. Each time, she examined the lump of glass as it was shaped.

Adam looked around the room. There were buckets of water, sand, and what looked like hot wax near where the two people worked. There were two wooden, floor to ceiling cabinets on the left wall furthest from the furnaces. He imagined they contained chemicals and tools.

The young woman's movements caught Adam's attention, and he watched as she pulled the glass out of the furnace and blew into the pipe forming a small bubble in the glass. She once again heated the glass inside the furnace, and then she removed it and carefully looked it over. She heated it again, and then she dipped the small bulb of glass into something in a container on another table. Adam glanced over at the man for an explanation.

"She is adding color to the glass," he replied in response to Adam's unspoken question. "The powder is finely ground glass."

She again returned the piece to the furnace and heated it. She inspected it and returned it to the furnace. She did this until she was satisfied. She turned and nodded to a young boy who placed a white clay mold on the floor and opened the two halves. The woman placed the glass into one side of the mold and the boy, wearing thick gloves, closed it. The woman then blew hard into the tube. She then nodded to the boy who pulled the two mold pieces apart and stepped out of the way. The glass was now an oval shape with bumps and lines in it. Adam watched in awe as she heated the glass again. This time, when she pulled it out of the furnace, she pinched the end of the glass not attached to the rod with a large pair of metal tweezers and twisted it swirling the glass.

The young, and Adam thought quite beautiful, woman worked the glass in and out of the furnace several more times. Then she walked over and dipped another pipe into the hole in front of the furnace and pulled out a lump of glass. She transferred the piece to another pipe with a snap causing Adam to jump. Then using the glass she gathered, she fashioned a dollop on the top of the ornament. She used a metal pointed tool dipped in the hot wax to poke a hole through the top making a hanger. She turned the piece from side to side and examined it, and then she detached the globe. The young boy, who still wore the thick gloves, took it, and he carefully placed the piece in an oven.

The woman took a deep breath, then she wiped her brow with a towel and turned around. Adam's breath caught when he saw her face clearly. She was indeed beautiful. She had soft delicate features, creamy white skin, and large, dark brown, doe like eyes. Her cheeks were red, and her forehead glistened with perspiration. A few tendrils of dark brown hair peaked out from under the cap she wore and curled around her face. Adam felt an overwhelming urge to reach out and tuck those pieces of hair behind her ears.

Shayla looked at the man standing near the wall, and then she looked at the younger man. "Jimmy, who is this? Why is he here?" she demanded. She set her hands on her hips and fixed Adam with a stare.

Jimmy opened his mouth to reply, but undaunted by her stance, Adam took a few steps forward and bowed. "I was told by Mr. Toselli that there was a back door through the workshop."

With narrowed eyes, Shayla took in the man's rather large frame. He was tall with short black hair and sparkling blue eyes. She thought he must be around thirty. He stood close to her, and Shayla felt more than just the heat from the furnaces. She shook her head. "Why do you need to go out the back door, Sir?"

"I was trying to avoid someone who was coming in the front door of the shop," he explained.

Shayla gave him a smirk and rolled her eyes. She was not certain she believed him. He was finely dressed and obviously a gentleman, so who was he avoiding?

Jimmy looked at her. "Shayla, this is…"

"Adam," the man said loudly cutting Jimmy off. "Please just call me Adam." Again, he bowed, "and, you are Miss?"

"Shayla Toselli." She stared at him and was not sure if she liked him or not, but she could not deny that he was quite handsome. He wore an expensive and well-tailored black frock coat that accentuated his broad, strong shoulders. The coat was unbuttoned revealing a dark grey embroidered waist coat. He had on a white shirt and cravat. His shoes had a high polish, and he held a hat in one hand and a hat box in the other hand. His smile was warm, and Shayla noticed that unlike some men, his smile extended to his eyes. Since he was being informal using his first name, she smiled and said, "you may call me Shayla. Everyone in the shop does."

Adam bowed his head slightly as he stepped closer. "It truly is a pleasure to make your acquaintance, Miss Shayla." He smiled as he shifted his hat to his other hand. Then he took her hand with his free one. He kept his eyes on her as he brought her hand up to his lips, and kissed her warm, soft fingers just below the edge of her gloves.

Shayla felt herself flush. She looked at him with wide eyes, and her breath caught in her throat. Why was she having this reaction to a man she just met? Yes, he was handsome, but there was something else about him that attracted her. Perhaps it was his confident manner and his deep inviting voice.

Adam felt her pulse quicken as he held her hand. He had to admit she stirred something inside him. This was a strong woman who did not bat her eye lashes at him and smile sweetly. Straightening up, he showed her a dazzling smile. "I was surprised to see a woman working in a glass shop."

Her expression became stern, and he instantly regretted his unfortunate choice of words. Her eyes flashed with anger as they continued to bore into him. "Tis true that in England, even in this more progressive time, women do not often work in glass shops, but in Ireland and France, it is not uncommon."

Adam caught the slight Irish accent. "My apologies. I did not mean to offend you." He smiled, and he saw that her expression softened just a tiny bit.

The burly man that worked at the other end of the shop came over and handed a glass globe to the boy who stood next to Shayla and Adam. The boy quickly ran to the oven and set the globe next to the one Shayla made. The man looked from Shayla to Adam and back to Shayla, and he smiled.

"Uncle Hal, this is Adam. He is looking for the back door," Shayla said without turning to look at him. She continued to look into Adam's eyes.

Hal opened his mouth to speak, but Adam turned his head and caught his eye. "Pleasure to meet you, sir," Adam reached out a hand. Hal shook his hand. He recognized the Duke's brother and wondered what he was up to. It was clear his niece had no idea who this man was, and he chuckled. When she found out, she was going to be mad, and Adam would hear about it.

Adam turned and smiled again at Shayla. "Would it be possible to watch you work a little longer?"

She placed her hands on her hips. "I thought you needed to leave?"

"I doubt anyone will come looking for me back here. I truly am fascinated with the work you do."

"I am not sure you should be in here." Shayla looked at the heavy jacket and the fine linen shirt he wore. Who is he, and why is he here? She wondered.

Adam took out a handkerchief and wiped his brow. "It is hot in here." He put down the hat box and took off his frock coat. "I really would like to stay and watch you make another ornament."

Shayla took a deep breath and looked at her uncle who shrugged his shoulders. She stared at Adam for a moment and then came to a decision. "Fine. You can stay and watch. Put the hat box and your coat in the other room. While you are at it, take off the cravat and everything down to that fancy shirt and trousers," she ordered.

Adam immediately complied with her directions.

"Jimmy, get the gentleman an apron and gloves," she instructed. She gave Adam a little smirk. "Sometimes the glass pops, and I would not want to ruin your fine linen shirt." She turned toward the furnace then turned back to Adam. "Oh, take off those gold cuff links and roll up your shirt sleeves. You do not want to wear anything metal while working with hot glass."

Adam did as she instructed. He may have wanted to stay and watch, but he also wore a worried expression on his face. Hal hid his laugh and went to stand by the door to watch.

Jimmy took an apron off the hook by the door and picked up a pair of fingerless gloves off the bench. He walked over and handed the items to Adam. He gathered up the clothing Adam took off, picked up the hat box, and left the furnace room.

Shayla looked over Adam to make certain there was no loose clothing on him. Loose clothing was dangerous when working with glass. She pointed to an area near where she planned to work. "Stand right there and watch," she directed Adam. She picked up a blow pipe and dipped it into the open furnace to gather glass on the end. "This is the crucible," she explained as she worked. "The glass is made in this furnace which is never turned off except for once a year when it is cleaned."

"That furnace is never turned off?"

"We add materials to make glass every night, so it is ready in the morning."

She twirled the glass and walked over to the other furnace to heat it. "This is the glory hole where we heat the glass while working it. Putting glass on a pipe is called making a gather." Next, she heated the glass in the furnace, then she rolled it on a cold marble table, and then heated it again. She continued the process until the piece took the desired shape. "The process of heating the glass and rolling it on cold marble is repeated until it is roughly the desired shape." Adam crept forward for a better view.

"What color do you like?" Shayla asked.

"I like blue."

She nodded and dipped the lump of glass into a container of blue powdered glass and then twirled it in the furnace. "You must continually turn the glass. If you do not keep it moving, it will warp and then fall to the floor."

After heating the glass again, she blew into the tube and a small bubble formed. "Would you like to try blowing?" she asked.

Adam's face lit up in a smile. "Yes, I would."

Her uncle, Jimmy, and Joseph stood and watched as Shayla heated the glass one more time. "Come stand right beside me." She worked the glass several more times. "Blowing into the tube is fairly simple, but you must be careful. Do not breathe in when your mouth is on the pipe, or you could die. Turn your head to the side and take a breath. Put your mouth on the pipe and blow out slowly. When I say stop, take your mouth off the pipe, and turn your head to the side before you breathe in. Do you understand?"

Adam nodded. Shayla heated the glass one more time. "Take a breath and slowing blow into the pipe."

Adam did as he was instructed. He forced air out of his lungs and through the pipe.

"Blow a little harder. That is enough. Stop."

Adam took his mouth off the pipe, turned his head, and took a breath.

"Very good. See the bubble is larger."

Adam smiled. "It is much harder than I thought to blow a bubble in the glass."

Shayla nodded. She heated the glass again. "Blow again and make the bubble bigger."

Adam blew several more times and each time the bubble grew.

"Blow again," she instructed. This time a larger bubble grew. "Good." Shayla detached the globe from the pipe, and she added a hanger the same way Adam saw her make one on the fancy ornament she made earlier. Joseph ran over, and Adam watched as she carefully handed the boy the globe, who then placed it into an oven.

"The glass must cool slowly in an annealing oven, or it will break," Shalya explained to Adam. "Small pieces take less time to anneal. Large pieces take longer. The slower the piece cools, the less chance of breakage. We generally let our pieces y cool overnight, so your piece will be ready tomorrow."

"My piece?"

"Of course. You made it, so you should keep it."

Adam looked at the pieces on the workbench. "Your work is beautiful, Miss Shayla."

"Thank you. I hope Duke Wellshore agrees with you. He is coming to the shop today to look at samples to give as favors at his Christmastide Ball."

Adam smiled at her. "I am certain he will be delighted with your work."

"Ready to make another?" Shayla asked.

"Yes," Adam replied eagerly.

She picked up another blow pipe and started the process all over again.

## Chapter 3

The little bell over the top of the door jingled, and Henry looked up. "Duke Wellshore, welcome," Henry bent into a deep bow.

Elliot nodded. "Good day, Mr. Toselli, I was to meet my brother here. Have you seen him?" Elliot looked around the shop but saw no sign of Adam. The tasks at the bank took considerably longer than he planned since it seemed everyone wanted to talk to him. He frowned. It was just like his youngest brother to take off. Adam was no doubt in the pub having a pint or two.

"Yes, Your Grace, he was here some time ago." With a pained expression on his face, Henry continued. "He went out the back door before Lady Justine and her daughter came in the shop," he informed the Duke.

Elliot let out a deep breath. "Ah, yes," he replied with a knowing nod. "Understandable and very much like my brother, I am afraid. It seems every eligible maid from here to London is hoping to catch the eye and hand of my brother."

Henry nodded he understood, but he thought it best to change the subject. "I have the samples ready for your inspection, Your Grace." He walked behind a counter, reached under, and pulled out the boxes. Henry carefully removed each globe from its box and lined up the five different ornaments on a thick piece of black velvet on the countertop. "These are the designs we thought you would like, but of course, we can modify any design to your further specifications, Your Grace."

Elliot took off his gloves as he walked over to examine the glass globes. His eyes widened as he looked them over. "Sir, your work is exquisite." Elliot picked up one of the delicate globes. It was made of very thin clear glass with the slightest hint of pink. The top was decorated with tiny pink and white flowers that cascaded down the globe. The flowers and vines were accented with delicate gold lines and accents.

Henry nodded. "Thank you, Sir, but these are the work of my daughter, Shayla."

Elliot looked up at Henry. "Your daughter, Sir?"

"Yes. My daughter has worked in the shop since she was a young girl. She is a third owner."

"An owner?"

"Yes, Your Grace. My brother and I drew up the papers making her an owner when she reached the age of majority."

"She is your only child?"

"She is."

Elliot nodded thoughtfully and set down the ornament he held. "It is wise to protect our daughters as well as our sons, Mr. Toselli. Securing more protections for women will be one of my priorities in Parliament next year." He picked up the globe again and looked at it carefully. "Well, she is quite talented." Elliot set the globe down and picked up another. It was similar with blue and white flowers and silver accents. "These are delicate and intricate. It is impossible to select one style." Elliot looked over the other globes. A third one had white lilies and was accented with tiny pearls, a fourth had green vines that twisted and turned around the globe, and the fifth was adorned with tiny red birds. Elliot stood shaking his head. "Remarkable," he muttered more than once. "The level of craftsmanship is amazing, and they are unlike any I have seen before. Even in Germany." Finally, he looked up at Henry. "I must meet your daughter and offer my congratulations on her fine work."

"She is in the workshop. I will summon her, Your Grace."

"I would enjoy seeing her at work, if that is acceptable, Sir."

Henry hesitated. The workshop was not a place for a duke who was dressed in a fine wool coat and trousers. He wore a silk cravat around his neck, and Henry saw the fine linen shirt under his waist coat. "Your Grace, the workshop is hot and dirty. It might be best if I bring her out here."

"Mr. Toselli," Elliot began politely but firmly, "I truly would like to see her at work."

Henry knew he could not refuse his Duke. He wished to talk to Shayla first, but that was not possible now. If the Duke of Wellshore wanted to meet Shalya and see her work, Henry had no choice but to bring him back to the workshop. He hoped Shayla would be on her best behavior. He knew all too well that she was sometimes sharp with people who interrupted her when she was working. He bowed. "As you wish, Your Grace."

Henry looked over at Brian, an older man who worked in the shop that day. Brian nodded, and Henry walked out from behind the counter. "Please follow me, Your Grace." He led the way out back. They walked down the hall toward the workshop. Elliot suddenly stopped. Alarmed Henry turned. "Is something wrong, Your Grace?"

Elliot looked up ahead and saw Adam. His brother held a rod with a lump of glass on the end. A young woman was instructing him, and although he was concentrating, he was smiling. "Mr. Toselli, it appears my brother is still in the building."

Henry turned and looked in the window. He saw Shayla instructing Adam. His mouth went dry, and he was at a loss for words. He had no idea how his daughter came to be teaching Captain Preston how to blow glass. He noticed his daughter looked happy as she placed her hands over Adam's and helped him turn the glass in the furnace. Shayla and Adam looked at one another and smiled.

Hal had moved out of the furnace room and now sat on a bench having coffee. When he saw Henry and Duke Wellshore, he stood up and began to explain. "Your Grace, your brother saw us working, and he wanted to learn glass blowing, so Shayla, Miss

Toselli, my niece, said she would instruct him. He catches on quickly. That is his second piece." Hal looked at Henry, and the two men exchanged nervous glances. "I have been here watching the whole time, Your Grace. Your brother is in no danger."

"Your Grace, may I present Hal Toselli, my brother and an owner of the shop as well."

The two men shook hands then Elliot looked back at his brother. "Adam does seem to be enjoying himself. Your daughter is very patient."

"She has her moments," Hal commented drawing a sharp look from Henry.

The three men stood and watched as Adam blew into the rod until a globe formed on the end. He smiled at Shayla who smiled back and nodded encouragingly to him. When he finished, Shayla took the rod. They walked over to the crucible, and Shayla expertly added a hook.

She walked over to the annealing oven and placed the globe inside just as the door opened wide, and Elliot, Henry, and Hal walked in.

"Elliot," Adam called, and Shayla turned around quickly. She was about to yell at whoever opened the door while she put the globe in the oven, but she stopped when she recognized Duke Wellshore.

"Elliot, this is amazing," Adam called to his brother.

Shayla's mouth dropped, as she looked from Adam to Duke Wellshore and back again. She glared at Adam with narrowed eyes.

Adam gave a nervous laugh and shrugged. "I forgot to mention he was my brother. Sorry," he casually whispered over his shoulder to Shayla.

"Forgot?!" Shayla demanded in a slightly higher voice, but she forced herself to smile and kept the anger she felt from showing on her face. It would not be wise to scream at Adam in public at any time, but certainly not when Duke Wellshore was here to commission ornaments. She had to keep her anger in check, but she would let Adam know she was upset privately.

The intensity of her stare told Adam that Shayla was going to tell him off when they were alone, so he smiled, shrugged his shoulders, and walked toward his brother.

Shayla looked over at Jimmy. "Did you know he was Duke Wellshore's brother?" she whispered.

"Everyone knew he was the Duke's brother," Jimmy whispered back. "Everyone but you."

Shayla glared at him.

"Glass blowing is fascinating, Elliot," Adam said as he shook his brother's hand.

"It warms my heart to see you so happy." Elliot clasped Adam on the shoulder.

Shayla took off her cap as she approached. More tendrils of hair fluttered around her face. She was so flustered that she tripped as she tried to curtsy. Adam caught her arm and steadied her. "Your Grace," she said as she straightened up. She frowned at Adam.

"Elliot, may I present Miss Shayla Toselli." Adam pushed her in front of him as if he were showing off a prized possession.

"Miss Toselli, let me express my admiration for your work." He took her glove covered hand, looked down and selected an area of her fingers, and gave them a quick peck.

Shayla blushed. "Thank you, Your Grace. I am honored." She lowered her hand and wished that for once she was clean when she met someone important. "Your Grace, have you looked at the ornaments and decided which design you would like for the ball?"

Elliot laughed a deeply appreciative laugh. "My dear, I cannot decide. They are all so lovely."

Shayla blushed lightly again and smiled. "Thank you. I can make other designs if you like."

"No, no. Actually, I would like you to make them all. Select designs and make as many of each design as you like, Miss Toselli. I defer to your excellent judgment."

Shayla started to speak but was at a loss for words.

"I would like to commission one hundred and sixty ornaments for the Christmastide Ball on Christmas Eve."

"Thank you, Your Grace," Shayla bowed her head then smiled at him. "I promise, you will not be disappointed." She knew her face was flushed with excitement, but she did not care. Her ornaments would be given to very important and influential people who would bring the ornament back to London which would bring in more business.

"Your ornaments will make my first Christmastide Ball as Duke a success. Thank you, Miss Toselli." He nodded his appreciation, and Shayla blushed again.

Henry and Hal shook hands. This was what they hoped for when Duke Wellshore approached them early in the Fall. The business they started fourteen years ago was more successful than they could have imagined. Henry looked at Shayla. A large part of their success was the work she did. Her talent and skill kept customers coming back. Her mother would be so proud, he thought sadly to himself. He wished Corrine were here to see her daughter's success.

Adam smiled at Shayla. He was surprised that his stomach did a flip flop when she smiled back at him. She was young and a little boyish, not at all polished and sophisticated like Lady Justine's daughter. Adam laughed to himself. That was why he liked Shayla. She was different than the high maintenance society women his sister-in-law Amelia planned to parade in front of him. No, this woman was the type of woman that appealed to him. Not that he was looking for a woman, but if he was looking, then Shayla was a woman he would be interested in. He stared at her and something inside him longed to get to know this enchanting young woman. He decided he needed to stay away from the estate as much as possible and spend time here with Shayla instead. Before he thought better of it, he asked, "can I help you in the shop, Miss Shayla?"

"You want to help?" She looked at him with narrowed eyes. She would never outwardly show it, but a part of her liked the idea of having him in the shop. There was something about him that she found very appealing. She started to smile, but quickly changed her expression.

However, Adam caught the excitement in her eyes before she narrowed them and pouted again. "My ornament making would slow you down, but I could do other things. I could load the oven, box the finished pieces, bring you water. I would like to learn about the business."

If either Shayla or Adam had been paying attention, they would have read the expressions on the faces of their family around them. Henry, Hal, and Elliot watched Shayla and Adam's exchange. Henry looked lovingly at his daughter, but there was concern in his eyes because she was bossy and pushy when she worked. Hal, on the other hand, gave them a sly smile because he saw the spark in Adam's eyes when he looked at Shayla, and he saw that Shayla had the same look for Adam. He rubbed his hands together in anticipation of giving them a little push should it be necessary. Elliot was overwhelmed with happiness. He smiled broadly at Shayla because Adam was finally showing interest in someone and something. Elliot was happy to see the vibrant brother he loved resurfacing, and he suspected Miss Shayla Toselli would challenge Adam at every opportunity.

The four men eagerly waited for Shayla to make the decision. She continued to stare at Adam with narrowed eyes. She was not certain having him work in the shop was a good idea, but she also knew she wanted to get to know him better. "Yes. You can help," Shayla replied quickly before she changed her mind.

Henry and Hal exchanged astonished looks, and Hal saw that she blushed very slightly as she said it.

She quickly recovered and took a step closer to Adam. "But you must be here early in the morning, and you must take orders. You must do as you are told without complaint. You will get no special treatment because you are a captain or the Duke's brother."

"Understood," Adam replied smartly. He sprang to attention. "I expect to be treated like any other worker in the shop. I will be here exactly at six in the morning, ready to work, and take orders." He then decided to salute her, and she blushed again.

Elliot picked up Shayla's hand and kissed it. "Thank you for being so gracious."

"Well," Shayla stuttered. "I am certain he will be a good worker." She looked up at Adam and blushed again.

## Chapter 4

Adam jolted awake early the next morning. His left leg was aching, and he was sweating. He reached down and rubbed the spot where he was shot and then got out of bed. The fire in his room was just embers, so he put on a robe then walked over and tossed on a small log. He had fallen asleep thinking about Shayla but had woken to a nightmare. He rubbed the back of his neck with his hand. He was having nightmares less frequently, but the horror of being shot twice in the leg often crept into his dreams. He knew he was fortunate to have kept his leg. Others were not so fortunate. He went to the basin on the table and splashed cold water on his face, and then he dressed and went downstairs to the dining room for breakfast.

The house was quiet. No doubt Amelia was still asleep. Elliot might be awake, but he would be in his study having coffee and maybe reviewing his schedule for the day. Adam remembered getting up early when he was a child. His father began his day early and went to his study to work before the rest of the house woke up. Even though Adam was the youngest, he was always the first to rise in the morning. He often went to his father's study and watched his father work. It was the only time he was truly alone with his father who enjoyed having his son for company in the early morning hours. Adam sat next to the desk and sipped hot chocolate while his father drank coffee and worked.

Adam took a seat on the side of the long mahogany table. He and his slightly older brother Colin played fort under this table when they were young children. Colin was still in the military and was due home for the upcoming holiday. This would be the first holiday the family would be together since his father's passing.

Mrs. Flannery, the cook, bustled in, set down the coffee service, and then poured him a cup. "Captain. You are up early this morning," she said as she also placed bread and butter in front of him. "Would you like eggs and ham for breakfast?"

"No thank you, Mrs. Flannery. This will be fine." He took a long drink of black coffee to steady him. "I do need a carriage this morning. I am starting a new position today, and I am afraid I will be up early every morning."

"In that case, I will have breakfast prepared early for you."

"Thank you." He smiled at her. Mrs. Flannery was a widow. She had no child and came to work in his father's household following the early death of her husband. She was a short sturdy woman who smiled often. Adam grew up with her in the kitchen, and while she still cooked occasionally, she also managed the domestic staff now that his brother was head of the household. She thought of Adam and his brothers as her own and pampered them, but she always addressed them formally despite the number of times they told her to call them by their given names. Propriety was very important to Mrs. Flannery even if she was a shoulder to cry on, a wealth of information, and motherly. She offered goodies to the children and always had a special treat ready for when someone had a bad day, but always there was the formality.

"A new position you say." She smiled at him as she buttered several pieces of freshly baked bread. She added a generous amount of jam to each piece and placed the plate before Adam.

"Yes, I will be an apprentice at the Toselli glass shop."

She raised her eyebrows. "Aye, that is a fine shop. Young Miss Shayla is quite a craftswoman."

"Do you know her?"

"I have been in the shop, and I see her from time to time in town. My cousin, Mary, went to work for her Aunt Margaret oh seven or eight years ago. The aunt and uncle live right next door. The poor girl lost her mother five or six years ago."

"Her mother is dead?"

"Aye. A carriage accident near London as I recall. The girl's father dotes on her. But, well, that is understandable. The poor thing is a tough young woman. Tougher than a young lady should be. Mary said Shayla took her mother's death very hard. The aunt is her mother's sister, and she tried to fill in, but Shayla's grief was great."

Adam looked down remembering when he heard the news his two eldest brothers had been killed in a carriage accident. "It seems we all have tragedy and grief in our lives."

Mrs. Flannery patted Adam on the shoulder. "Tis true, we all have tragedy. It is the way of life. But we heal from those unfortunate events by making new, happy memories." She patted his shoulder again. "I will have fried apples and pork when you return from your labors."

"You are a gem." Adam picked up her hand and kissed it.

She laughed a hardy laugh. "I will summon the carriage and pack food for your midday meal."

"I did not think about food. I thought I would go to the pub." Then he laughed. "I do not think Miss Toselli goes to the pub for lunch."

"That I am certain," Mrs. Flannery laughed. "It will be good for you to be busy. It is not wise to be lazy too long." She patted his arm and retreated to the kitchen to prepare food.

Adam poured a second cup of coffee, and he realized that he was nervous. Why should he be nervous? He was a seasoned soldier. He made life and death decisions. Men looked up to him. But this was different. Shayla was not one of his men. No indeed she was a woman. A fine woman. Her hands were soft. Even with gloves on, he noticed how soft her fingers were when she placed her hands over his to show him how to rotate the pipe in the furnace.

The clock struck half past five waking him from his daydreams of Shayla. He ate the last piece of bread and swallowed down the remainder of the coffee. He took a deep breath. He was ready.

Elliot walked into the dining room and sat down.

Mrs. Flannery came out of the kitchen and placed a small bundle on the table next to Adam. "That should sustain you until the evening meal." She poured Elliot a cup of coffee. "I will get your breakfast, Your Grace."

"No hurry, Mrs. Flannery. I wanted to see my brother off on his first day of work."

She bobbed a small curtsy and went back to the kitchen.

"Are you ready?" Elliot asked.

"As ready as I can be. I have a feeling I am going to work hard today."

Elliot laughed. "Yes, of that you can be certain." He studied his brother. His eyes were brighter this morning. "This will be a good opportunity for you to ease back into civilian life." As the eldest brother, Elliot knew it fell to him to see that Adam was well placed in a business situation, and working in the glass shop fit the bill, at least for now.

"Military life is not that much different. You do the job and don't ask too many questions."

"But you have been a captain. You are accustomed to giving orders."

"And it will be good to not have people's lives hang on my decisions."

Elliot nodded. "Garret's death is not your fault, Adam."

"I gave the orders."

"And you were wounded saving the life of one of your other soldiers."

"Being a hero is easy. Living with the what ifs is more difficult."

"Well, you will not have to make any life and death decisions today."

Adam stood up, poured a little more coffee, and drank it down. "I don't know," he pondered, "if I upset Miss Shayla, I may have to make a decision to run for it or kiss her."

"Kiss her?!"

"When she narrows her eyes and pouts at me, I have this desire to kiss her."

"Be careful, Adam," Elliot laughed, "you sound like a man who is falling in love."

"No. Just a man who is intrigued. She is quite a woman. Wish me luck." Adam put the food in his bag, strode out of the house, and stepped into the waiting carriage.

When he arrived at the glass shop, work was already underway. Several boys were checking the furnace temperature and sweeping the workshop floor. They laid out tools and stacked towels.

Hal leaned against the doorway drinking coffee. "Adam. Welcome. You are on time." He extended his hand, and Adam grasped it firmly.

"I could not be late on my first day of work." He craned his neck and looked around. "Is Shayla here?"

"Aye," Hal gave a hearty laugh and jerked his head toward the office on the other side of the wall. "She is having a cup of tea and sketching the globes she plans to create today."

"I think I will say good morning to her."

"Be careful. She is not always pleasant when she is working," Hal laughed again. "We have an ice box for food."

Adam nodded and in several long strides crossed the room. He put his food away, and then he knocked lightly on the open office door. Shayla looked up from drawing. Whenever she saw Adam, her heart seemed to beat just a little faster. It was exciting, but it also annoyed her. How could a man excite her in such a way by simply being in her presence, she wondered?

"Good morning, Shayla."

Shayla felt her face get warm. "Good morning, Adam." She looked up at the clock. "You are on time." She quickly looked back down at her drawing.

Adam smiled. It pleased him to see a blush color her cheeks when he spoke to her. It showed him that she was feeling something for him just as he was feeling for her. He pulled out a chair next to her and sat down. He leaned over, and they both felt the heat rise. They turned and looked at one another. They were inches apart, and Adam breathed in the soothing lavender scent that she wore. She captivated him, and he wondered how she would feel in his arms.

Shayla cleared her throat and quickly looked down again at her drawing.

Adam composed himself. She intrigued him, and he felt a burning need to get to know her. "You are going to make globes with holly today?" he asked as he studied her sketches.

Shayla added dots for berries and swirls she intended to highlight with gold to complete the design. She looked up. "Duke Wellshore said he trusts my judgement, but do you think he will approve this design?"

Adam studied the drawing for a few seconds. He looked into Shayla's eyes. "Yes. It represents Christmastide." They stared into one another's eyes, and time seemed to stop for each of them. Their lips were so close, it would only take a small shift for their lips to meet. Adam thought about what it would be like to savor her lips. They were naturally red and looked luscious and full. Oh, he just knew her lips would be soft, and he wished to feel them under his, but he could not touch them. He knew it was inappropriate considering they met only yesterday, and they were in a workshop. Yet, he longed to take Shayla in his arms and feel her body pressed against his. She was young and sweet and innocent, and his stomach knotted. He cleared his throat. What on earth was he thinking?

Shayla felt heat travel through her body to her cheeks. She felt lightheaded sitting only inches from Adam. She stared at his face. And for a fleeting moment, she imagined him kissing her. She let out a tiny gasp. She never felt like this in the presence of a man before. Not when she danced at parties or talked with a young man. But Adam was not just any man. He was mature. He had been to war. He was a worldly man, and Shayla thought a man like him would not be interested in a young woman like her. She was not worldly or sophisticated.

The moment passed and Adam leaned back. "When do we start?"

"Now." Shayla stood up, took an apron off the hook, and handed it to Adam. As he put it on and tied it, she led the way. As they crossed the small preparation room, she stopped and took a pair of heavy gloves off a shelf and handed them to Adam. "Watch and learn."

"Good morning, Jimmy," Shayla said brightly as she and Adam opened the door and stepped in the furnace room.

Adam noticed that Jimmy's eyes followed Shayla and turned cool when Jimmy looked at him. No doubt Jimmy hoped that he would one day court her.

"Jimmy watches the furnaces and oversees the young boys in the shop," Shayla explained. "He also is quite a good glass blower."

"Let me check the furnace for you," Jimmy said in a casual manner that told Adam that he knew Shayla very well and was comfortable with her. He went to the furnace and checked the temperature. He nodded to her that the furnace was hot enough to begin work. She picked up a blow pipe and opened the front door of the furnace. Shayla turned to Adam and took his hand to show him how to turn the pipe to evenly heat the glass. Adam glanced up at Jimmy and saw despair in his eyes. He was right, Jimmy had feelings for Shayla. Well, Jimmy had years to act on those feelings, and now it was his turn.

"Jimmy," one of the boys called. Jimmy took one more longing look at Shayla and went to see why he was needed.

Adam turned back to Shayla and leaned in close to her.

Shayla let Adam do more of the work today. He asked questions, and he concentrated on learning the techniques. Finally, she let go entirely and watched as he heated the glass and then blew into the pipe. The bubble formed. She instructed him to heat the glass again, which he did. He removed it from the furnace and blew again. He repeated the process until he had a small globe.

"I will put the hook on this time," Shayla told him as she took the pipe and globe out of his hands. "Watch, but this is tricky." She detached the globe, gathered glass from the crucible, and with a few twists expertly attached the hanger. She smiled at him.

"How did he do, Shayla?" Hal asked as he opened the door and walked over to them.

"He did very well. He is a quick learner." She patted her brow with a towel. Her face was hot and not just from the heat of the glass furnace.

"Only because I have the very best teacher," Adam added.

Hal shook his head at the game they were playing. "Well, come with me, Adam. Shayla has globes to make for your brother's commission, and I want to show you how the rest of the factory works."

"You can make another globe later," Shayla said to Adam.

"I look forward to it." Adam bowed to her. They were never formal in the workshop, but Adam was formal with Shayla, and although she denied it, part of her was flattered that he was so polite when he interacted with her. It made her feel…special.

Hall looked at Adam and then he caught Shayla's eye and smiled. She felt her face get warm.

"Come on, Adam. Follow me." Adam reluctantly turned to follow. Shayla watched him as he walked away, and then she picked up another pipe and got back to work.

While Shayla blew globes, Adam learned about the workings of a glass factory. The small area where Shayla, Hal, and occasionally other glass blowers worked was a small part of the overall factory. It was not the biggest glass factory he had seen, but it was substantial. In this part of the building, bulk glassware was made. Adam felt the heat on his face from the many furnaces, and he began to sweat. Men worked the glass into goblets, bowls, bottles, and other items while boys ran between the men taking glass off pipes, loading the ovens, and keeping the area clear of broken glass and of tools. Shayla had one boy working with her, but here in the main factory, there were many boys working alongside the blowers.

"Normally, I spend most of my day here supervising the blowers and helping out wherever I am needed. I also make certain the glass is inspected before it is packed and shipped." Hal explained. He walked over to a table and inspected a row of glassware that a boy was taking out of the annealing oven. Adam looked down the row at other men inspecting the pieces after they annealed. Older boys then packed pieces of glassware into crates.

"This is the commercial part of the business." Hal looked at Adam and grinned. "Not as glamorous, is it?"

Adam was fascinated. He watched as two men blew glass goblets. When the cup portion of the piece was completed, the man handed the piece off to an older boy who added the straight stem and bottom. Then the completed piece was handed off to a young boy who loaded it in the oven. Meanwhile, the blowers dipped their pipes in the crucible, gathered glass, and began the process all over again.

Hal watched as Adam took in the scene around him. "Henry deals with the distribution of the finished pieces as well as running the front shop and supervising the clerks. Shayla mostly completes special commissions, but she too works in the front shop, and when necessary, she works on the floor here as well. We all oversee the finances, but we have a money man who keeps the books and pays the workers."

"You all?"

"Shayla is a third owner."

"She is?" Adam did not attempt to mask his surprise.

Hal nodded as they walked down the row of workers and back. He put his hand on Adam's shoulder in a fatherly gesture because he liked Adam. "Shayla has been working in the factory since she was a young girl."

"Most fathers would not allow their daughters to work."

"Henry is not most fathers. Your brother is young and progressive. I like that he is interested in promoting women's rights. Shayla is like a daughter to me, and I worry about her future."

"My mother and my sister-in-law make certain Elliot Preston the Duke of Wellshore promotes women's rights," Adam laughed, but then he turned serious. "I believe my brother chose the right wife. I know I would rather have a wife who has her own interests, knows her own mind, and shares her thoughts than a wife who says nothing."

"Aye. If I had a wife, I would want one who speaks her mind." Hal laughed to himself and wondered if Adam knew just how attracted he was to Shayla.

"This area runs so smoothly." Adam stated as he stopped and looked around in awe. "

Hal laughed. "It does until all hell breaks loose."

"Does that happen often?"

Hal shook his head no. "Usually everything runs smoothly, but it is a working factory." Hal clapped Adam on the shoulder. "Are you ready to get to work?"

Adam spent the rest of the morning assisting in the factory. Hal believed the only way to learn a business was to learn every job firsthand. Adam was no stranger to hard work. He was a soldier and spent days marching, fighting, and clearing land when necessary. He enjoyed working, getting his hands dirty, and like Hal, he believed a man had to know all aspects of a job in order to succeed at it.

A few hours later, Adam closed the back of the furnace and pulled off his gloves. He wiped his forehead with a towel. His shirt stuck to his body, and he made a mental note that he needed to bring an extra shirt with him tomorrow.

"Lunch time, Adam." Hal called. "Did you bring enough food?" He gave a hearty laugh.

Adam realized he was starving. "I will bring more food tomorrow that is certain," he said as they walked back to the small glass workshop.

Chapter 5

Shayla sat at a bench working at a flame making a small bird figure that could be attached to larger pieces or stand on their own. She heard the door open and smiled as Adam walked out of the factory excitedly talking to her uncle. She finished the piece she was making and put it between thick layers of heavy, white material. When she stood up, one of the boys came over, took the material, and went to the annealing oven.

Adam stepped into the room and peered over the boy's shoulder as he carefully lifted the top layers and took out several birds and a small rabbit then placed them inside the oven to anneal. He turned to Shayla. "Those are beautiful."

"Thank you." Shayla pulled off her hat and gloves. Her hair was in a messy bun on top of her head. Several long tendrils escaped the bun and framed her lovely face. The tip of her small nose and her cheeks were rosy from the heat of the workroom. What did you think of the factory?"

"Impressive. I did not realize there was so much to it."

"We produce a great quantity of glass," Shayla said proudly.

"Have you had your noon meal, Shayla?"

She shook her head. "Not yet." Together they went into the side room and walked over to the ice box. "Mrs. Lawry brought sandwiches for our noon meal, and she brought extra for you too, Adam."

"That was nice of her. Mrs. Flannery packed food for me, but I am quite hungry. Let us see what we have."

Shayla handed him several packages. Henry came in from the front shop to join them. "It looks like we have a feast today."

They unwrapped the packages and set out the food. There were brown bread sandwiches, sliced cheese, and cut up figs. They sat at the table and began eating. Adam sat next to Shayla. She took a somewhat large bite of her sandwich of cheese and meat. She swallowed and took another big bite. Adam smiled. He liked that she had a good appetite. Afterall, she worked all morning too. She was so different from the women that tried to attract his attention. They were all "proper ladies", but they were not real. They adjusted themselves to suit a man. However, Shayla was a woman who knew the meaning of work and enjoyed it. She would not conform to her husband's wishes and would be a handful, but he would love it. He cleared his throat and took a drink of tea. What was he thinking? He did not need a wife.

Shayla looked over at Adam. She seemed conscious of the way she was eating and set her sandwich down. She took a sip of tea then dabbed the corners of her mouth with her napkin before returning it to her lap. She was sure that he was accustomed to dining with young women who picked at their food and ate little. She tapped the sides of her mouth again and took a slightly smaller bite.

"May I refill your tea?" Adam asked.

"Yes, thank you kindly." Shayla felt heat spread up her neck and into her cheeks. Whenever she was near Adam, she did not feel like herself. She blushed, and she never blushed. She felt fluttering in her stomach that she never felt before. Her breath caught when he leaned close to her, and she could smell the scent of him. Spice and man. "Would you like another sandwich?" she asked in a higher than normal voice.

"Yes, thank you."

Shayla unwrapped a sandwich while Adam poured them more tea. They smiled at each other and resumed eating.

Henry and Hal watched them, but neither made any comments. When they finished eating, they took their leave and left the room.

"What will we work on this afternoon," Adam asked.

"I have more flame work to do. I will make flowers and birds for the globes."

"What can I do to help?" Adam knew he could not make tiny glass flowers. "Are you the only one who does flame work?"

Shayla shook her head. "I am not the only one, but I do almost all of it. Flame work is tedious, and many people do not have the patience for it; although Uncle Hal is very good at it and my father is as well. The pieces are small, so they can cool between layers of thick material for some time, and then they can finish in the annealing oven to ensure their strength."

After cleaning up, they went to the furnace room, and Shayla sat down at the bench. She lit the burner and started forming small flowers.

"I need another white rod," she called over her shoulder to Adam.

He went to the rack that held rods of various thicknesses and colors. He located the bin of white rods. "What size do you need?"

"Bring over two or three that are very thin."

Adam selected the three thinnest rods and brought them to her. He placed them within her reach and stood back and watched as she worked. Her fingers continuously moved the glass. She used small metal tweezers to pull shapes, and Adam watched as she formed delicate flowers and leaves. She pulled longer strands of glass and twisted and pulled them to form bows. As she finished a piece, he opened the layers of white material, and she placed the piece in a soft bed of fabric. He closed the top over the hot glass so it would not cool too fast or get a shock. When a bat was full of small pieces, Shayla attached the pieces to the waiting globes that she made the day before. She added glass ribbons and added gold and silver accents. When she was satisfied with the composition, she handed the globe to Adam who loaded it in the annealing oven and then returned to Shayla's side awaiting another more.

Hours later, she finally turned off the burner, Adam was quite tired. Shayla stretched her arms over her head and arched her back. "That is all for today," she said as she stood up. "What do you think after your first day?"

Adam looked at the time. Hal told him Shayla generally finished between three and four o'clock and it was half three. He handed her a glass of water. He leaned against the counter and took a long cooling drink. "It is hot work. The heat drained me, and I feel more tired than I think I should feel."

Shayla nodded. "The heat is tiring. It is much worse in the Summer."

"I can imagine." They hung up their aprons, took off their gloves, and went into the preparation room. They sat down and finished their drinks. "My carriage will be here shortly. May I take you home, Shayla?"

She looked down, and she twisted her hands together. "No thank you. I have my bicycle today." She slipped off her work boots and stuck her feet into a pair of flat shoes. "I will see you tomorrow morning at six. Good night, Adam."

"Good night, Miss Shayla." Adam bowed to her, and she walked down the hallway to the shop. Adam heard her say good-bye to her father. He picked up his bag and went outside to wait for the carriage that would take him home.

## Chapter 6

Adam sauntered into the parlor after work early Thursday evening. His brother and sister-in-law were sitting side by side on the piano bench playing a duet. He watched for a few moments unnoticed. Elliot married for love. That was how it should be, Adam thought to himself. He hated the idea of arranged marriages for political and financial gain. His father's first marriage was arranged, but when he married a second time, it was for love. He suspected that was why his father never tried to force an arranged marriage on any of his sons. Of course, his two older brothers never married, but at least they were not in loveless marriages, and Elliot and Amelia, who had been married just two years, were very much in love.

Amelia turned around and smiled warmly at Adam. "Good evening, brother."

Elliot turned around. "Adam, how was your day at the glass shop."

"I had a rather busy day. Shayla is hard at work creating the ornaments for your Christmastide Ball."

"The ornaments are so beautiful. She is quite a talented young woman," Amelia commented.

"She is amazing," Adam whispered, and Amelia watched as Adam seemed to get lost in his thoughts.

"We have guests coming for dinner at seven," Elliot reminded him.

"Yes, I have you seated next to Colonel First's lovely daughter, Harmony. I am sure you will find her engaging," Amelia informed him.

"Another one," Adam muttered. He sighed. Amelia was intent on finding him a wife. He did not need to find a wife; he had already found Shayla. She was someone he could love. Adam swallowed hard. Love? He just met her. He could not possibly love her. At least not yet. Still the image of Shayla popped into his head when he thought about love and a wife. He took a deep breath to steady himself. "I shall go upstairs, wash, and dress for dinner," Adam replied with a deep bow to his sister-in-law.


Throughout dinner, Adam did his best to engage Harmony First in conversation. Quite honestly, she was intelligent and well read. She was polite, never interrupted him, and smiled at him often. However, Adam found himself thinking about Shayla at the oddest times.

"Captain?" Harmony called his name softly.

"Forgive me, Miss First. I have had a long day." She smiled at him, but she did not inquire further as it would be rude to ask him questions. Surely, Shayla would have asked about his day, but Harmony, being a well-bred lady, would not ask no matter how interested or curious she was. She would wait for him to offer an explanation if he cared to explain. He liked that Shayla asked questions and spoke her mind. Adam found himself explaining why he was tired. "I began a position at the Toselli glass shop this week."

"Oh, that sounds like an interesting position," Harmony replied with interest.

Adam was not sure if she was truly interested, or if she thought her interest was expected. He knew from experience that many women molded themselves to their love interest. He preferred simple honesty. He was not interested in someone he knew was molding herself to his desires. He cleared his throat. "It is an interesting position. However, it does require me to be up very early in the morning."

"Oh, how dreadful," she replied and clutched her throat.

That was an honest response, Adam thought to himself.

After dinner, the ladies gathered in one parlor while the gentlemen had cigars and brandy in another. Adam watched the clock until several card games began, and then he took the opportunity to leave. He returned to his room and undressed.

His valet hung up his clothes and poured him a brandy. "Thank you, Thompson. That will be all tonight."

"Good night, Sir."

"Good night."

Adam sat in front of the fire. He leaned back and sipped brandy. He knew he needed to move out of his brother's estate. While he was there, he had no choice but to attend the many dinners and social gatherings his brother and sister-in-law hosted.

It was not supposed to be this way, Adam thought. He, Elliot, and Colin were his father's sons by his second wife, Grace. Adam and his brothers were not destined to inherit a title.

James and Jonathan, their father's first and second born sons by his first wife were the heirs to the Dukedom. They were attending the university when their father married Grace who was his junior by twenty plus years. James and Jonathan were rakes in every sense. They drank too much, they womanized, and they gambled. Then five years ago, their father became ill and died, and James inherited the Dukedom. The brothers were poor administrators, and they refused to give up their long engrained rakish ways.

Grace moved into the Dowager's house, but she spent most of her time in the smaller of the London townhouses. Adam and Colin were in the military, and Elliot had invested wisely in the railways for himself and his brothers. Then in early February of this year, James and Jonathan were killed when the carriage they were driving slid on ice and crashed. Jonathan was killed instantly, and James died a week later. Elliot, as the next eldest son, became the Duke of Wellshore.

Adam finished his brandy and got into bed. He rubbed his injured leg. How quickly his life changed. He was wounded and shipped back to London during the Summer. Now he was out of military service, and at nearly thirty years of age, he was starting a new phase in life. He thought to remain a bachelor for some time, but he often found his thoughts drifting to marriage and Shayla. Tonight, just like many other nights of late, she was on his mind as he fell into a deep sleep.

When Adam arrived at the glass shop early the next morning, he looked for Shayla, but she was not there. He helped Jimmy set up for the day, and then he watched as Joseph emptied the oven. Hal came into the small shop and started to make a set of goblets. "Where is Shayla this morning?" Adam asked. He tried to sound casual, but he was not certain he succeeded.

Hal raised his eyebrows and smiled. "She went to pick greens for the windows this morning."

Adam stood up straight. "Alone?"

"She is not far. She often goes to the grove of fir trees near the rails to pick greens. She likes to watch the trains too. She goes there a couple of times a week."

Adam did not understand Henry and Hal's attitude regarding Shayla. She often went out alone, and right now it was dangerous. Elliot told him there was a kidnapping several days ago. The young woman was held for ransom. Her father paid, and the woman was safely returned, but the police had not apprehended the culprits.

"She will be here soon," Hal informed him.

"Hal, Shayla really should not venture out alone as she does."

"Believe me, Adam, Shayla can take care of herself. She will return shortly."

Adam nodded. "Hal, can you assist me with a project while we are alone in the workshop?"

"Oh course."

The two men got to work on the project Adam had in mind. It did not take very long, but when he finished, Shayla still had not returned. How long did it take to gather a few greens? No one seemed concerned that Shayla had not returned, but Adam was worried. He went outside to watch for her. If she did not come along in a few minutes, he was determined to find her. It was morning, and with so many people coming and going, he knew she was relatively safe, but what if something happened to her. He would be devastated. The woman who was kidnapped was out in the early evening walking her dog when she was taken. The woman had a maid with her which did not help in the least. He wiped his hands nervously on his trousers.

Adam's ears perked up at a loud noise that sounded like gunshots, but he was not certain because of the noise from the train coming into the station. He stood for a few moments listening for more shots but did not hear anymore. That was it. He needed to find Shayla. He walked quickly toward the railroad tracks where Hal indicated she liked to go. He was a short distance down the road when he saw her riding her bicycle toward the shop, so he stopped and waited for her.

Her face was flush from riding. She wore a dark blue cycling suit and boots. Her hair was pulled back and gathered at the base of her neck, and on her head was a small, blue hat.

"Hi," Shayla called brightly to Adam as she stopped the bicycle. She stepped off it. "Are you looking for me?"

"Yes. I was."

"Is anything wrong?"

"I was just worried about you."

Shayla gave him a smirk. "I can take care of myself."

"So your uncle tells me."

They walked back to the shop. Shayla leaned her bicycle next to the building, and then she detached a large basket full of greens.

"Let me carry that for you." Adam reached for the basket.

She detached her umbrella from the bicycle's handlebars. "I hope I picked enough. I want to entice customers in with a festive window display."

"Did you hear gun shots while you were picking the greens," Adam asked.

"What?" Shayla whipped her head around.

Adam looked at her. Shayla's eyes were wide, and her breathing hitched when he asked the question. There was definitely an edge to her voice, and Adam wondered if she was scared. "I was outside earlier, and I thought I heard shots."

"Over the sound of the train?" Her voice was high, and her face flushed with color.

Adam nodded. "That is why I am not certain what I heard."

"I am not certain if I heard anything unusual." She moved quickly toward the front door and opened it.

Adam brought in the basket of greens, and he set them down near the window.

"I will start making garlands and join you in the workshop soon. You can help Uncle Hal if you would like," she said.

Adam noticed Shayla did not make eye contact with him as she usually did when she spoke to him. She kept her eyes on the greens and began fashioning them into garlands. Adam nodded and went to the workshop.

Chapter 7

Later that afternoon, Shayla, Henry, and Adam dressed the front windows. Adam helped Henry hang globes on various length ribbons from the garlands Shayla made from the greens she picked earlier in the day. Below them, on the bottom of the windows, Shayla laid a bat of pure white material over several boxes to resemble snow. She set out small trees made of greens, and around the trees she set glass pieces. She placed several bowls, a number of vases, and delicate perfume bottles on the soft material. The windows had new gas lights, and the light reflected off the surfaces of the glass. Next, she handed another garland of greens up to Adam who strung the garland and attached it in several places.

Shayla stood back then made a few adjustments. She went outside and smiled. The front windows surely would attract customers. She rubbed her arms from the cold as she went back inside. "The windows look inviting," she informed them, she placed a few more pieces in the windows, and then reached up a hand to help her father down from the ladder.

"You did a good week's work, Adam," Henry said as they folded up the ladders. "Come have dinner with us tomorrow night."

Shayla looked at her father with wide eyes.

"Thank you. It will be my pleasure." He turned to Shayla. "I look forward to socializing in your home."

Shayla blushed and nodded her head. "You honor us."

Adam carried the ladders to the workroom. When he was down the hall, Shayla looked at her father. "Dinner at our home?"

"Why not? He is one of us now."

Shayla took a deep breath. "What will I wear?" she mumbled, but her father heard her.

"Maybe you should shop for a new dress, Shayla." If his daughter was interested in what she would wear, he wanted to make certain she had something new.

"No. No, I have many nice dresses, Papa. I was just wondering out loud which one I should wear." She looked down at her masculine work trousers. Styles for women had changed. Many women were wearing athletic clothing now because it was more practical, especially for a woman like herself who bicycled. However, Shayla knew the women in Adam's class always wore fancy dresses, and she was determined to show him that she was every bit a woman. She was not sure why she needed to show him, but she felt it was important for him to see her in a fancy dress and not the work clothes she wore every day.

"I think I will go home now, Papa."

"As you wish. Tell Uncle Hall about dinner, and when you arrive home, tell Mrs. Lawry that we will have a special guest for dinner tomorrow evening. And please tell your Aunt Margaret that she and your Uncle James should come to dinner as well," he added.

Shayla nodded. She walked out back and bid everyone a good night.

"I will see you tomorrow evening, Shayla," Adam said as he gave her a small bow.

"Yes. I am looking forward to the evening."

Hal looked on. "Uncle, Papa would like you to come to dinner tomorrow evening."

"I will be there."

"Well, I am off. Good night."

"Good night," Adam replied, and Shayla wrapped herself in her coat, put on her mittens and hat, and left the shop. She hopped on her bicycle and peddled home.

"Mrs. Lawry, Papa invited Adam to dinner tomorrow evening," Shayla announced as she strode into the kitchen. There were gingerbread cookies cooling on the counter. She took a deep breath of the delicious aroma. "May I have one?"

"Of course, dear." Mrs. Lawry went back to basting the meat for the evening meal. She was a short, rather round woman with grey hair. She wore a white apron over her dress. She put the meat back in the oven, and then she worked cutting out biscuits. "Adam?" she asked.

"Duke Wellshore's brother and our newest employee." Shayla sighed and took a bite of cookie. "I am uncertain what I will wear," she mumbled with her mouth full.

"Oh, I see." Mrs. Lawry smiled. Shayla normally was not very concerned about what she wore. She also seemed nervous which was unusual. Obviously, the dinner, or more specifically the guest, was important to her. "What dress are you considering wearing, dear?"

Shayla looked up. "I was thinking my periwinkle dress. What do you think?"

"A fine choice. I will get it ready for you."

"Thank you." Shayla took another cookie, walked out the back door, and over to her aunt's home. "Aunt Margaret," she called as she opened the back kitchen door and went inside. Her aunt and uncle had more domestic staff than she and her father. They had two butlers, a maid, a cook, and two coachmen. She and Papa only had Mrs. Lawry and a part time man who was a coachman and groom. Usually, they drove themselves where they wanted to go.

"Hello, Miss Shayla," Mrs. Stewart, the cook, said.

"Hello. Is my aunt in?"

Graves, the butler, saw Shayla and bowed. "She is. This way please, Miss." Graves led her to the small front parlor. "Miss Shayla, Madam," he announced.

Aunt Margaret looked up from her needlework. "Thank you, Graves."

He bowed his way out of the room, and Shayla walked up to her aunt.

"Shayla, love." She stood up and hugged her niece.

"Aunt Margaret, you look well."

"As do you," she replied. She indicated Shayla should sit down in the chair beside her. Shayla looked at her aunt's work. She was stitching an alphabet border, likely something for someone's new baby. Her aunt was quite skilled with a needle, something Shayla had little patience for. Shayla thought her aunt was the perfect wife. She was pretty, delicate, smart, and she had impeccable manners. Margaret was her mother's much younger sister, and she was only nine years older than Shayla herself. Margaret loved Shayla very much, but Margaret's hair was red, like Shayla's mother, and she had green eyes, also like her mother. Aunt Margaret painfully reminded her of her mother, and she thought that was why she did not spend a great deal of time with her aunt. She shook her head to clear it. "Papa would like you and Uncle James to come to dinner tomorrow evening."

"We would love to. What is the occasion?" Aunt Margaret asked without looking up from her work.

"No occasion. Papa invited, Adam Preston, who now works in our shop to dinner."

Margaret stopped and looked at Shayla. "Adam Preston? Duke Wellshore's brother?"

Shayla sighed. "Yes, that is the one," she said with a roll of her eyes. Honestly, why did everyone make such a fuss over the man?

Margaret smiled. "He would be an excellent match for you, Shayla." She leaned back from her needlework stand.

"No," Shayla replied a little too quickly. She shifted uncomfortably in her chair and looked at her aunt.

Margaret gave her a small smile. "Why not?"

"I am not interested in marriage. I plan to stay an independent woman." Shayla sat up straighter. "I do not need a man."

"Every woman needs a man," her aunt replied softly.

"I can provide for myself."

"Financially yes, but men take care of a woman's other...needs."

Shayla chose to ignore her aunt's comment and stood up. "Well, I must get back home. Mrs. Lawry may need my help with dinner." Not that she usually helped Mrs. Lawry prepare dinner, but she did not want to have this uncomfortable conversation with her aunt.

Unphased, Aunt Margaret started to stitch again. "What dress do you plan to wear?"

"I have not decided. I will find something in my closet no doubt."

"Um hum." Aunt Margaret smiled. "Well, dear, I am here if you need help selecting a dress."

"Thank you." Shayla bent down and kissed her aunt's cheek then quickly left the parlor.

Chapter 8

Saturday morning, Shayla went to the glass shop as she usually did. Only some of the blowers worked a half day on Saturdays, so the workshop was quiet. Her father and uncle spent the day in the front shop because of the number of shoppers. It was getting close to Christmastide, and families were out and about in town. She did take a commission when she first arrived at the shop, but now, she took a cup of tea and stood in the doorway watching. A young mother took her son's hand and pulled him away from a display of goblets. The father picked the child up and showed him the hanging birds that fluttered over the counter.

Adam was not working today. She found her thoughts went to Adam often, and she did not like it. She meant what she said to her aunt. She did not intend to marry. She planned to be a new modern woman. It was coming up on the turn of the century, and women were fighting for the right to vote. Women wanted independence, and Shayla wanted to be a woman who took care of herself. A woman who took care of the business her father and uncle started. She knew it would be difficult, and she knew people would gossip, but she did not care. She thought about the women who were fighting for women's rights. That was a worthy cause and an important pursuit but putting together dinner parties and being the perfect hostess was not.

Shayla walked back to the workshop, set her teacup on the table, and put on her gloves. Jimmy had the furnace heated so she could work. When they were children, they joked that one day they would marry. He was a good man, but he was only a friend. It annoyed her that society expected a woman to have a husband, especially in business. It was unfair, and she resolved to join the fight for women's rights in the new year. But now, she needed to get to work.

She took a sketch out of her bag. She woke up with the idea in her head. A short piece that swirled and twisted around the sides. In blue, she thought. Yes, cool blue, like the ocean. A swirl of glass that blended and twisted as it rose up in a sweeping arch from the base. She pulled her hair up and stuffed it under her hat.

While the image swam in her head, she made the first dip of the pipe. It took time, and she worked the glass, adding color here and there. She heated and rolled the glass, added more color, and heated it again. The form began to take shape. She transferred the piece to a pontil and pulled at the top with tongs to widen it then returned it to the furnace to heat it. On a whim, she added course white frit and swirled the piece contouring the top. It took quite a few trips to the furnace to get the piece the way she wanted it, and when she looked at her creation, it reminded her of the ocean: blue, swirling and rolling. Shayla kept the piece moving. Never stopping. She added gold luster liberally. She heated the piece slightly then walked over to the covered workbench and detached it. She smiled. It was perfect. It was a piece Shayla decided to keep for herself. She slid on thick gloves and carefully loaded it into the annealing oven. She picked up another pipe, gathered glass from the crucible, and began blowing more globes.

Mid-afternoon, Shayla put a globe in the oven and closed the door tight. She stretched her arms over her head and stretched from side to side. "Good night, Jimmy," she said as she put on her coat and slipped into her boots.

"You goin' to the dance tonight?"

She stopped and made a face. "Oh, I forgot about it."

"Well, come. It will be fun."

She left out a breath. "I cannot. Papa invited Adam and my aunt and uncles over for dinner tonight."

Jimmy looked crestfallen. He was two years her senior, and they had worked side by side in the shop for years. They danced sometimes at parties or at the town's public dances, but their relationship never evolved beyond friendship.

Jimmy forced a smile. "Ok. Well, have a good time."

"Thanks, Jimmy. Have fun at the dance." Shayla walked down the hall and went out the front door. She hopped on her bicycle and peddled home for a hot bath before dinner.

The delicious smell of roasting meat was making Shayla hungry as she put on her dress. She reached behind her and tried to fasten the buttons to no avail. She let out a sigh and went to the door to call Mrs. Lawry for help. She jumped and let out a small squeal when she opened it.

"I figured you needed help," Mrs. Lawry said as she entered the room. Shayla nodded, pulled up her hair, and turned around so Mrs. Lawry could fasten the buttons of the dress. She let down her hair and turned to face the cheval glass. The dress had a u-shaped neck and frilly white accents on the bodice. The periwinkle blue showed off her long dark brown hair which Shayla curled and left down. It tumbled over her shoulders and down her back.

"Wear your locket and gold earrings, dear, they will look nice with the dress," Mrs. Lawry suggested. Shayla nodded and put them on. She looked at herself in the glass again. "You are a beautiful young lady." Mrs. Lawry touched her cheek then turned and left the room.

Shayla sat at her vanity and brushed her hair again. She touched the small perfume bottle and thought about wearing a dab of the perfume it contained but decided against it. Instead, she reached for another bottle and dabbed a few drops of its contents behind her ears. She adjusted the pins in her hair and added a gold filigree comb. When she heard the rumble of a carriage approaching, she looked out the window and saw a magnificent carriage bearing the Duke's crest on the door stopping in front of the house. Adam. She could not stop the smile that spread across her face or stop her heart from racing. She picked up her shoes and sat on her four-poster bed to put them on. When she heard the knock on the door, she smoothed the front of her dress, reached over and turned off the light on her dresser, and went downstairs.

Adam stood in the foyer. He handed Mrs. Lawry his overcoat and hat then he looked up and smiled when he saw Shayla coming down the stairs.

"Good evening, Miss Toselli." He walked to the stairs and extended his hand.

Shayla placed her hand lightly in his. "Good evening, Captain Preston."

Henry stood in the doorway to the parlor and looked at his daughter with her hand in Adam's hand. He suddenly realized that she was no longer a child, but a grown woman. A woman that another man looked at with desire in his eyes. Henry stared at them as Shayla smiled and looked at Adam as he never saw her look at a man before. He sighed and walked into the foyer. "Please, come into the parlor," Henry said, and Shayla startled at hearing her father's voice. Adam bowed and extended his hand indicating that Shayla should enter before him. She nodded and walked into the parlor.

Henry made the introductions. "Captain Preston, may I present Mr. James Oliver and my sister-in-law Mrs. Margaret Oliver."

"A pleasure to meet you, Mrs. Oliver," Adam said to Margaret as he took her extended hand and kissed it. He shook hands with James and then turned to Hal. "Good evening, Hal."

"Evening, Adam." They shook hands.

Aunt Margaret caught Shayla's eye and signaled she should sit on the settee. Shayla complied. Adam sat down next to her. Henry poured drinks and passed them around and then sat down. The conversation was something about the glass shop, but Shayla did not really hear it. She looked at Adam in his dress uniform. He was so handsome. Somehow, he looked taller in it.

"Shayla?" she heard her name and looked up. "How are the ornaments coming along, dear," Aunt Margaret asked quietly.

The question snapped Shayla back to reality. She was a glass blower, and Adam was a Captain. Granted a Captain that had just left the service, but also, he was the brother of their new Duke. He was older and much more worldly than she. She took a breath. She needed to get a grip on herself. "I made good progress this week."

"What else were you working on today, girl," Hal asked.

Typical that her uncle would notice, Shayla thought to herself. "Oh. A blue and white vase. The idea came to me in a dream last night, and I had to make it this morning before I could concentrate on the ornaments."

"Do you often get ideas in dreams?" Adam turned his full attention to Shayla. He noticed a little hitch in her breathing and smiled to himself. She was quite beautiful, and the scent of her filled his senses.

"Sometimes," she whispered when she caught her breath.

"She also gets inspiration when she is mad at something," Hal laughed, and Aunt Margaret gave him an admonishing look. "We can tell when she is upset. She uses a great deal of red glass," Hal snorted and emptied his glass.

"Dinner is ready," Mrs. Lawry announced.

Adam stood and held out his arm. Shayla stood. She placed her hand on his arm, and when he laid his hand over hers, Shayla felt warmth radiate up through her body. She never felt that connection before, and it scared and excited her. Why was she attracted to a man she could not have? Why would he want a craftsmen's daughter when ladies of the aristocracy were dangling themselves in front of him? But a voice in her head said, then why was he hiding from one of those very ladies in your workshop?

He led her to the dining room. Shayla stood at her chair and waited as he pulled it out for her. She nodded her head in thanks, pulled her skirt to the side, and sat down. The others took seats around the large cherry table, so Adam took the seat next to Shayla.

Mrs. Lawry put the stuffed goose on the table. It was a beautiful bird, lightly browned with crispy skin. Arranged around the bird was an assortment of potatoes and carrots. Shayla knew from experience that it was juicy and tender.

"It looks delicious, Mrs. Lawry," Adam said to her.

Shayla smiled. She liked that he was not stuffy and spoke to everyone. He was more like an ordinary person. She sighed. He was not ordinary. No, he was extraordinary. She longed to be with him, but she remembered her promise to herself. She would not fade into the background for any man. Even if that man was gorgeous with a firm and muscular body, dancing eyes, and curly hair she longed to run her fingers through.

"Captain, Shayla tells me that you are learning the glass craft quickly," Aunt Margaret said with a smile.

"It is entirely due to her excellent teaching," he replied with a nod and smile to Shayla that made her heart flutter.

"He learns quickly," Shayla praised him.

Adam watched as she cut the meat on her plate. He knew her hands were strong, and he wanted to feel those hands pull him close. He closed his eyes for a moment. He needed to keep his mind off such thoughts. He took a large drink of wine to steady himself.

Dinner was a combination of discussion and a great quantity of food, and when they adjourned to the parlor, Shayla relaxed and found herself engaged in conversation with Adam. "Tell me about your first time blowing glass," he asked her.

Shayla rolled up her sleeve. "See this?" She held out her arm for him to inspect. Adam looked closely and saw a small but distinct scar.

He looked up into her eyes. He hated to see anything mar her skin. Skin that was soft and fragrant. The scent of flowers surrounded her. He leaned down and kissed the scar. He knew his actions would not go unnoticed. Shayla shuddered at his touch which he also knew would be noticed. Why was he being so bold? He wanted Shayla. They knew each other only a short time, but Adam felt so comfortable with her, with the entire Toselli family because they were warm and welcoming. "So, tell me what happened?"

"Everyone was taking a break. I had watched them work so many times that I thought I knew what I was doing. So, I opened the furnace and dipped in the pipe. I blew a small bubble. Nothing big really, but I was thrilled. I detached it from the pipe and reached in the oven to set it on a self and accidently touched my arm to another piece."

Hal had walked over unnoticed. "And boy did she scream," he laughed, and Shayla was startled to see him standing beside her. "We realized it was time to teach her the craft. The next day, we got her small gloves and began training her. She learned quickly too."

Aunt Margaret and Uncle James stood up. "I am afraid we must retire early tonight," she said. "Henry, thank you for a wonderful evening." She kissed Henry's cheek, and he returned the kiss. Hal walked over and kissed her cheek. Shayla embraced her aunt and uncle. Adam watched their exchange. His family was always properly formal when they were out in public or had guests at the estate. He liked the open and warm affection Shayla's family showed one another whether it was at home or in the shop.

Adam stood up and kissed Margaret's hand. "It was a pleasure meeting you, Mrs. Oliver." He shook hands with James and then held his arm out for Shayla, and they walked out of the parlor. They said their goodbyes, and Aunt Margaret smiled at them which made Shayla flustered under her stare.

Not having a butler, Henry opened the door. "It is snowing," he called back to the others as Margaret and James stepped out the door.

"It is?" She looked out the door. A very light snow was falling. "I love snow!" Shayla sounded excited.

"Would you like to take a walk?" Adam asked.

"I would. I will get my coat." She rushed up the stairs. Shayla pulled on her long dark overcoat and put a fur trimmed matching bonnet on her head. She took her mother's white scarf and thick gloves out of the bottom drawer of her dresser and hurried back downstairs. Adam had his overcoat and gloves on. He looked up as she came down the stairs. He groaned. She looked so young and innocent. She was delightfully enthusiastic, and he never met anyone like her. He took her hand and assisted her down the last few steps.

"Your daughter is safe with me, Henry."

"I know she is," Henry replied.

"Good night, Adam," Hal extended his hand. "See you Monday at work."

"Good night, Hal." Adam shook his hand.

Hal walked out with Adam and Shayla, but he turned the other way at the end of the walk and went to his home down the street. He looked back and saw Henry still in the doorway watching Shayla and Adam strolling away. Shayla had her arm hooked in Adam's arm. Then he heard his niece laugh. It was a good sound. She needed more laughter in her life. Hal caught Henry's eye and they both nodded their heads in understanding.

The night was serene and picturesque with the falling snow. Adam and Shayla walked down the street to the square. The only sound was the squeaking of snow under their boots. When they reached the square there were several other people out for a walk in the first snow of the season. Several small children made snowballs and threw them at one another. Large flakes fluttered down to the ground, and they were beginning to stick to the road.

"Do you think we will get a lot of snow?" Shayla asked as they walked.

"It is early for a large storm, and the temperatures are not very cold, but maybe."

Shayla took off her glove, held out her hand, and caught a flake. It melted quickly. "When we were children, my friends and I caught snowflakes on our tongues."

"We did that as well."

Shayla looked at Adam with a mischievous grin then she stuck out her tongue and caught a snowflake. "That was fun," she laughed.

Adam gave a hearty laugh. "Ok, you cannot have all the fun." He stuck out his tongue and caught a snowflake. They laughed and caught snowflakes as they walked along.

"Oh look. The dance is still on." Music poured from the open doors of the dance hall.

"Shall we dance, my lady?" Adam asked with a flourish of his hand.

"Yes." Shayla took Adam's hand, and they walked to the door. A polka was just ending. No one was at the door since the public event was close to ending. They went inside just as the last dance was called. They took off their coats, and Adam laid them on an empty chair.

"May I have this dance, Miss Toselli." Adam bowed.

Shayla curtsied. "You may, Captain."

Adam took her hand and led her to the dance floor as the first notes of the waltz began. Adam placed his hand at Shayla's waist and held her other hand delicately. His head was up, and he looked over her shoulder. Shayla took a breath and held her head high, and then they began the intricate and quick movements of the waltz.

When she was younger, Shayla did not want to learn to dance, but now she was very glad that her mother insisted. They moved smoothly around the dance floor with the other couples. They smiled as they danced; their heads held high. Their movements were fluid but crisp. And when the last note sounded Adam bowed low and Shayla curtsied. Their cheeks were rosy from the dance and their hearts beat fast, and perhaps not only from dancing. Adam took Shayla's hand as they straightened up, and they looked into each other's eyes. He wanted to kiss her so badly, but it was inappropriate and scandalous to do so in public. He saw her desire for him in her eyes, and he could still feel her in his arms as they moved across the dance floor.

Reluctantly, they moved away from one another. They put on their coats, went out the door they came in, and began the walk back to the Toselli home. Shayla tucked her arm in Adam's, and he steadied her on the slippery road which was now covered in snow. Suddenly, in his heart, Adam knew Shayla was the only woman for him, but was he the man for her? He was not sure he knew the answer to that question, but he intended to show her that he was the man who could make her happy.

Chapter 9

Henry was busy restocking the shelves of the shop when the bells on the door jingled as it opened. He straightened up and adjusted his waist coat. A footman held the door open, and the Duchess of Wellshore and her maid entered the shop. Henry quickly went to greet her. He bowed low. "Good morning, Duchess. It is a pleasure to have Your Grace in my shop."

"Thank you, Mr. Toselli," she replied cheerfully. The footman closed the door and waited by the carriage with the coachman. The Duchess took off her bonnet and slowly looked around at the many glass pieces on display in the shop. "You have quite a lovely selection of merchandise, Mr. Toselli, and I have to express my admiration for the work you do. The ornament my husband brought home for my inspection was beyond words."

"My daughter Shayla's work," Henry told her proudly.

"Yes, my husband told me your daughter is the creator of the exquisite globes. You must be exceedingly proud of her."

"Yes, Your Grace. Shayla is quite talented." Henry nodded in acknowledgement.

The Duchess walked around the shop and looked at various items. She stopped in front of a glass case of pens. Henry went behind the counter. "May I take something out for your inspection, Your grace?"

She looked over the pens. "I would like to see the purple one please, Mr. Toselli."

Henry took out the pen and laid it on a velvet covered cushion on the counter. "We also have holders and ink wells to match." He took out the items to show her. She picked up the pen. It was well balanced. At the end of the pen was a tiny elephant.

"Would it be possible to get another animal or a bird perhaps on the pen?"

"Yes, Your Grace. Anything you desire."

The Duchess continued to look at various items. She lightly touched a blue glass desk lamp. "This is beautiful."

"Thank you kindly."

"I see this one has more gold accents." She pointed to a black lamp next to the blue one. "Can more gold be added to this one?"

"Yes, Your Grace. Any item can be made to your specifications."

Amelia considered the lamp. She looked back at the pen that still sat on the counter. "Very good. I believe I want the blue lamp but with more gold accents for my husband's study. It is to be a gift, so not a word."

"Very good, Your Grace."

"I would like to speak to Miss Toselli about the details for my husband's present."

Henry nodded. "Of course. I will get her."

"No, no. I will go to her. Like my husband, I too am interested in seeing her work. I am told it is fascinating to watch glass blowing."

Henry hesitated. Taking Duke Wellshore into the shop was one thing, but the Duchess was another matter. He stepped forward. "Your Grace, the workshop is hot, and dirty, and dangerous. It is best if I bring Shayla out to you."

"I would appreciate seeing her work, Mr. Toselli. My husband and brother-in-law told me she is a remarkable craftswoman." She stepped a little closer to Henry. "We need more women stepping into new roles. Do you not agree, Sir?"

"Yes, I believe my daughter can do anything, Your Grace."

"More men need to think that way, do you agree?" Henry bowed his head and nodded. "And I really would like to see your daughter at work."

Henry sighed. He knew he would not win, and she would have her way. "As you wish." Henry pointed to the door at the back of the store. "Please follow me." He led the way, and as he went, he moved things out of the aisle to make room for the Duchess because her dress was rather wide. "Please be careful, Your Grace," Henry pleaded.

"Do not worry, Mr. Toselli. I am quite sure on my feet." Amelia followed Henry, and her maid followed her closely as they made their way down the hallway. When they entered the preparation room, Amelia stopped by the window and watched Shayla, who was hard at work. Today, Shayla was making delicate flowers and leaves for the ornaments at the flame. One by one, she attached the tiny flowers and stems to one of the globes. She drew out thin strands of glass to form ribbons. She worked quickly and soon the globe was decorated. Amelia was fascinated as she watched Shayla work. Then Shayla handed the globe to Adam, and he placed it in an oven.

"What did Adam do with the globe Miss Toselli just finished," The Duchess asked Henry.

"After Shayla adds the decorations, the piece must go into the annealing oven overnight. The piece is very slowly cooled. This tempers the glass to strengthen it and keep it from breaking easily," Henry explained.

"Fascinating." Amelia leaned closer to the glass to get a better look. Shayla and Adam were so engrossed in their work that neither looked over and saw her standing at the window.

"Your Grace, I will summon my daughter."

"Mr. Toselli," Henry looked at her, "please do not tell Adam I am here. I wish to speak to Miss Toselli alone."

"Of course. This way, please." Henry led her and her maid to the office. "If you would wait here, I will get Shayla, Your Grace."

He closed the office door then went in and asked Shayla to come out to speak to him.

Shayla followed him out of the furnace room. "The Duchess of Wellshore wishes to speak to you about a commission," Henry whispered.

"The Duchess?" Shayla asked. Henry nodded.

Shayla took off her apron and hung it on a hook by the door. She removed her cap and pushed her hair back, then smoothed her shirt and the front of her trousers.

Amelia smiled when Shayla entered the office. "Your Grace," Shayla said as she curtsied.

"Miss Toselli. It is a pleasure to make your acquaintance."

"You honor us by visiting our establishment." Shayla executed a perfect curtsy. She practiced her curtsy every night just in case Duke Wellshore came to the shop again. Shayla wanted to do everything she did well, including executing a flawless curtsy. It simply was not acceptable for her to do any less than her best.

"Excuse me, Your Grace. If you do not need me, I will return to the showroom out front."

"Of course, Mr. Toselli. I am very sorry to have kept you so long. Thank you."

Henry bowed and then turned to Shayla. "Be certain to walk Duchess Wellshore back to the showroom," he said quietly to his daughter. "Be good," he added.

"Of course, Papa," Shayla whispered back. Henry bowed to the Duchess again, and he left the office closing the door behind him.

Shayla smiled then looked over at the maid who stood silently waiting to do the Duchess' bidding. She smiled at the young woman, but the maid's expression never changed.

"Your work is, to use my husband's word, exquisite, Miss Toselli."

"Thank you, Your Grace." "I am happy you both are pleased with the ornaments."

"Miss Toselli. I would like to discuss a commission for my husband."

"Of course, Your Grace."

"Come, let us sit down and talk." Amelia pointed to the small table and chairs where Shayla often sketched. Amelia sat down, and Shayla took the seat next to her.

"Please, call me Shayla, Your Grace."

Amelia smiled. "Very well, Shayla. I must say, I am impressed with your skills and talent. I am also impressed that you are teaching Adam to work glass." She glanced at the closed door. Adam had not yet realized she was there, and Amelia hoped he would stay in the workshop until she finished talking to Shayla.

"He catches on quickly, and he seems to enjoy the work," Shayla said proudly.

"He has been somewhat withdrawn since his injury and subsequent departure from the military. I am happy to see he is finding a great deal of joy and a new pursuit. You must be a good teacher."

Shayla felt herself blush.

"He speaks highly of you, Shayla, and Adam is sparing in his praise of anyone."

Shayla looked down, and the Duchess smiled because she sensed that Adam and Shayla had feelings for one another. She was also certain that neither would admit it.

"You said you wanted a commission?" Shayla asked changing the subject.

"Yes, I would like the blue lamp on display in the shop, but I would like more gold accents like on the black lamp. It is a gift for my husband's study," Amelia explained.

"I would be honored to make it for you. I will make a new lamp and add the gold accents that you desire."

"Good. Thank you. I know it will be beautiful." Amelia gave Shayla an appraising look. "I admire you, Shayla. You work in what is typically a man's profession, and you excel at it."

"Thank you, Your Grace. My mother was also a glass blower. She learned as a girl in Ireland. It is not uncommon for women to work glass in Ireland."

"Your mother was Irish?"

"Yes."

"Well, I certainly hope it will become common for British women to work glass."

"I can have the lamp finished for you at the end of the week, Your Grace. I will have a boy deliver it to you on Saturday morning."

"I would like you to bring it to me on Saturday, Shayla."

"Of course."

Amelia clasped her hands in her lap. "I am having a small party Saturday afternoon to make baskets for the poor. Some early Christmastide charity work. This will be followed by games, dinner, and a bit of dancing. There will be many young people there. I think you will enjoy it."

Shayla's heart started beating fast. She did not want to go to a party. She needed to refuse, politely. "Thank you kindly for the invitation, but I must work on the ornaments for the Christmastide Ball."

Amelia frowned. "All day on Saturday? I commend hard work, but surely you can make time for other activities, and this is for a very good cause."

Shayla stuttered. "I really do not think I would fit in, Your Grace."

"Nonsense. You are young and single. Your family is prosperous. It is time for women like you to be introduced into society. This will also give you an opportunity to meet eligible men."

The color drained from Shayla's face and her expression startled Amelia.

"Surely, you intend to marry one day?"

Shayla cleared her throat. "Actually, Your Grace, I do not."

"Why ever not?"

"My father and uncle have only me to take over the business. As a maid, I have more autonomy. I am a third owner."

Amelia was surprised but not entirely shocked. "My dear, I understand that now that women were being accepted in the workplace more and more, many young women like yourself chose to make their own way in the world. Right now, it may appear the law is more favorable to a single female heir than to a married woman, but you have heard of the Married Women's Property Acts? You keep whatever you inherit, and the money you earn while married is your own. These are new laws, and more are coming in the new year to protect women such as yourself."

"Yes, I know of the laws, but many men do not want their wives to work. And I am not a woman to sit around the house and show off my husband's wealth." Shayla took a deep breath and continued. "I have seen what has happened to my friends after they married. Their husbands want them to stay home, have children, and run the house. Their lives are social visits, purchasing items they do not need simply because they are expensive, and they seem to lose all sense of themselves." Shayla shook herself and wrapped her arms around her body.

Amelia looked wide eyed at Shayla. She took a deep breath. She had to be cautious, and she chose her words carefully. "What you say is true, many men do not wish for their wives to work." She nodded her head. "It is status and ego that makes men want their wives to stay at home. I might add that running a household is quite demanding and important work. However, more and more women are working outside the home. Some do it for economic reasons, but others work because they want to work. The number of women who own businesses is increasing and that includes married women. A married women who owns a business can have her children with her which is something she may not be able to do if she worked for someone else."

"Oh, well, yes," Shayla stuttered. "My mother was able to work and take care of me. Because this was her shop, she made the rules."

Amelia continued. "Women are demanding equality and many men, my husband included, recognize that equality between the sexes is necessary for a well-functioning society. These forward thinking men are working tirelessly on strengthening and expanding women's rights."

Shayla gasped. "Your Grace, I am sorry. I meant no disrespect to you or Duke Wellshore." She was flustered, and her face turned red. "I am certain he is doing everything he can for the status of women."

Amelia reached over and touched Shaya's hand. "My dear, no offense was taken. I am simply pointing out that not all men are possessive of a woman or intimidated by a woman who is independent." She stopped again and looked at Shayla. "Your father and uncle, my husband, his brothers, all are men who respect women as persons in their own right would you not agree?"

"Yes. Yes, that is true." Shayla thought for a moment. Adam seemed to be the kind of man who was not possessive. He was genuinely impressed with her and her abilities. Of course, her father and uncle treated her as an equal  They trained her and encouraged her to work with glass. She began working in the shop when she was only twelve years old. She worked as hard as any boy and learned every job. Then she began blowing and shaping glass, and she excelled at it. Her father and uncle also trained her in finance and running the shop in the hopes that one day she would take over the business. The men in the factory also respected her and her abilities, and she never had any difficulties when she worked on the factory floor.

Amelia smiled when she saw the subtle change in Shayla's expression as if she just realized the possibilities. "Yes, it is decided. You will come to the party on Saturday, and you will see that there are many progressive men who do not simply want to possess their wives."

Shayla started to protest, but a look from Duchess Wellshore told her she lost this battle. There was no choice. She was going to attend the party on Saturday. She bowed her head. "As you wish, Your Grace."

"Good. I will speak to your father. Do you need help selecting a dress? As your mother has passed, I would be happy to help you."

"Thank you, but I can manage. Mrs. Lawry can help me as well as my aunt, my mother's sister."

"Very good. I will expect you and your maid at two o'clock."

Shayla looked at the Duchess. "I do not have a maid, Your Grace."

"No?"

Shayla shook her head no. "Not that my father has not wanted to hire a maid," she added quickly. She did not want the Duchess to think her father could not afford one. "I just have never felt the need of a maid."

The Duchess smiled. "Very well. I will expect you at two o'clock Saturday afternoon. Come in an afternoon gown, and after we fill baskets, I will assign a maid to help you dress for dinner and dancing." She stood up and took Shayla's hands. Shayla stood up. "It was a pleasure to meet you, Shayla, and I look forward to getting to know you better."

"Thank you, Your Grace. Let me show you back to the front shop."

"Shayla, I was wondering where," Adam cut off when he saw his sister-in-law walk out of the office behind Shayla. "What are you doing here?" he asked.

"Adam!" Shayla exclaimed as she reached out and touched his arm, but she smiled at him, and he smiled back at her.

Amelia cleared her throat, and they both stepped back and looked at her. "And a pleasure it is to see you too, my dear brother-in-law," Amelia retorted. She looked from Adam to Shayla and knew they had feelings for one another. "If you must know, I am here commissioning Shayla with a present for my husband." She smiled at them. "Well, I must be off."

"Yes," Shayla stuttered, "let me show you out, Your Grace." She led the way back down the hallway to the front shop.

## Chapter 10

Shayla arrived at the workshop early the next morning and was surprised to see Adam already at work. He and Jimmy were emptying the oven and setting out tools. She stood in the doorway and watched Adam work. He was part of the aristocracy, but here he was working hard side by side with commoners and enjoying it. He talked with Jimmy easily as they carried glass rods in and put them in the rack.

She watched as Adam picked up a heavy box of glass. His hands gripped the box tightly, and the muscles in his arms tightened visibly beneath the thin shirt he wore. She never met anyone who made her heart flutter the way seeing Adam did. His commanding presence felt confident and accomplished but not overbearing. He was masculine and strong, but also caring and tender. She saw his tenderness in the way he interacted with the young boys who worked in the shop. He never raised his voice when he spoke to them, and he always had a compliment or encouraging word when he worked with them. Perhaps the Duchess was right, and she could find a man who would support her and not restrict her. Afterall, her father was not an overbearing man. Her mother worked and was not suffocated by him. Suffocation, that was what scared Shayla the most. She did not want a man who controlled her and made her feel like property instead of a unique individual.

Adam set the box down, turned, and saw Shayla watching hm from the doorway. He liked the way her eyes brightened when he looked at her. He saw contemplation in her eyes and maybe desire. He did not know how to tell her that he thought about her whenever he was not with her. She seemed to always be in his thoughts. He walked over to her. "Good morning," he said in his deep seductive voice that made her knees weak.

"Good morning. You are here early."

Adam noticed her voice was a little high sometimes when she talked to him. He also liked seeing the light pale rose that often colored her cheeks when she was with him. "It is going to be another busy day," he commented.

"It is. I want to make the lamp for the Duchess' commission first thing this morning."

"I heard she talked you into coming to her party on Saturday," Adam grinned.

"Coerced is what she did." Shayla shook her head remembering the Duchess would not take no for an answer.

Adam let out a deep laugh. "Amelia is exceptionally good at it."

Shayla tried to look disinterested, but she had to ask. "Will you be at the party on Saturday?" She felt her face get hot. She hoped he would be there.

"She coerced me too. Did she tell you about the party games?"

Shayla nodded yes.

Adam's heart thrilled at the thought of playing games and dancing with Shayla. She was so beautiful, and more importantly, she was genuine. He liked that she said what was on her mind. He was just unsure how to tell her or show her what she meant to him. He wanted her to be his, and in some ways that scared him, but not being with her also scared him. He thought this party might be a way to show her how he felt about her, and he got an idea. "We can help each other," he suggested.

"Help each other? How?"

"When we have to pair off for a game or other activity, we can be partners."

Shayla smiled. "I would like that."

"Good." Adam went back to work, and Shayla walked over and picked up a glass rod. She sat down in front of the bench and lit the flame. Suddenly the thought of a party did not seem so bad. Adam kept looking over at her while she worked, and Shayla glanced over at him as well. They smiled when their eyes met.

Henry came into the preparation room to pick up an order. Hal stood by the window drinking coffee. Henry stopped next to him and watched for a few moments while Shayla worked at the flame making a small glass animal. She cut it off the glass rod and placed it on a cloth bed. Adam immediately picked it up and carefully placed it in the oven. Adam watched her intently as she continued to work. Then Shayla looked up at Adam and smiled warmly at him, and he returned the smile. Henry sighed. "I saw it at dinner Saturday. How long have they had eyes for one another?"

Hal took a long drink then looked at his brother. "From the first moment they met."

Later that day, Henry poured a cup of coffee and sat down next to Shayla as she worked at the table in the preparation area.

"Papa," Shayla began, "I think we should apply for a coat of arms."

Henry lowered his mug. "You do?"

Shayla nodded. "Queen Victoria has granted royal warrants to tradesmen. It is a sign of quality products. Our products are of the highest quality, and I believe it would give customers increased confidence in our glass."

Henry thought for a moment. "Then we should apply for a royal warrant." He took a sip of coffee. "I am certain Hal will agree." Henry knew his brother would agree to anything Shayla wanted. "It could give us the edge on the competition."

"Exactly, and if the Duke is happy with his commission, as I know he will be, we should be able to secure one."

Henry nodded. "What are you working on?"

"Sketches for a commission for the Earl of Huntington." She turned the paper so he could see that she drew a large vase made of yellow glass. The lip curled and twisted back down the front of the vase. At the end of each tendril was a delicate white lily. "It is for his granddaughter for Christmas."

"It is lovely." Henry sipped his coffee. "Adam is picking up the trade quickly."

Shayla nodded eagerly. "Yes. He is a quick study."

"I like him. He is a good man."

Shayla stopped working and looked up at her father. "He is a good man." She knew that despite her belief that she would never marry, she had been thinking she might enjoy marriage with Adam. He was fun to be with and very supportive and understanding. They worked well together too. Unlike some men, Adam was not intimidated by her skill, and he was happy to assist her.

Just then, Adam walked in. "Hello, Henry. Good afternoon, Shayla." Adam smiled broadly.

"Hello, Adam."

Henry saw his daughter's eyes flutter ever so slightly and her cheeks blushed softly. "Well, it is almost quitting time." Henry stood up. "Would you like to come to supper, Adam? Mrs. Lawry always cooks plenty."

"I would love to." Adam and Shayla smiled at one another.

"Good." Henry left the room. As he started to walk down the hallway, he looked back at Adam and Shayla. Adam leaned close and looked at her drawing. Then he whispered something, and

Shayla laughed. Henry groaned at the loss of his little girl, but he also smiled. He wanted her to be happy.

# Chapter 11

The morning of the Duchess' party, Shayla was nervous. She wrapped herself up in her dressing gown and went downstairs to eat a hearty breakfast. She knew that young women ate very little at parties. "Good morning, Papa." She kissed her father's cheek. "Good morning, Mrs. Lawry."

"I made eggs and sausage for breakfast. Be careful how much you eat at the party," Mrs. Lawry warned.

Shayla stuck her hands on her hips. "Why is it that men can eat whatever they want, but women must appear to have no appetite? It is unfair."

"Life is not always fair," Mrs. Lawry replied as she loaded a plate for Shayla.

"It is customary to arrive by carriage, so Mr. Jones will drive you to the estate," Henry informed her.

Shayla sighed. "I suppose it is necessary."

"He will stay and wait to bring you home."

"You and Mrs. Lawry do not need the carriage today, Papa?"

"We can use one of the wagons if need be."

Henry folded the newspaper and looked at Shayla. "There will be many eligible men at the party, today. Perhaps you will meet someone you fancy."

Shayla shrugged. "Maybe, but Papa, I am not interested in finding a husband, especially a man in the aristocracy." She ate everything on her plate and poured a second cup of tea.

"Shayla, you are young. You should be interested in romance."

She shook her head. "Anyway, Adam and I have a plan."

"A plan?" Henry and Mrs. Lawry asked at the same time.

"Yes. Whenever we must pair up for a game or activity, Adam and I will be partners. We will appease the Duchess, and we will get through the party together." She ate another biscuit and drank the rest of her tea. "I am going to bathe."

When Shayla was upstairs, Mrs. Lawry looked at Henry. "They have a plan," she chuckled.

"The best laid plans often go awry," Henry replied.

Later that day, Henry carried Shayla's evening gown downstairs while Shayla made certain she had everything she needed. "Parties are so complicated," she said as she went downstairs. Mr. Jones, one of her aunt's coachmen, took her cases and her gown and put them in the carriage.

"Have a good time," Mrs. Lawry kissed Shayla. "Remember your manners," she instructed. "We will see you when you return."

Henry took Shayla's hands. "Be well, and please have a good time." He hugged Shayla tight. He leaned back and looked at her. "Your mother would have been excited for you. It is an honor to be invited to a party at Duke Wellshore's estate. She loved you very much and wanted you to be happy."

Shayla hugged him. "I love you, Papa."

"And I love you."

He walked her outside. Uncle Hal, Aunt Margaret, and Uncle James were waiting near the carriage. Aunt Margaret embraced Shayla. "I am so happy for you. To be invited to a party with the Duke and Duchess. You mother would be so proud." She kissed Shayla.

The mention of her mother made Shayla sad. She missed her dearly and wished she were her to give her advice and guidance. Perhaps it was true that her mother wanted her to enter society. Shayla had attended only a handful of house parties when her mother was tragically killed. Since then, no one pushed her to accept party invitations, and she was happy to decline them. She only attended the Earl of Huntington's parties because he was a very sweet old man and a good customer. Well, no one forced her to accept an invitation except for the Duchess.

She hugged each member of her family and stepped into the carriage. She took a deep breath and waved as the carriage pulled out onto the street.

Fortunately, the ride to Wellshore Manor was not long. Shayla stared ahead, and her ears were tuned for any strange sounds. She disliked carriage rides since her mother's accident. She preferred her bicycle, but it was unacceptable to arrive at the estate on a bicycle.

As soon as the carriage stopped, Shayla opened the door. The footman who was waiting for the carriage lowered the step and helped her out. Other men came to take her gown and cases, and the groom instructed the coachman where to put the horse and carriage.

Shayla took a deep breath and looked up at the expansive mansion. It stood three stories high and had a façade of cream colored stone which contrasted with the red shingles on the roofs. Both ends of the mansion featured prominent rounded towers, and one side had a small building extension. She made her way up the long walk to the stately black front door.

It opened immediately, and she was greeted by the butler. "Greetings, Miss Toselli," he said with a deep bow. An under butler took her traveling cloak. "Your belongings will be brought to your chamber, Miss."

"Thank you."

"Is that for the Duchess?" the butler asked looking at the box Shayla carried.

"Yes, it is."

"Her Grace has instructed me to have it brought directly to her chambers." He signaled to a maid who came quickly down the hallway.

Shayla nodded and handed the box to the butler. He handed it off to the maid with instructions on where to place it in the Duchess' chambers, and then he stepped forward. "Announcing Miss Shayla Toselli."

All eyes turned and focused on her, and Shayla felt queasy. She entered the parlor. There was no formal receiving line, so she walked over to where Duke and Duchess Wellshore stood talking with a few guests.

"Welcome, Miss Toselli." Duke Wellshore bowed.

"Your Grace." She curtsied.

"I am so happy you are here." The Duchess took Shayla's hands. "Excuse us, husband. I wish to introduce Miss Toselli to our other guests."

"Of course."

The Duchess ushered Shayla to the other side of the room. "I gave the box with the lamp to the butler," Shayla whispered. "I do hope you are satisfied."

"I cannot wait to see it. I am certain it is wonderful."

"I am awed by your confidence in my abilities," Shayla replied politely.

Amelia steered Shayla toward Adam who stood alone sipping a drink by the hearth. He adjusted his position to watch Shayla since she entered the parlor.

"Miss Toselli, you of course know my brother-in-law, Captain Preston."

"An honor to see you again, Miss Toselli." Adam bowed, and she curtsied.

"Adam, would you kindly introduce Miss Toselli to the other guests?"

"It would be my honor." He took Shayla's hand and kissed it. He turned and offered her his arm. "Come, let me introduce you to the others."

The Duchess walked toward her husband who was conversing with several ladies. He excused himself and joined her. "I see you are up to your tricks," he whispered quietly in her ear. Amelia just smiled and took his arm.

Adam led Shayla around the room. There were primarily women in attendance, and Shayla recognized a couple of them from attending Earl Huntington's parties, so she struck up a conversation with Miss Caroline and Miss Faith. Waiters passed silver trays on which sat crystal glasses filled with punch and tiny pastries. Shayla was relieved that the party was much more relaxed than she expected.

Once everyone was assembled, the Duchess called for everyone's attention. "Ladies, let us go arrange baskets for the poor." She walked over to the door which led out of the parlor and led the women down the hall and to a large room. There were piles of goods, including dried fruits, smoked meats, confections, and staples such as flour and sugar. "We will be arranging these goods into large baskets. Now, I do not want any of the ladies to pick up the filled baskets. That is the men's job. We will fill the baskets, tie up the cloth, and add a festive bow. The men will move the basket, so you can begin filling another. Let us get started."

It was a pleasant task. A young man serenaded them on the piano while they worked. He played several Christmas carols, and everyone joined in the singing. Waiters came by with cups of wassail to sustain them in their work. Shayla smiled when Adam came to remove the basket she had filled. He was always quickly by her side as she finished, so no one else had an opportunity to assist her.

When the baskets were filled, the ladies adjourned to their chambers to rest and change for dinner. Shayla's maid was Bridget who was just a couple years younger than her. Bridget helped her out of her afternoon gown. Shayla was unaccustomed to having a maid, and she was not sure she could get comfortable with one. Bridgett poured her a cup of tea, and Shayla sat by the generous fire blazing in the hearth to rest before getting ready for dinner and the party.

The room was elegant. Fine silk in a very pale pink covered the walls on which hung several paintings of flowers. The windows were dressed in long velvet curtains in a darker shade of pink. The furniture was made of walnut, but the pieces were distinctively feminine.

"Would you like to lie down, Miss?" Bridgett asked when Shayla finished her tea.

"I might as well. The bed looks comfortable." Bridgett turned down the coverlet, and Shayla laid down on the soft feather bed.

"I will wake you in half an hour."

"Thank you." She closed her eyes, but she knew she would not sleep  It was enough to just lie there and rest.


Adam was in the parlor with his brother and several other men. They talked and played cards. He was losing, so when the hand finished, he stood up, walked over, and poured himself a drink. He looked around the room and then sat down on the sofa to talk with Elliot.

"I noticed you did not let anyone get near Miss Toselli this afternoon," Elliot commented.

"Really? I had not noticed."

Elliot snorted. "Of course, you did." He took a sip of his brandy. "Are you interested in her?"

"Interested?" Adam swirled the liquid in the glass he held. "I guess I am."

"Is she interested in you?"

Adam thought for a moment. "I think she is, but I also think she does not want to be. She is quite intent on remaining an independent woman."

"So my Amelia has told me." Elliot took a sip of his drink and smiled over the rim of his glass. "Amelia has taken an interest in Miss Toselli. And in you."

Adam sat up straighter. "Elliot, that may scare Shayla off."

Elliot assessed his brother carefully. He always looked out for his brothers. It was obvious to everyone that Adam and Shayla had eyes only for each other. "Perhaps it will not scare her off. It is possible she just needs a little encouragement?" Maybe you also need encouragement, Elliot thought, but he did not say the words out loud.

"No. I believe it would scare her. Please tell Amelia to not interfere."

"Ah!" Elliot laughed. "I have no control over my wife when she decides to do something."

"You are duke, Elliot. Make her listen to you."

"That is another aspect of marriage that you need to learn, Adam. When your wife sets her mind on something, it is easiest if you let her do it." He tipped his glass to his youngest brother.

Shayla looked at herself in the beautiful gilded cheval glass in the room. Bridgett helped her put on her mother's thin gold necklace.

"You look pretty, Miss."

"Thank you, Bridget. Do you know what type of games we will play?"

"Sorry, Miss. I do not."

"Well, I guess I am ready."

Shayla walked down the hallway, down the grand staircase, and entered the parlor. She took a glass of wassail and walked over to talk to Florence, a woman she met earlier in the day. She noticed that several other men had arrived, but there was less than thirty people at the party.

Adam watched Shayla as she entered the room. She was gorgeous dressed in a floral gown with dark purple trim. The bodice was fitted with a wide neckline and short puffy sleeves. A single gold chain encircled her neck. Her lustrous dark brown hair was curled and pulled up in front and piled on top of her head. Long curls cascaded down her back. He wanted to loosen those pins in her hair and see it tumble down her naked back.

Shayla smiled when she saw Adam watching her intently. Florence also noticed and excused herself. Adam, who had eyes only for Shayla, walked to her in a most predatory way which captivated Shayla.

When he reached her, he bowed, and kissed her hand. "You are exquisite, Miss Toselli."

"Thank you, Captain." Shayla appraised his attire. Tonight, he wore black trousers which made him look taller. He wore a white shirt under a brocade dinner jacket, a dark grey vest, and a white cravat. They sipped their drinks and continued to stare at one another.

"Shayla, the lamp is perfect," the Duchess whispered as she walked up to Shayla and Adam. "I know my husband will love it. I plan to give it to him tomorrow morning with another surprise I have for him." She blushed ever so lightly.

"The first game shall be charades," the Duchess announced a little louder as she addressed the crowd. She broke them into groups. Adam stood next to Shayla, and Amelia selected them for the same team.

They started with simple two syllable words and progressed to short phrases. Shayla was quite competitive, and she and Adam, who was also competitive, were very good at guessing the other person's words.

"Christmas Tree," Adam blurted out.

"Yes!" Shayla shouted.

They moved on to longer phrases, and eventually, they were the last pair. "Partridge in a pear tree," Shayla guessed.

"Yes!"

"We won," Shayla said excitedly.

"That we did."

A butler held up a small basket of prizes. Shayla reached in and pulled one out. "A swan."

Adam reached into the basket. "A swan," he laughed. "What are the odds?"

The second game was a scavenger hunt. Adam and Shayla paired up again. Each pair selected a slip of paper from a basket. On it was written five items. They had to find the items in the order listed and return them to the parlor. The first pair to find all the objects was the winner.

They looked over their list. "A spoon. The dining room," Adam said, and they set out for the dining room. He opened the buffet and pulled out a spoon. They rushed back to the parlor and placed it beside a card with their names.

"Second, Shakespeare's Sonnets," Shayla informed him.

"The library," they said together, and they ran out the door and down the hallway toward the library." They passed several couples as they ran. The Sonnets were up on a high shelf, and Adam drew over the ladder to get to the volume. They raced back to the parlor.

They next found a piece of twine and then an orange. The last item was mistletoe. This was harder to find. "I saw a clump on the way to the library," Shayla said as she pulled Adam down the hallway. They came to a sudden stop. Another pair had already found the mistletoe and were heading back to the parlor.

"We need to find more." They hurried from room to room. "There!" Shayla shouted. She pointed to a clump in one of the parlors.

Adam stretched up. "That is very high up. I do not think I can reach it."

Shayla pushed a table over and positioned it under the Mistletoe. "Put that footstool on top of the table," she directed Adam.

"You are not seriously climbing up on that."

"Oh, yes I am." She stepped up on a chair then up on the table. Very carefully, she stepped up onto the footstool. "Almost." She stretched a little higher. "Got it." Her sudden movement made the stool kick out, but she jumped to the table and then off it onto the floor. "We must hurry." She ran from the room. Adam caught up to her. "Oh no, it looks like Miss Scott and Sir Tamworth have their last item too." She picked up one side of her skirt and ran faster.

They passed the other pair and slid into the parlor. Shayla slapped down the mistletoe and turned to Adam. "We won!" She exclaimed and bounced up and down on her toes.

"You are very competitive," Adam remarked with a smile.

"Yes, I am."

"Well, it seems Miss Toselli and Captain Preston are once again the winners." Several of the girls glared at Shayla. "Your prize." Shayla's mouth dropped as the Duke and Duchess held the mistletoe over their heads. "And make it a good kiss."

Adam bowed. "Miss Toselli, I believe we must uphold tradition."

Shayla felt the heat rise up her neck to her face. She knew her cheeks were bright red, but she straightened up. "Yes, Captain, we must uphold tradition."

Adam grinned as he leaned forward and captured her lips. They were soft and warm, and he wished they were not standing in front of the all the guests. Shayla enjoyed the kiss, and she leaned closer. When Duke Wellshore started clapping and everyone joined in, Adam and Shayla stepped back.

"Well, now that everyone has worked up an appetite, let us adjourn to the dining room." The guests left the room and walked as a group down the hall to dinner.

"Shall we?" Adam held up his arm, and Shayla lightly placed her hand on it as they followed the others.

Adam shot Amelia an angry look because Amelia did not seat him and Shayla together. Baron Fitzgerald was seated to

Shayla's left and was engaging her in conversation much to Adam's annoyance. He glared down the table at his sister-in-law who smiled at Shayla. Obviously, Amelia was interested in giving Shayla options. He turned and engaged the woman next to him in conversation so as not to appear rude, but he kept glancing at Shayla. At one point their eyes met. He gave her a small nod, and she smiled.

The Baron escorted Shayla to the ballroom after dinner. Guests stood in groups talking while the three piece orchestra played soft music. No one would step onto the dance floor until Duke and Duchess Wellshore opened the dancing. Shayla stood next to several of the other ladies.

"There are so many gorgeous and capable men here tonight," Miss Claire Grey commented. She surveyed several of the men standing together talking. "Do you not agree?" she asked.

Shayla looked around. "I suppose."

"You and Captain Preston seem to be on very friendly terms."

"He currently is employed in my family's glass shop."

"Hum," Claire responded.

The Duke and Duchess Wellshore swept into the hall, and the musicians began to play a waltz. Duke Wellshore held his wife in his arms, and they smiled as they danced. They moved across the dance floor gracefully. Shayla thought they looked well matched. She had light hair to his dark hair. She was shorter than him but not overly so, and she seemed to fit perfectly into his arms. Shayla took a breath, what brought on those thoughts. She looked over and saw Adam watching her intently.

When the dance ended, he made his way to her side. Adam bowed to Shayla and extended his hand. "May I have this dance, Miss Toselli?"

Shayla nodded and placed her hand in his, and they took their places on the dance floor. The music started, and they began to dance. Because this was a small, somewhat informal party, there were no dance cards or strict rules, much to Shayla's relief. However, during the evening, Shayla danced with several other men that were present.

Sometime later, Shayla finally had time with Adam. "All this formality really is a bother," she said to him as they slowly strolled around the room. "That is why I rarely attend parties."

"I agree."

"You do?"

"Yes, I find the formality bothersome. I, however, must abide by the rules while living in my brother's home."

When they returned to the spot where they began, Adam bowed. He knew he could not monopolize Shayla's time or her dances, or they would be the talk of the party, more so than they already were having paired up in the games. "May I have the pleasure of the last dance, Miss Toselli?"

"Yes, Captain." She inclined her head, and Adam bowed again and left.

Shayla talked with several of the other girls at the party. She danced a few more times. Adam watched but chose to lean against a post most of the evening.

"Amelia would like you to dance with Miss Grey," Elliot said when he walked over to Adam.

"Of course." Adam walked over to the young woman and asked her to dance.

Shayla saw Adam dancing with Claire and her stomach tightened in a knot. He can dance with whomever he chooses, Shayla reminded herself. She told herself that it did not matter. Afterall, she was dancing with someone too, but she felt a pang of jealousy.

When the last dance was announced, Adam bowed, took Shayla's hand, and led her to the dance floor. The music began, and they danced another waltz. Shayla did not think she was a great dancer, but Adam was very good, and he led her around the floor with ease. As one, they turned and moved together. They smiled as they danced, and when the song ended, Adam bowed, and she curtsied. He offered her his arm. Light refreshments were served including hot chocolate which Shayla favored, and then guests began to depart.

Adam walked Shayla outside to her waiting carriage. "The evening went well, but no more pretending, Shayla." She looked at him and nodded her head. Afterall, the party was over, and they made it through the events together. At the carriage, Adam kissed her hand then helped her inside. "Good night, Miss Toselli."

"Good night, Captain."

He closed the door, and the coachman moved the carriage down the driveway. Shayla leaned back and rested her head on the carriage wall. What was she feeling? Did she have real feelings for Adam? She enjoyed his company. Well, she enjoyed it more when they worked together where they could relax and be themselves. She did not think she could live with so much formality every day. She sighed. The evening was much better than she thought it would be, but thankfully, it was over. She could not wait to get home, get undressed, and get into her warm comfortable bed.

## Chapter 12

Henry and Shayla were adding new merchandise to the shop windows when the bells over the door tinkled, and a young woman dressed in a dark blue coat with white trim and a matching bonnet walked in.

"Hello, Mr. Toselli." Sarah waved and gave a small curtsy.

"Hello, Miss Williams." Henry reached up and helped his daughter step down off the ladder.

"Hi, Sarah," Shayla said with obvious delight in her voice.

"Are you terribly busy today? Can you go to town and shop?" Sarah asked hopefully.

"I do not know, Sarah. Papa is working the shop alone today."

"Shayla," Henry put his hand on her shoulder, "go shopping with your friend. You need an afternoon off."

She looked at him. "You are working alone. Everyone is off today."

"Jimmy is out back if I need help, and Brian will be here soon. I will be fine. Go."

Shayla smiled and turned back to Sarah. "I will meet you at the tea shop."

"I can wait and bring you in the carriage."

"No. I will bicycle and meet you. I need to change my clothes."

Sarah nodded. "Good-bye, Mr. Toselli." She opened the door and left the shop.

"Thank you, Papa," Shayla stretched up and kissed his cheek.

"You deserve it. You have worked very hard."

"Duke Wellshore's commission is nearly finished. I will work on it tomorrow." She practically skipped as she went out back and changed into her bicycle suit which had a short overskirt. The outfit was new and was a little dressier than her normal attire. Shayla put on her coat and shoes and said goodbye to the boys who were busy cleaning up the workshop.

"I am off, Papa. I will be home for dinner." Henry took her hand and placed money in it. "Papa, I have money."

"I want you to buy yourself something nice. If it is not enough, tell the shop keeper I will be in to pay the rest."

"You spoil me." She kissed his cheek.

"You are my child. Of course, I do. Now, go. Have fun with your friend. You need to spend more time with your friends."

"My friends are all getting married and having children."

"You are of the age."

"I plan to stay with you, Papa." She put her hat on and went outside. She moved her bicycle away from the wall, hopped up on it, and took off down the street. Henry stood in the doorway and watched her until she was out of sight.

Shayla pulled up in front of the tea shop, secured her bicycle, and then went inside. The shop was crowded. Finally, she saw Sarah and made her way through the tables of people having tea and cakes to where Sarah sat. The tea shop was warm and fragrant and smelled of sugar and spices. Small doily covered tables were scattered throughout the room and each had a pretty China tea set in the middle. Sarah sat at the table covered in a pink cloth with a delicate white lace doily on top of it and a tea set decorated with tiny pink roses. The walls of the tea shop were lined with many shelves which held tea sets, silver sets, and tins full of teas from all over the world. A generous fire blazed in the hearth.

A young woman walked over when Shayla sat down to take their order. She smiled at the two friends. "What would you like today ladies?"

"Should we order petit fours?" Sarah asked softly. Shayla nodded her head eagerly. They were her favorite cakes, pretty and sweet. The waitress nodded and left.

Shayla and Sarah immediately began to talk at the same time. It had been a while since they had time to talk for more than a few minutes after church or when they saw each other in town, and they had much to discuss.

Shayla thought it was nice to have tea with a friend. She had not taken the time lately to be with her friends. The weeks leading up to Christmastide were very busy in the shop.

"I saw Captain Preston in town earlier this week. My he looks fit and strong," Sarah commented as she batted her eyes.

"You saw Adam?" Shayla felt another pang of jealousy. Why did she feel jealous? It was not like they were courting, but she did not like that Sarah noticed that Adam was handsome and strong.

Sarah looked at her friend. "You call him by his given name?"

"Of course," Shayla snorted. "He is working in the shop. There is no place for formality in there."

"Still, he is Duke Wellshore's brother."

"Aye, and he is also learning the craft. Our shop is informal. So, what are you shopping for today?" Shayla asked changing the subject.

Sarah frowned. She did not think Shayla fully appreciated the opportunity she had to get to know Captain Preston. Every woman in town noticed him, and yet Shayla, who saw him regularly, did not appear to be interested in him at all. But then she knew Shayla was not interested in a husband. They grew up together, and Sarah knew that sometimes there was no changing Shayla's mind, so she sipped her tea, and changed the subject. "I want a new dress for the Christmas tree lighting festival and dance," Sarah said excitedly.

"Oh yes. The festival is coming up," Shayla remarked casually. She took a bite of a chocolate frosted petit four with tiny blue flowers on top and savored the rich flavor.

"I was hoping Joseph would ask me to favor him with a dance, but he has not." Sarah took a nibble of one of the little cakes.

"I thought his family was going to London to visit his mother's family."

"I heard they are going in the new year instead."

The two girls talked as they drank tea and ate the tiny cakes. By coincidence, Mrs. Grant, Joseph's mother, and her sister came into the shop and looked around. Sarah watched them for a few moments. "Should I go talk to her?" Sarah whispered to Shayla. She inclined her head toward the two women as they looked at tins of tea on the shelf near the front of the store."

Shayla shrugged her shoulders.

Sarah made her decision, stood up, and walked over to the women. Shayla watched from her seat and drank her tea. The shop was small, and she could see and hear Sarah. "Mrs. Grant. How lovely to see you," Sarah said in her sweetest voice. Apparently, Mrs. Grant approved of Sarah because she smiled warmly at her. All that formality gave Shalya a headache. She took a bite of another cake when just then who should walk in but Joseph. His eyes actually sparkled when he saw Sarah. He bent low and kissed her hand while his mother and aunt looked on and smiled, and Sarah blushed and looked flustered. Shayla watched with a mixture of annoyance and envy as Sarah laid on the charm, and Joseph seemed to hang on her every word. She straightened up when they walked over to the table.

"Miss Toselli, a pleasure to see you." Joseph bowed.

"And you, Mr. Grant." Shayla resisted the temptation to roll her eyes. She held out her hand, he grasped it, and gave it a peck.

"Mr. Grant is shopping with his mother and aunt," Sarah informed Shayla who thought that was obvious. "But he can sit a minute; is that right, Mr. Grant?"

"I am honored to sit with such beautiful ladies." He smiled and held the chair for Sarah. He then reached over for a chair from another table and sat down. The conversation immediately turned to the upcoming festival and dance.

"Miss Williams, I would be honored if you would favor me with a dance at the tree lighting festivities." Joseph smiled at her.

"I am honored to save you a dance, Mr. Grant," Sarah replied in a high girlish voice.

Shayla did roll her eyes this time. The two of them had known each other since they were children in school. They saw each other in town and in church regularly, yet here they sat being formal with one another like they just met. The charade annoyed her, and she grumbled and drank her tea straight down.

Joseph took Sarah's hand, and then as if remembering they were not alone, he looked at Shayla. "Miss Toselli, will you be attending the festival?"

"I have not decided yet," Shayla replied with a fake smile. Joseph looked at her, and she could see his mind turning. He was going to try and fix her up with one of his friends. "Advent is a very busy time in the shop," she added quickly. "I am completing a commission for Duke Wellshore, and I am certain other orders will be placed."

"You cannot get away for one evening? Do you not have people who work in the shop?" Sarah asked.

"We do, but we all help out at this time of year."

"Surely, your father will not require you to be in the shop during the festival," Joseph added.

"Of course, he will not demand I be in the shop, but we often have customers come in asking for custom designs, and I like to talk to my customers directly."

"Shayla, you must go to the festival. The tree is going to be lit with electric lights for the first time," Sarah pleaded.

"I will see it either way."

Sarah and Joseph looked at her. Neither understood her attitude, but then this was Shayla. She was not very sociable sometimes. Joseph stood up still holding Sarah's hand. He bowed and kissed her fingers then turned and took Shayla's hand and kissed it too. "It was a pleasure talking with you, ladies, but I see my mother and aunt are ready to continue shopping."

The girls smiled and nodded.

"May I call on you tomorrow, Miss Williams."

Sarah blushed and giggled. "I look forward to it, Mr. Grant." Joseph bowed again and left the shop.

Sarah let out a huge sigh. "I am so excited. You know, Joseph is working with his father at the bank now that he has returned from university."

"That is good." Shayla picked up the last petit four and ate it knowing Sarah would not be eating much of anything until the festival. Her thoughts turned to Adam. Since the Duke was presiding over the Christmas tree lighting, surely Adam would attend. It would be nice to watch the tree light up with Adam, she admitted to herself. What are you saying? she heard a voice in her head scream. She closed out the voice, and she wondered if Adam would want to dance with her if she did attend. Or maybe he would escort someone else. Shayla felt sick to her stomach at the thought of Adam with another woman.

The girls put on their coats, and Shayla was still lost in her thoughts of Adam and the festival when they left the shop and walked up the street. They entered a dress shop, and Sarah tried on a few dresses, but Shayla did not try anything on. In the next shop, she looked at a pretty silk scarf but decided against it.

A half hour later, Sarah had several packages, and Shayla only had a small bag of candy. "You have not seen anything you like as of yet?" Sarah asked in an exasperated tone.

Shayla shook her head. "Not yet." They entered the shop that still displayed the lavender gown in the window. She liked the merchandise in that shop, and Shayla tried on a dark navy skirt and a floral silk blouse with long sleeves and a scoop neckline. She stood in front of the cheval glass and looked at her reflection.

"That is a good color for you," Sarah commented as she turned to look at herself in the glass. She glanced over at Shayla. "The skirt is not very full though."

"I prefer the newer more streamlined style, but I am not sure I need this outfit."

Sarah laughed. "Shopping is not about necessity. It is about getting something pretty."

Shayla could not help but laugh at that. "This is pretty, and Papa said I should get something."

"I like it, but it is not dance worthy," Sarah replied.

Shayla moved back and forth as she looked at her reflection. "I have a birthday next week. I could wear it then, and it is fine for the tree lighting festival."

Sarah shook her head. "It is not sexy enough for a dance. You need something that shows off your figure and bosom."

"Sarah!" Shayla laughed.

"Well, why not? You are thin and have a good figure. You eat everything, and I wish I could eat as much as you and still be thin."

They made their purchases and were laughing and talking when they exited the shop, turned the corner, and saw Adam and another man. The two men crossed the street and walked toward Shayla and Sarah. Shayla felt her heart beating faster as she watched Adam walking toward her.

"Miss Toselli, Miss Williams," Adam said with a low bow. Shayla sighed. Of course, he would be very formal.

She almost retorted and called him Adam, but she decided to play along. "Captain Preston. So nice to see you." She and Sarah curtsied.

Adam smiled. He recognized Shayla's sarcasm. "Miss Toselli, and Miss Williams, may I present Captain Shawn Atkinson."

Captain Atkinson bowed low. "Ladies, it is indeed a pleasure to meet you both." They responded by curtsying to him. Sarah giggled softly, and Adam chuckled to himself when he heard Shayla's sigh of annoyance. He knew she preferred informality, but a little formality was fun and besides necessary and expected on a public street.

"Shopping this fine afternoon?" Adam inquired with a nod to the packages they carried.

"Oh yes," Sarah replied eagerly in a high pitched excited voice. "Christmastide is approaching. Will you be attending the town's Christmas tree lighting festival this year, Captains?"

"Regrettably, I must return to London before then," Captain Atkinson replied.

"And you Captain Preston? The whole town is very excited. Duke Wellshore said the tree will be lit with electric lights this year instead of candles," Sarah sounded excited.

Adam smiled at Shayla. "Will you be attending the festival, Miss Toselli?"

"I have not yet decided," she replied quickly. Adam fixed Shayla with a stare. He wanted to ask her to save him a dance, but they had just pretended to be interested in one another at his sister-in-law's charity party. She might think this was a continuation of the pact they made. He knew he should tell Shayla how he felt about her. He hoped she felt the same way about him. They got along superbly. They talked while they worked and at lunch. They sometimes took walks, and when they danced, he felt that Shayla enjoyed his company and being held in his arms. But he also saw the turmoil in her eyes. Either she did not know how she felt about him, or she was conflicted in her feelings. He laughed to himself. He was sure it was part attraction and part annoyance.

Shayla was the first to break eye contact. "Well, we should continue our shopping, gentlemen."

Captain Atkinson bowed again. "Lovely to make your acquaintance, Miss Toselli, Miss Williams."

Adam bowed. "Ladies, enjoy this glorious afternoon." He looked at Shayla then picked up her hand and kissed it. "Miss Toselli, a great pleasure to see you as always." Shayla stood staring at him. She was at a loss for words. He smiled at her lack of response and released her hand.

"Good day ladies," he tipped his hat as he and Shawn walked toward the pub. Shayla stood glued to the spot and watched them walk away. Her hand remained held up in front of her. She still felt the touch of Adam's lips on her fingers. It sent tingles up her spine. Her eyes were slightly dazed, but then they hardened over. What was his game? she thought to herself. There was no reason to keep up the charade of last weekend's activities.

"Oh, he is dreamy," Sarah cooed breaking into Shayla's thoughts. "Tall, muscular, handsome. He fancies you."

"No, he does not," Shayla replied back quickly.

"I saw the look he gave you. And he asked if you are going to the Christmas tree lighting festival. Shayla, you have to attend."

Shayla shook her head. She was confused. Adam had said, no more pretending, so what was he doing? They talked in the shop on Monday and decided that their plan worked brilliantly over the previous weekend, but it was over now. Well, if that was not pretending, what was it? Deep down, Shayla knew she was not entirely pretending at the party. She cared for Adam. Too much. She never met a man she even considered marrying. She did not want to marry. Yet she could not deny that she thought about what life would be like with Adam many times over the past weeks. He would have family business to tend to, but sometimes they would work side by side in the shop. At night, they would sit by the fire and talk. For a second, she saw a small child sitting on the floor playing with blocks. She shuddered. Why was she having these thoughts?

"And Captain Atkinson is really good looking too," Sarah said.

"I guess so."

"You did not notice?" Sarah smiled. She knew then that Shayla liked Adam because Captain Atkinson was quite handsome.

"Come on," Shayla said firmly. "I want to stop in the candle shop."

The two young women wiled the afternoon away shopping. They talked and went to several shops where they tried on clothes, they tried on shoes, and they tried on accessories. Shayla pushed thoughts of Adam from her mind and started to enjoy the shopping trip. They had multiple shopping bags on both their arms when they walked back to the tea shop late in the afternoon.

"That was fun, but I am exhausted," Sarah said as she leaned against a lamp post. The sun was setting, and the lamplighter was making his way toward them. Sarah's carriage pulled up, and the coachman got down and took Sarah's bags from her. "I can take you home, Shayla. Mr. Morgan can tie your bike to the back of the carriage."

Shayla stared at the carriage. Her mouth went dry. She rode in carriages when it was necessary, but this was not necessary. She could still get home before deep darkness fell. "I will ride my bike. You go home, Sarah."

"Are you certain? Shayla it is getting dark," Sarah pleaded.

Shayla nodded her head. "Yes. I will be fine." She unhitched her bike and draped her bags over both sides of the handlebars.

Sarah frowned. She knew Shayla avoided carriage rides, so she did not push her friend to get in the carriage, but she worried about her. Sarah stepped up into the carriage and waved as the driver pulled away from the curb.

As Shayla adjusted her parcels and stepped up onto the pedal of the bike, she heard her name. She stepped down and turned in the direction of the sound. Adam and Captain Atkinson were striding purposely toward her. She sighed.

Adam walked up to Shayla and put his hand on the bicycle's handlebars. "Why did you not get in the carriage. It is nearly dark."

"Yes, and I need to get home." Shayla started to get on the bike again, but Adam stopped her.

"No. Shayla, I will call for a carriage and take you home. Let me carry something for you. You know you really should not be out all by yourself. Your father should get you a maid. And why are you not using a carriage of your own?"

That did it. Shayla stiffened. Anger flared in her eyes. "Why do I need a maid? Or a coachman? I am not helpless." She glared at him. "I am a grown woman, and I am perfectly capable of getting myself home, thank you, Captain Preston."

"Shayla," Adam pleaded. He did not mean to offend her. He was just worried about her safety. Canterbury Corner was a relatively safe town, but there had been increased crime in recent weeks. "Please, Shayla. I worry about you," he said quietly but firmly, and he did not let go of the handlebars. "You do not want a maid fine, but it is late, and you should not be riding your bicycle alone."

She narrowed her eyes and put her hands on her hips. "I will have you know that I am nearly three and twenty and well over the age of majority. I am also a businesswoman, and even in your social class, a working woman is allowed some freedoms. I do not need a maid to chaperone my activities." She swatted his hands away which took Adam completely by surprise. Before he could stop her from leaving, she hopped up on the bicycle, and peddled away. The two men looked dumbfounded at her retreating back.

"Feisty little thing," Shawn said as they watched her go down the street and then turn toward her home.

Adam let out a sigh. There was nothing he could do now. "She is feisty," Adam replied. His voice was tinged with annoyance. He narrowed his eyes, "I think there was more to her not getting in the carriage than just independence and determination to get herself home."

Shawn nodded. "I am certain you will discover the reason." Adam looked at Shawn who shrugged. "You like to fix things."

"I do not need to fix her," Adam replied. "She is perfect just as she is."

"Perfect, you say?" Shawn raised an eyebrow. He knew Adam for many years, first at the university and then in the military, and he never once heard him refer to anyone as perfect.

Adam nodded his head. Shayla was perfect, but she was also afraid of something. He shook his head. "That woman works with molten glass in a hot furnace, yet she looked terrified to get in the carriage. She does not want help, not here, not in the glass shop, not at home, but there is more than independence going on here."

"Well, since the damsel does not require or want our help, shall we take ourselves back to your honorable brother's estate?" Shawn asked.

Adam let out a sigh. "Yes, we better get back. Did Amelia say who was coming to dinner tonight?"

Shawn shook his head. "I have lost track. She keeps parading women in front of us. I did not know there were so many eligible women in this town. Maybe you should choose one and get married? It will make your sister-in-law happy."

Adam barked out a laugh. "Maybe you should choose one?" he suggested, and Shawn shuddered.

## Chapter 13

On Saturday midday, Adam stopped at the factory.

"Adam, are you here to work today?" Hal bellowed from down the line of workers.

"No, I am helping my brother with arrangements for the town's Christmas tree lighting festival, but I wanted to pick up the gift I made for Shayla."

"I have it here." Hal walked over to the office in the production area and brought out a small box. "When it came out of the oven, I put it in a box just in case Shayla came in the office. I did not want her to see it and ask questions."

"Is she here today?" Adam kept his voice as casual as possible.

"She is in her workshop."

Adam hesitated, but he needed some answers, and Hal was the best way to get those answers. "I saw Shayla shopping in the town center with Miss Williams yesterday afternoon."

Hal smiled. "Good for her. The girl works too hard." His niece spent far too much time working. She was young and needed to get out of the shop and have fun like other young women her age.

"Do not let her hear that," Adam grimaced as he looked around in case Shayla was nearby. "She does not like to be told what to do."

"That is very true," Hal roared. "Do not worry, she will not come in here. She is finishing the ornaments for your brother's commission. She has quite outdone herself. By the way, we will need your help boxing the ornaments on Monday morning."

Adam nodded. "I need a beer. Join me for a pint and lunch in the pub?" He knew the way to get Hal to talk was to fill him with good food and drink.

"Aye, I could use a pint." Hal walked to the rack and picked his jacket off a hook. "Jimmy, I am going to the pub for lunch," he called down the row, and Jimmy waved acknowledgement.

The two men went outside and got into Adam's waiting carriage. Hal settled himself on the plush seat for the short ride to the town center. The pub was crowded since it was Saturday afternoon and so close to Christmastide. People were bustling from shop to shop, and carolers walked up and down the street. Large evergreen wreaths decorated with holly and ribbon hung from the light poles.

They walked in the front door of the pub and took seats at a table near the window. This was an old pub. The wooden floors were uneven, and the walls were lined with paintings of Canterbury Corner's buildings, the sea, and London. Fires blazed in the two hearths in the room, and a man seated off to one side played a fiddle.

The barmaid, dressed in a white shirt with large puffy sleeves and a multi-colored and multi-layered skirt, sauntered up to the table. She recognized Hal and Adam, and she smiled at Adam then bobbed in a part curtsy. "Captain, Hal, what is your pleasure this fine day?" she purred.

"The house stew?" Adam asked Hal.

"Aye."

"Two pints of ale and two bowls of stew, please."

"Right away." The barmaid did another bob and went to the bar. She returned quickly with the pints.

"Thank you, love," Hal said with a smile. He was a frequent visitor to the pub. She smiled at him and went to the kitchen.

She returned and placed bowls of stew in front of them and placed a plate of bread in the middle of the table. "Eat hearty."

"Thank you," Adam said, and she bobbed yet again before leaving them.

They started to eat. "The stew here is quite good." Adam took another spoonful.

"Aye." Hal reached for a slice of bread and dropped it in his bowl. "You say you saw Shayla yesterday." He had a feeling that Adam wanted to discuss something with him.

"I did. She and Miss Williams were out shopping, and they seemed to be enjoying themselves." Adam took another spoonful of stew. "It was late and getting dark when they finished shopping. Shayla would not let Miss Williams' coachman take her home or allow me to take her home. Hal, maybe it is not my place, but she bicycles by herself when she should be taking a carriage."

Hal took a swig of beer. "I wondered when you would notice. Shayla does not ride in carriages often."

"She came to the estate last weekend in a carriage."

"Aye, she will ride in one when she has no other choice."

"Why?'

Hal drank down his beer. "Shayla's mother, Corrine, was killed in a carriage accident six years ago."

"Yes, I heard about the accident," Adam informed him.

"The story is Corrine went to London to visit with her great aunt who was ill. Shayla was to go with Corrine, but at the last minute, a large commission came in, and Shayla stayed home and worked with me and Henry instead. Margaret and James were in London at the time, so Margaret and Corrine helped care for the aunt. Corrine stayed a few days longer than Margaret, and she hired a driver and carriage to take her back to London to get the train home. On the way, another carriage barreled into the one that she rode in."

Adam stared wide eyed at Hal. He knew Shayla's mother was killed in a carriage accident, but this was not merely an accident. "Why did the driver of the other carriage hit them?" Adam asked.

"The bloke had kidnapped a young woman and planned to hold her for ransom. He botched the job and was fleeing police when he crashed. The young woman in his carriage, Corrine, and her driver were all killed. He was gravely injured, and when he recovered, he was prosecuted, and hanged for murder."

Adam nodded. People were being held accountable for recklessness and accidents. This was essentially homicide. "At least all of you had justice for your loss."

Henry looked at Adam. It was hard for him to talk about it as well, but he wanted Adam to know, so he could understand Shayla better. "Margaret was hysterical after Corrine's death, and she was so upset, she was sick for months. Shayla was distraught, but she kept too much bottled up inside her. Henry does not like to talk about Corrine's death. We did have a bit of justice when Shayla, Henry, and I attended the hanging in London."

Adam stopped the pint halfway to his mouth. He set in on the table. "Shayla attended the hanging in London?"

"Aye."

Adam shook his head. "A hanging is not something for a young lady to see."

"Well, no one would have stopped her from going. She and Henry went to the trial too, and she was determined to see the murderer hang."

"But Hal," Adam began and stopped. He did not know what to say. He felt sorry for Shayla, for the whole family.

They finished their stew in silence. "Another pint, Hal?" He nodded, and Adam waved to the barmaid and held up two fingers. She nodded then brought fresh pints to their table.

"To this day, Shayla is uncomfortable riding in carriages," Hal explained.

"Thank you for telling me. It explains Shayla's reluctance to get in a carriage."

Hal took a long drink. "Shayla feels guilty because she did not want to go to London with her mother."

"But she likely would have been killed too."

"That does not rid her of guilt."

Adam knew the guilt soldiers sometimes felt after a battle when they lived, and others died. He supposed it was the same regardless of the situation. The survivor wondered why he lived, and another did not? Shayla should have been with her mother, but she did not go, and so she lived, but her mother died. "I understand her more now. Thank you, Hal."

"You needed to know, Adam." He took a long drink from his pint and nearly emptied it. "Shayla enjoys your company."

"Not enough to allow me to assist her yesterday."

"Aye, she is a stubborn and capable woman. That is why she rides her bicycle. She likes the independence." He finished his drink. "Shayla needs a strong man who will give her freedom but will also stand by her. I see how she looks at you, Adam. She enjoys eating her lunch with you."

"I enjoy her company as well, but why do you say that?"

Hal laughed. "Well, for one thing, she sits and eats like a young lady. She used to draw while she ate quickly, so she could get back to work. I have never seen her sit, place a napkin in her lap, and eat slowly at lunch before. Do not misunderstand me. Shayla is well mannered, but at the shop, she is focused on one thing: work."

Adam smiled. "She is a remarkable woman, Hal. I have never met anyone like her."

"She is one of a kind."

Adam took a drink, set his mug down, and took a deep breath. He needed Hal's advice. "I think you know I am interested in courting her."

"I do."

"I do not want to scare her away."

"Henry likes you, and he has told Shayla that he approves of you. She greatly values her father's opinion."

"As she should."

"You must be cautious and take it slow. Show her that you are interested in her and that you value her. She needs to know that you will not stop her from working in the shop or try to possess her. She is afraid that she will lose herself in a marriage."

"I love her as she is, Hal. I do not want to change her."

"That is what you need to prove to her."

## Chapter 14

Shayla woke up, dressed, and then went downstairs to breakfast.

"Happy birthday, Shayla." Henry kissed his daughter. "Three and twenty today, and I remember when you were born like it was yesterday."

"Thank you, Papa."

"Happy birthday," Hal called as he walked in the kitchen. He kissed his niece. "You are more beautiful with every passing year."

"Happy birthday, Shayla," Mrs. Lawry hugged Shayla.

"Thank you all."

"We will have a big celebration tonight, but for now, I made your favorite, hot cakes, for breakfast, Shayla." Mrs. Lawry put hotcakes on a plate and set it before her.

"With strawberry jam?"

Mrs. Lawry nodded and set a jar of strawberry jam on the table.

"Oh, yummy. Thank you." Shayla beamed at her family.

Henry and Hal sat down at the table and filled their plates. Henry watched his daughter sip her tea. She was as beautiful and talented as her mother. Henry wished Corrine were alive to see the woman their daughter had become. Shayla was accomplished and independent, and she deserved to have a special bond with a man just as he had with Corrine. Someone who would love her, support her, and stand by her side through the good and the bad times.

"Papa, are you ok?" Shayla set her teacup down.

Henry smiled. "Yes." He reached over and covered her hand with his. "I want this to be a special day."

Hal knew what was on Henry's mind. Shayla was the child he never had, and he too wanted her to be happy.

After breakfast, the three of them left the house. Shayla hooked one arm with Henry and one with Hal, and the three of them walked to the glass shop. She knew she was lucky to have her father and her uncle. They were special men. Shayla felt light and happy as they walked in the brisk morning air. On the way, they passed a few neighbors who wished them a good day. It was a bright and sunny day for December which reflected Shayla's mood.

They went into the shop, and Shayla opened the curtains to the front windows. Henry turned the sign around to read welcome, and Hal went out back to check on the furnaces.

"Happy birthday, Shayla," Jimmy said when she went in back to get ready for the day. He handed her a wrapped present.

"Thank you, Jimmy." She opened it. "Oh, Jimmy, it is beautiful. Thank you." She held up a glass mug decorated with pink and white flowers. "I will have my tea in it this morning."

"You are welcome." Jimmy looked up and saw Adam coming down the hallway carrying flowers, so he left the room.

"Happy birthday, Shayla." Adam handed her a tussie-mussie of ivy and white roses.

She looked at him. She knew ivy meant fidelity and white roses meant you are heavenly. "Adam. Thank you." She smiled and her cheeks filled with color. She held the flowers near her heart. "They are beautiful."

Adam smiled at her acceptance of his flowers. Shayla smiled, held them under her nose, and took a deep breath. "They smell heavenly."

They looked into each other's eyes, and finally, Adam took her hand. He continued to hold her gaze as he lingered over her hand breathing in the clean, fresh scent that surrounded her. He felt her pulse quicken, and he kissed her fingers. He longed to hold her in his arms and taste her lips. They would be soft and sweet. He looked back up into her eyes and saw surprise and desire. In time, he thought to himself, but he did not want to wait long.

"I will get everything ready for you." Adam kissed her hand again and went to the furnace room.

Shayla watched him and then took one of her own vases off a shelf and put the flowers in water. She bent down and smelled them again. They were lovely.

The morning went by quickly. Shayla did a careful last inspection of each ornament for Duke Wellshore's commission. Each ornament had a gold hanging ribbon and was nestled inside a black velvet lined gold, silver, or red decorative gift box. Shayla and Adam carefully placed the gift boxes into several crates, and Jimmy and another boy stacked the crates in the front shop.

When they finished, Shayla went into the office and changed into the skirt and blouse she bought on her shopping trip with Sarah. She combed out her hair and checked her appearance in the small cheval glass that hung on the office wall. She walked out into the preparation room and stopped to smell the flowers from Adam.

"You look beautiful."

Shayla turned and saw Adam leaning against the door frame. His arms were crossed, his shirt was open at the collar. His sleeves were rolled up revealing strong forearms. Shayla longed to be held in his arms. Her heart fluttered every time she saw Adam which both excited and scared her. She knew she was falling in love with him. She sighed. Correction. She had already fallen in love with him. "Thank you," she replied sweetly.

When the Duke of Wellshore arrived a short time later, Shayla, Henry, and Hal met him in the shop. Jimmy had several boys carry the crates out to the waiting wagon. Shayla handed him a box. "To commemorate your first Christmas as our Duke and Duchess, Your Grace." She curtsied.

"Thank you." Elliot looked at the box. "May I."

"Of course, Your Grace."

Adam came into the front shop, leaned against the counter, and watched as Elliot took the lid off the box. He smiled at his brother's astonished look. Elliot held up a large iridescent white globe inscribed with the year and Duke and Duchess of Wellshore in gold. A pair of delicate white doves adorned the top and very thin gold and white ribbons twined around the entire globe.

"Miss Toselli, you truly are a master craftswoman. I have no words to describe my admiration for your talent. Thank you."

Shayla bowed her head. "You are most welcome, Your Grace."

Elliot replaced the ornament in its thick velvet cushion inside the box and put on the lid. He took three envelopes out of his breast pocket. "Your invitations." He handed the envelopes to Henry. "My wife and I look forward to hosting you at our Christmastide Ball on Christmas Eve."

Involuntarily, Shayla looked at Adam. He smiled back at her. She smiled and took a deep breath. She was going to the ball, and Adam would be there.

A light snow began to fall when Adam walked home with Shayla, Henry, and Hal. Shayla carried the flowers he gave her. She smiled at him as they walked. Henry opened the front door and a delicious smell wafted through to them. "Mrs. Lawry has been hard at work," Henry remarked.

"Welcome home." Mrs. Lawry bustled over to help with their coats when they came inside. "Dinner will be ready shortly." She looked at the flowers Shayla held and smiled then hurried back to the kitchen.

There was a knock at the door, and Aunt Margaret and Uncle James walked in. "Happy Birthday, Shayla." Aunt Margaret hugged her. "Oh, I remember when I first held you when you were born." She dabbed at her eyes with her handkerchief. She thought of her dear sister. She missed her sister terribly and wished Corrine could celebrate with them. She wiped more tears from her eyes. It seemed everything made her weep lately.

"Let us have a drink in the parlor," Henry announced breaking the silence. He poured six glasses of brady. "To my beautiful daughter on her birthday. Three and twenty years ago, your mother and I welcomed you to this world. She would be so proud of the woman you are today." Henry paused and smiled at his daughter. "On this day, we celebrate your birth and wish you good health and long life. To Shayla."

"Shayla," they repeated.

"Thank you," Shayla said in reply, and they sipped their brandy. They all took seats.

Aunt Margaret once again indicated that Shayla should sit on the settee. She smiled sweetly at her niece and held out a gift. "From Uncle James and me." She twined her arm in her husband's and watched as Shayla opened the box.

"Oh, thank you." Inside was a pair of pearl hair combs. "They are lovely. Thank you so much." She stood up and gave them each a hug and kiss and sat back down on the settee.

Adam sat down next to Shayla and handed her a beautiful gold box with a gold and white ribbon bow. "Happy Birthday, Shayla."

"Adam, you gave me those beautiful flowers this morning."

"I made this for you."

Shayla smiled and looked at the box. It was decorated with two swans with their necks entwined. She lifted the lid and inside was a piece of cranberry red pressed glass. Red was a difficult and expensive color to make. A rose was pressed into the glass and highlighted with gold accents. It hung from a gold ribbon.

"Oh, Adam. Thank you. It is beautiful." She held up the ornament, and the light in the room highlighted the design. "Truly. It is beautiful. I will treasure it, forever." She smiled at him.

"Hal helped me mix the color, but the thought was all mine."

"It is lovely." Shayla leaned over and gave Adam a delicate peck on the cheek. They looked in each other's eyes. He took her hand and kissed it. Shayla took a steading breath. She stood up. "I will hang it on our Christmas tree, and after the holiday, I will hang it in my bedroom window." She walked over to the tree, reached up, and placed the ornament in a prominent spot on the front of the tree near the top.

Adam walked to her side. "Did you make all of these ornaments?" he asked as he looked at the array of glass ornaments that hung from the tree's branches.

"Almost all." She pointed to a Santa Claus figure. "This is a German made ornament that I purchased at one of the Christmas Village booths last year."

Adam looked into her eyes. "I believe, I prefer your ornaments."

"Thank you." They walked back to the settee and sat down.

"Now, your Uncle Hal and I have a gift for you." Henry went to a cabinet and took out a box. He handed it to Shayla.

"Thank you." She carefully opened it. Inside was a pearl and gold necklace and earring set.

"Oh," she gasped. "They are gorgeous." Aunt Margaret smiled at the gift and stood to help her niece put the necklace and earrings on. Shayla looked in the oval glass that hung over the buffet. "They are breath taking. Thank you both so much." She hugged and kissed them.

Shayla smiled at her family. She realized that she thought of Adam as family. "You are all so good to me. Thank you." Shayla wiped the happy tears from her eyes.

"Dinner is ready," Mrs. Lawry announced. "I made broiled halibut, your favorite, Shayla."

"Come we will feast." Henry put his arm around Shayla's shoulders and led the way into the dining room.

Much later, after the others left, Adam's carriage arrived to take him back to Wellshore Manor. Shayla walked him to the door.

He wrapped his scarf around his neck. "Miss Shayla, would you save me a dance at the Christmas tree lighting on Saturday?"

Shayla knew she should say no. She was attracted to Adam, but she was not certain she wanted a man in her life. "I would be honored to save you a dance, Adam," she replied.

"Good night, Shayla." He took her hand and examined it. Her hands were strong but delicate. He saw a few small nicks from the glass she worked with, and he kissed them. Still holding her hand, he looked into her eyes.

"Good night, Adam," she breathed.

He kissed her hand again then released her and put on his gloves. He smiled and went down the walk to the waiting carriage. Shayla raised a hand and waved. Adam tipped his hat to her, and the carriage pulled away.

Shayla closed the door and sighed. What was she doing? Falling in love was not part of her plan. She thought she was a modern woman. A businesswoman. But she also was realizing she was a woman. A woman who was attracted to a very handsome and engaging man. She walked upstairs to her bedroom. She breathed in the scent of the roses Adam gave her and began undressing. She had not planned to be attracted to Adam, but she was, and it was Christmastide, and she was happy. What was the harm in enjoying the company of a very handsome man, she thought as she got into bed and drifted off to sleep.

Chapter 15

Now that the Duke's ornament commission was completed, and the special orders they had thus far were also completed, Shayla had time to work on her own projects. She took her drawing paper and sat at the table while she ate a sandwich.

Henry came in and took a sandwich from the ice box. "What are you drawing, Shayla."

"I have an idea for a vase." She had one leg under her as she leaned over the paper.

"What is the inspiration?" Henry looked at the sweeping lines. There almost seemed to be two nondescript figures that emerged from the bottom and twisted and turned together reaching toward the top of the vase which flared out and seemed to turn back on itself.

"I am unsure. Just something in my mind."

"Is something wrong?"

"No," she replied with a shake of her head. She took a bite of her sandwich.

Henry ate his sandwich and watched her. She concentrated on her sketch, and she bit her lower lip as she drew. Without looking at what she was doing, she took another bite of her sandwich. "We have been having more formal lunches of late," Henry said.

"This is better. Like it used to be. We are too formal when Adam is around." She took a long drink of cider.

"Not having a cup of tea today?"

Shayla shook her head.

"Adam is not formal with us, so you need not be formal with him. Just be yourself."

She stopped what she was doing and looked up. "I feel like I have to be formal with him."

"Why ever would you feel that way?"

She took a deep breath. "He is used to fine manners, and the women he knows are all proper and sophisticated. He expects women to be that way."

"You do not know what he expects."

"Well, the women he knows are like that, so he likely expects a woman to behave in a certain manner."

Henry looked at his daughter. "Shayla, I love you, and you are proper and sophisticated too. You are a fine young woman, and Adam is not a stuffy and pretentious man. He is a military man. He knows what it means to be loyal, and he knows how to work hard. I am certain he sees through the façade many women project with him. Not all men want a woman who molds herself and pretends to be something is she not. You are kind, genuine, and hardworking, and I believe Adam appreciates those qualities."

Shayla looked at her father. This was the most open he had ever been with her. She knew he loved her, but to hear him say he thought she was sophisticated surprised her. "Thank you, Papa." She sat down on the chair and took a deep breath.

Henry smiled at his daughter. Her mother should be the one talking to her, but Corrine was gone, and Henry needed Shayla to understand her special qualities. "A marriage should be a partnership. Your mother and I were partners, and we worked through the hard times and enjoyed the good times, and together we made you."

Shayla took another steadying breath. She missed her mother who would know just what to say and do. She knew her father did his best, and she appreciated his efforts, but it was not like talking to her mother. She smiled at him. She loved her father, and they had a very special bond. "I know you both love me, and I miss Mama too."

"You need a man who has ambition, Shayla. Someone who will do things for you rather than you having to do everything for him."

"Someone like you, Papa."

"I did my best to be a good husband."

"And I want a relationship with a man like you and Mama had."

"As you should. Marriage should be a partnership." He reached over and placed his hand over hers. "Adam has broad shoulders, and he has already shown that he can work alongside you and not overshadow you."

Shayla nodded. What her father said was true. Adam was a good man. He never expected her to be someone she was not. He accepted her for who she was, and he seemed to like her as she was even when she was bossy, but she was still frightened of her feelings for him.

Henry finished his sandwich. "Have you considered that perhaps you simply like being formal with Adam."

She shrugged, finished the remainder of the sandwich, drank down her cider, and picked up her sketches. "I do not know. Maybe I do. See you later, Papa." She put on her gloves and went back into the furnace room.

Henry watched her and wondered if she knew that she was already in love with Adam. No, he thought to himself. Perhaps she did know, but she had yet to accept that she was in love. He drank down the remainder of his cider and stood up. We walked to the window and watched as Shayla shaped the glass on the marble table before heating it again. He shook his head. Or perhaps she knew she loved Adam and was intentionally fighting her feelings.

Later that afternoon, Henry poked his head in the workshop. "Shayla, finish up. It is time to go home and get cleaned up if we are going to be on time for the Christmas tree lighting festival."

She nodded and inspected the vase she was forming. This was a new commission for Mrs. Bartlett who recently came to the countryside for Christmastide. This vase was to be a gift for her daughter-in-law to be who was spending the holiday at the Bartlett country estate. She looked at it from all sides. Using tongs, she pulled up a gather of glass. The colored glass was sandwiched between clear glass and formed a unique design. Again, she blew into the glass and reformed the shape. She transferred the piece to a pontil and heated the glass again. She dipped tongs in water and using the tool and the steam from the water she enlarged the opening. Shayla returned the piece to the furnace to heat it while Joseph made a gather. He handed it off to Shayla, and she merged glass with glass to add decorative swirls to the rim. She lengthened and slimmed the glass. The pipe never stopped moving in a controlled and steady movement. She heated, shaped, and reheated the glass. Finally, she was satisfied that it was completed. She flattened the bottom with a paddle and took it over to the workbench. With a sharp rap, she broke the glass off the pontil. It was a spectacular piece. The inner and outer walls of glass merged and flowed together. The color was delicate. She handed off the piece to Joseph.

"Are you excited about the Christmas tree lighting?" she asked the boy as he closed the oven door.

"Aye. Are you?"

"Yes, I am. Good night, Joseph. Hurry home so you will not miss it." The boy put on his hat and coat and ran out the door.

Henry and Shayla took the wagon home. Shayla washed and dressed in a teal colored dress, which had been her mother's. She thought of wearing a red dress for the tree lighting festivities, but this dress was much fancier. It had long sleeves and the bodice was completely covered in delicate lace. The full skirt fell to the floor and had lace along the bottom. It was an elegant dress for dancing. Shayla thought about dancing with Adam, and she felt a rush of desire fill her. She longed to be held in his strong arms. She shook her head to clear it and looked in the cheval glass. Why had she started to think about Adam holding her in his arms? Oh but, she could not stop thinking about it. She shook her head again, picked up her reticule, and went downstairs. She put on her dark grey cloak. She thought about the white cloak with the white fur trim she saw in the shop downtown. Maybe she should purchase it, or something like it.

"What is it, Shayla?" Henry asked.

She was startled at his voice then shook her head. "Nothing, Papa."

Henry, Shayla, Uncle Hal, and Mrs. Lawry sat up on the bench seats. Henry maneuvered the open wagon and joined the line of carriages and wagons making their way down to the town green where the tree stood waiting to be lit. Henry tied up the horses, and they walked the short distance to the Christmas Village and bandstand. This was always Shayla's favorite time of year. Her birthday, advent, the Christmas Village, and the tree made it a fun and exciting time. Together, they walked around and looked at the various huts selling a variety of goods for Christmastide shoppers.

Mrs. Lawry bought a bag of walnuts in one of the huts. "I plan to make a walnut cake for Christmas," she told Shayla.

"Papa will be happy." Walnut cake was one of his favorite types of cake.

As Shayla walked down one of the long rows of village huts, she looked around, but she did not see Adam. She did not want to make it obvious she was looking for someone, especially a man. That was not a very ladylike thing to do. However, she spotted Sarah walking with her family. Sarah was dressed in a bright yellow dress and had a wrap around her shoulders. Sarah saw Shayla, and she and her brother walked over to say hello.

"The shops are filled with so many wonderful items, would you agree, Shayla?" Sarah asked excitedly.

"They are," Shayla replied.

Sarah's brother, Robert, bowed. "Good evening, Miss Shayla," he said as he kissed her hand.

Sarah rolled her eyes behind her brother's back, and Shayla had to stifle a giggle. "Good evening, Robert. How are you faring at the university?"

"Very well. I am on the crew team this term," he informed her as he proudly puffed out his chest.

"Congratulations," Shayla replied.

Sarah took Shayla's arm. "I want to show you something," she said as she pulled Shayla away from her brother.

"Sorry, Robert," Shayla called as Sarah walked away with her in tow. Robert frowned at his sister, but Sarah never turned around to look at him. They went into one of the little huts. Sarah looked back and made sure her brother could not hear her. "Sorry," she began, "Robert has been snooty since he returned from school."

"He is proud to be on the crew team."

"I know."

"Did you actually want to show me something?"

"I did." Sarah led Shayla to a rack of shawls. My father gave me money for a new shawl. Which one do you like?"

The two girls looked through the selection, and Sarah tried on several.

"Is it for any particular dress or occasion?" Shayla asked.

"No, nothing special," Sarah mumbled as she looked at another rack.

"Oh," Shayla said as she pulled a white and gold wrap off the rack.

Sarah looked over as Shayla took off her dark cloak and put the white and gold wrap around her shoulders. "That is beautiful, Shayla."

Shayla looked at herself in the small cheval glass that stood to one side of the rack of shawls. It was not as warm as her cloak, but it was pretty. "I have to have it," Shayla told her friend with a laugh. "You are such a bad influence," she laughed again.

Aunt Margaret walked into the hut. "Shayla, that is beautiful on you."

"Hello, Aunt. I just told Sarah I have to have it."

"As you should. It is stunning with your dress tonight." Her aunt adjusted the wrap on her shoulders. "You are a vision."

The salesclerk hovered nearby, and Shayla looked at her. "I would like this wrap. I will wear it, and you can package up my cloak, please."

"And I will take this one," Sarah informed the woman as she handed her a deep blue shawl that shimmered with strands of silver and gold.

The woman nodded and smiled. The girls paid for their items, and the three women went to find the others.

"There they are," Shayla said when she spotted her two uncles and her father standing at one of the pub tables having an ale.

The women walked up to the table. "Where is Mrs. Lawry?" Shayla asked.

"She saw several women from her knitting circle," Henry explained. "That is a pretty wrap."

"I just purchased it."

"It does look beautiful on her, does it not, Henry," Aunt Margaret added.

Sarah reached into her bag. "I am going to wear my new shawl too." She put it on.

"It looks nice," Shayla complimented her friend. To be honest, Sarah was more in tune with fashion than she was, and Shayla often relied on Sarah for wardrobe advice.

"Oh," Sarah looked down the aisle. "I have to go; my mother is waving to me. Bye."

"Bye, Sarah."

Sarah walked toward her mother, and Shayla looked around at the crowd. People were going in and out of the village huts. Most of them carried multiple packages. The mood was festive with the musicians playing holiday tunes. Carolers serenaded shoppers in the village, and people smiled and laughed as they walked along the rows of huts.

"Should we set up a shop in the Christmas Village next year?" Shayla asked her father and uncle. Across from them was a shop that sold imported German glass ornaments.

"Our shop is not far away from the center of town," Henry replied. He took a long drink of beer. "Do we want the expense?"

"True our shop is close-by, but just look at all the shoppers here at the village." Shayla spread her arms wide. Henry and Hal looked around and nodded. "Our shop is not even open tonight."

"It is the tree lighting tonight," Henry commented. "The Christmas Village is likely not this busy on other nights."

"But there is ice skating nearby, and it is not far from downtown," Shayla pointed out.

"Perhaps we should set up a small shop," Hal added. There were a great many people making purchases. He thought it was likely they missed out on sales by not being part of the Christmas Village. "We could sell smaller items here and direct customers to the shop for custom pieces or larger pieces."

"I agree," Shayla said excitedly. "We could decorate the booth with greens and hang glass icicles from them. Then set up a tree to display a variety of ornaments." She eyed the German ornaments in the nearby hut. "We could light the hut with our own lamps. We could also sell bowls, mugs, and glasses, and pen sets with ink wells. I think it would increase sales."

"It is fine with me if you two want to set up in the village next year," Henry replied. "We could hire a few more salesclerks."

"I love the idea," Shayla hugged her father. "Thank you, Papa."

"Good evening," a deep seductive voice said.

Shayla knew that smooth voice, and she turned around and saw Adam standing near them. He was dressed in his military uniform tonight. He shook hands with Henry, Hal, and James, and then he bowed to Margaret and kissed her hand. They in turn greeted him.

"It is nice to see you, Captain," Aunt Margaret said softly. Shayla thought maybe she should have told her aunt that she promised Adam a dance, but she knew her aunt would make a big deal of it. Shayla took a deep breath. That fluttery feeling, she so often got in Adam's presence went through her entire body. She shuddered, and she pulled her wrap a little tighter, but she was not cold. In fact, she felt quite warm.

Adam turned his attention to Shayla. "Good evening, Miss Toselli," he said as he bowed to her.

Aunt Margaret smiled at Shayla and nodded her head encouragingly.

"Good Evening, Captain Preston." She executed a perfect curtsy.

Adam came to attention and took her hand gently in his. He bowed again and leaned down and kissed her hand without ever breaking eye contact. It felt like they were the only two people in the world. The sounds around them seemed to stop when they smiled at each other and looked into one another's eyes. Without letting go of her hand, Adam turned to Henry. "I would like to ask your permission for Miss Toselli to stand on the bandstand stage with me and my family as the tree is lit," Adam asked Henry very formally. "The Duchess of Wellshore will chaperone," he added.

Shayla narrowed her eyes and looked at him. "We do not need a chaperone," she mumbled so only he could hear.

"It is Shayla's decision," Henry replied.

Adam turned to Shayla. "Miss Toselli, what is your answer?"

Shayla smiled at Adam and nodded her head ever so slightly. Ok, if he wants to be formal, I will be formal, she thought to herself. "Yes, Captain. It would be lovely."

Aunt Margaret took Shayla's package from her. She smiled at her niece and tears once again came to her eyes.

Adam bowed to Henry and the rest of her family, and then he held out his arm for Shayla. She gently laid her hand on his arm, and Adam escorted her to the bandstand stage. As they walked through the crowd, Shayla felt all eyes turn to look at them. So many people in the town were gossips. She held her head high and avoided making eye contact with anyone. They reached the platform, and Adam held her hand as she made her way up the stairs then he led her to where the Duke and Duchess stood behind a screen which shielded them from the crowd. Adam bowed, and Shayla dropped into a low curtsy.

"We will be announced soon," the Duchess said to Shayla. "I am very excited, are you?"

"Yes, Your Grace."

The mayor's assistant came over and bowed. "The ceremony is about to begin, Your Grace," he said.

"We are ready."

The assistant nodded and left. Adam and Shayla took their places to the side and behind the Duke and Duchess. Shayla placed her hand lightly on Adam's extended arm. He placed his hand over hers and smiled.

"Good evening," the mayor of Canterbury Corner said loudly. The mayor was largely a ceremonial position, and he relished occasions such as this when he was the center of attention. Everyone eventually stopped talking and turned to listen. "Welcome everyone." There was a splattering of applause. "Welcome to Canterbury Corner's Christmas Tree Lighting Festival. This is a very special year because this year, through the generosity of our Duke, the tree will be lit with electric lights for the very first time." There was loud cheering and whistling from the crowd.

When the applause quieted down, the mayor loudly said, "Announcing the Duke and Duchess of Wellshore." The crowd clapped loudly and cheered. The Duke and Duchess walked out to the front of the stage. Adam and Shayla followed behind them. The mayor bowed. "Your Grace," he said as he extended his hand. The Duke acknowledged the mayor, and then he stepped forward to address the crowd.

Shayla felt the entire town staring up at her, and she hoped she would not bobble or worse fall. She knew everyone in town was wondering why she was accompanying Captain Preston and standing on the bandstand stage with the Duke and Duchess of Wellshore. There would definitely be a great deal of town gossip.

Adam kept his hand over hers to reassure her. He smiled at her, but Shayla stared ahead and took a deep breath. Finally, she looked at Adam, and he felt her relax a little. She looked out over the crowd. She saw several people she knew, but she only made eye contact and gave a discrete nod to Sarah who was so excited she was practically jumping up and down. Joseph Grant stood next to her, and he stared up at Shayla with an unreadable expression on his face. Her brother, Robert, stood a few steps away from Sarah. He too looked up at her, and Shayla clearly saw disappointment on his face. She continued scanning the crowd, and finally, she saw her family. They stood proudly in front of the bandstand smiling up at her. She smiled back, and she felt Adam's hand squeeze hers.

"The Duchess and I are happy to see so many of you here this evening," the Duke said to the crowd, and there was more loud clapping. "For the first time, we have a town Christmas tree illuminated with electric lights." There was a great deal of clapping and hooting from the crowd. "Our lovely Duchess will pull the switch to light the tree." She stepped to her husband's side.

Duke Wellshore held up a finger and the crowd counted, "One, two, three!" The Duchess grasped the switch and pulled it down with both hands. The tree burst into light. Gasps and then cheers and clapping erupted from the crowd.

Shayla gasped. The tree was stunning. The colored lights twinkled and the star on top shone brightly illuminating the night sky. She never saw anything so wonderful in her life. Adam watched Shayla's reaction. The lights reflected in her eyes and illuminated her face.

She looked over at Adam and smiled. "This is wonderful."

"Yes, it is."

"Happy Christmas," the mayor announced, and the Duke and Duchess waved to the crowd. The conductor stepped up on a stool and raised his arms. The crowd quieted down, and the musicians struck up a waltz. Elliot bowed to Amelia who curtsied. He took her hand, and they started to dance.

Adam bowed to Shayla. "What are you doing?" she asked between gritted teeth. She had to keep a smile on her face, and she hardly moved her lips. She knew all eyes were on them.

"You did say you would save me a dance," Adam replied. He could not help smiling from ear to ear.

"Yes, but."

"So, let us dance." Adam took her hand and circled his left arm around her waist, and he started to move. Shayla concentrated on the dance steps so as not to stumble. The bandstand was small, and at first Shayla was nervous, but Adam was graceful, and together they glided around the stage. She felt his hand firmly at her back and knew she was safe. He delicately held her hand, and she rested her free hand lightly on his shoulder. Their heads were held high, and they smiled as they danced. The twists and turns of the waltz brought their bodies close together, and eventually, Shayla felt herself getting caught up in the joy of being so close to Adam.

The crowd below watched as the two couples moved gracefully around the stage. Shayla became so comfortable in Adam's embrace that she forgot she was dancing in front of the entire town. She saw only Adam, and she felt herself relax and enjoy the dance.

Adam watched Shayla's face as he led her around the small area. He felt the tension melt from her body as she relaxed and let him guide her. He wanted to always be by her side which surprised him because he never thought he would feel that way about a woman. He wanted to spend every minute with Shayla. He wanted to share in her laughter and comfort her when she was sad. He wanted to walk side by side with her and have a family with her.

The last notes of the song played, and the women dropped into low curtsies, and the men bowed. Then they stood up to thunderous applause. Adam kissed Shayla's hand, and she smiled at him. Elliot and Amelia waved to the crowd, and then they turned and descended from the bandstand stage. Adam and Shayla followed them down the stairs and out into the crowd that gathered to greet them.

While the Duke and Duchess greeted people, the musicians began playing again, and many people started to dance in front of the stage on a makeshift dance floor. Adam took Shayla's hand again for a second dance, and together they moved gracefully to the music.

Henry watched Shayla and Adam. They looked well matched, and they clearly had eyes only for each other. He watched them move in the intricate pattern of the waltz. Shayla's eyes sparkled, and she smiled at Adam, and Adam looked at her with tenderness and love.

Aunt Margaret stood next to Henry, and she dabbed her eyes. "She looks happy."

Henry smiled at his sister-in-law. "She does."

As they danced, Shayla saw Sarah dancing with Joseph. Sarah smiled as they made eye contact, and Shayla knew that she and Sarah would have a lot to talk about when they were next alone together.

She turned her head and smiled at Adam. "I like country dances better than formal dances," Shayla said to him as they moved close to one another in the dance step.

"Why is that?"

"Because there are no silly rules about not dancing with someone more than twice."

"I would dance with you all night," Adam replied with a smile, and despite what people might say, he planned to dance only with Shayla.

They danced again and then took a break to get refreshments. They watched couples dance, and they talked to friends and family. They danced several more times, and Shayla never wanted the night to end. She never had so much fun at a dance before. When the festival began to wind down, Adam walked Shayla back to where Henry waited.

"May I call on you tomorrow, Miss Toselli?" Adam asked formally.

"I look forward to your visit, Captain Preston."

"Until tomorrow. Good night." He kissed her hand.

"Good night."

Henry did not say anything as he and Shayla walked to their wagon. He never saw his daughter beam with happiness as she did right now. All he wanted was for her to be happy, and he could tell that she was very happy.

"Where are the others?" Shayla asked when they reached their wagon.

"Aunt Margaret and Mrs. Lawry were tired, so Uncle James took them home. Uncle Hal went to the pub." Henry helped his daughter up onto the wagon's bench seat, and then he settled beside her and started the horses toward home. "You seemed to have a great deal of fun tonight, Shayla."

"Oh, Papa, I did." She hooked her arm in her father's and laid her head on his shoulder. "It was a wonderful night."

Henry kissed the top of her head, and they drove silently home.

# Chapter 16

"Papa, I need to shop for a dress for the Christmas Eve Ball," Shayla announced one morning at breakfast.

"Yes, you do."

"It is such an honor to be invited to the Duke and Duchess' Christmas Eve Ball." Mrs. Lawry refilled Henry's cup with coffee. "If you two are settled, I will take the wagon to the market."

"Thank you, Mrs. Lawry, we can manage."

"Good. I will see you both later."

"Bye." Shayla waved as Mrs. Lawry put on her coat and walked out of the kitchen. She sipped a cup of tea and took a bite of a scone. "It was nice having Adam visit yesterday. Do you agree?" She kept her voice as casual as possible.

Henry looked over the top of the newspaper he was reading. "It was quite pleasant."

"I like when we can be ourselves and not have to worry about appearances." Shayla thought about Adam's visit. They spent the afternoon in the parlor playing board games and sipping hot chocolate by the fire while it snowed outside. They talked about their lives and discovered much about one another. As the youngest of five, Adam had to learn to stick up for himself from an early age. That was so foreign to Shayla because she was an only child, and there was no one to compete with growing up. After dinner, they took a walk in the snow.

Shayla had a faraway look in her eyes, and Henry lowered his paper and cleared his throat to get her attention. "As the Duke's brother, he has responsibilities to his family. The Duke is new to his position, and they must all make a good impression on the people. I believe Duke Wellshore wants to reassure the community that he cares about the people of Canterbury Corner."

Shayla nodded. "Yes, Adam said something like that yesterday when we took our walk. He said it was important for his brother to show the people that he is a good and trusted administrator." She took another sip of tea. "It is interesting that we rarely saw our Duke before His Grace, Elliot Preston, became Duke. Why did the others avoid the people they governed?"

Henry took a breath. "The older Duke was active in our community when you were young."

Shayla buttered another scone. "Yes, I remember seeing the Duchess, Adam's mother, in the Christmas Village."

"However, as the Duke aged, it was easier for him to stay in London, so they came to the country less and less. When his sons took over, they were more interested in their own pleasures and rarely left London. However, I believe our new Duke plans to spend more time in his country estate, and he wants to be in touch with the people. He is young and progressive, and I believe he will be a good administrator."

Shayla nodded. "Yes, the Duchess told me he was very interested in women's right when she visited our shop."

Henry finished his tea and folded the newspaper. "Shayla, I know you prefer to be informal, but it is not bad to be formal in a relationship. In fact, a little formality is good in a relationship."

"It is?"

"Yes. Observing a few formalities keeps a relationship from becoming too casual. It helps a couple appreciate one another."

Shayla sipped her tea. She thought about her parents and how they interacted with each other. Her mother insisted on a fancy Sunday midday meal most weeks. She wore a lavish dress and jewelry, and her father wore a cravat and a dinner jacket. He always complimented her mother and often gave her flowers. He held her chair when she sat down at the table, and after dinner they had brandy in the parlor. Shayla remembered that when she was young, she thought it was fun to dress up. Her mother let her wear one of her necklaces and sometimes even dabbed a drop of her perfume behind Shayla's ear.

Henry watched Shayla. He could see her mind turning. He hoped he gave her something to consider. He felt a little sad though. If Shayla and Adam's relationship progressed, his daughter would marry and move away from his home. Of course, he knew that was normal, but it also made him a little sad. He straightened up and checked his emotions. He knew he could not show that sadness to his daughter. or surely it would influence her decisions. "So, you need a pretty dress for the ball." He picked up his newspaper again.

"Yes, I do. I saw a dress in one of the shop windows at the town center," Shayla told him. She buttered a roll and then took a bite. "I think I better ask Aunt Margaret to shop with me." She looked at her father. "Do you think she would mind?"

Henry smiled at her and set his paper down again. "I think it would make her very happy to help you select a dress."

"I am going to ask her." Shayla jumped up, kissed her father, pulled on her coat, and ran next door to her aunt's house.

"Hello, Mr. Roberts. Is my aunt awake?" Shayla asked.

"She is in the parlor having a cup of tea, Miss."

"Thank you." Shayla did not wait for him to announce her. She walked to the front parlor. "Good morning, Aunt." She walked in and sat down in a chair opposite her aunt.

Aunt Margaret set her teacup down. "Shayla, what a pleasant surprise. Would you like a cup of tea?"

"No, thank you. I have a favor to ask."

"Anything."

"Come shopping with me this morning? I need a gown for the Christmas Eve Ball at Wellshore Manor."

"Captain Preston invited you?" her aunt asked excitedly.

Shayla was annoyed that her aunt's only thought was that Adam invited her, but she did not show her annoyance. "No," she replied calmly. "The Duke himself invited Papa, Uncle Hall, and me to the Christmastide Ball on Christmas Eve."

"Oh. Your father did not mention the invitation, but Captain Preston will be there?"

"Well, yes. He lives there."

"He is such a fine man. When you danced with him, you looked well matched."

Shayla shook her head. "We are not a match, Aunt. He is learning the craft with us, but we are not a couple."

"No? You looked like a couple at the festival."

"Oh, well, no. We are not courting."

"Well, maybe not yet, but you could be with a little effort on your part. I saw how you looked at one another when you danced."

"No. We are not courting."

"Why ever not?"

"He is the brother of a duke and a soldier. He has many beautiful aristocratic women falling at his feet."

Margaret smiled at her niece and recognized her lack of confidence. "He is the brother of a duke yes, but he is no longer a soldier." She paused. "And as for women falling at his feet, it was you he asked to accompany him at the Christmas festival, not any other woman."

"Yes, I know but," Shayla sighed.

"You sell yourself short, Shayla. You are beautiful, well mannered, and now a successful businesswoman."

"Exactly. I am successful because of my own actions. I am not interested in marriage, and Adam knows it. No. We are just enjoying one another's company." Shayla could not help but think about their charade. Although Adam said no more pretending, Shayla was certain they were only friends. Afterall, why would he want a woman without a title. She might be a business owner now and reasonably wealthy, but she still was not in his social class.

Her aunt simply sipped her tea and smiled. Her niece did protest too much, she laughed to herself. "Well, I am happy to help you shop for a gown."

"I will get dressed and come back to get you. Thank you for helping me."

"I will have Mr. Logan prepare the carriage to take us to the town center."

Shayla nodded. She knew if she wanted her aunt's help, she would have to ride in the carriage to the town center.

A half hour later, the coachman took the two women down to the shops. Margaret took a deep breath and let it out slowly. "Aunt, are you well?" Shayla asked.

"It is just a bit of motion sickness. It will pass." She held a handkerchief to her mouth, and Shayla studied her. Her aunt did not look well and that was worrisome.

Once in town, they strolled along the street and looked at the window displays. They browsed in several shops. Margaret insisted they look at the new styles that were available. She wanted her niece to look spectacular. However, in the end, Shayla tried on the lavender dress she saw in the front window of the dress shop.

"What do you think, Aunt Margaret," Shayla asked as she stood in front of a huge cheval glass. The seamstress fluffed out the gown's skirt.

"Oh my. You are a vision." Margaret stood up and walked around her niece, but she suddenly felt dizzy, and she sat down.

"Are you alright?" Shayla asked. She was alarmed to see her aunt perspiring despite the chilliness of the day.

"Oh yes. I just stood up too quickly."

"Should we return home?"

"No. I am fine," Aunt Margaret replied as she straightened up. "You were right about that gown. It is perfect for you," she said changing the subject.

"It needs only a few alterations," the seamstress commented as she put pins in the dress to cinch in the waist. "See how that shows off your figure, dear." She made several tucks and suddenly Shayla had a very distinct and small waist.

"I love this color." Shayla stared at her reflection and held still as the woman continued to pin and tuck.

"And it is lovely with your hair," the seamstress added. "May I suggest sliver slippers and reticule to complete the outfit?" Shayla nodded eagerly, and the woman went to get them.

Shayla slipped on the dancing slippers. "The dress is perfect."

"You will be the belle of the ball," Aunt Margaret beamed.

"I will make the adjustments and have the dress ready for you in two days," the seamstress said as she wrote up the sale.

A short while later, they left the dress shop and walked to the tea shop. "Aunt, are you certain you are feeling well?" Shayla looked at her aunt's pale face.

"It will pass," she said, "but I could do with a little something to eat." They ordered tea and biscuits. Shayla kept looking at her aunt. She knew something was not right. She feared something happening to her aunt, and Margaret could tell her niece was worried. She leaned forward and covered Shayla's hand. "How do you feel about being a godmother?"

"What?" Shayla gasped and her mouth fell open.

Margaret smiled and nodded her head.

"You are with child?"

"I am. The doctor confirmed it just yesterday." Aunt Margaret beamed with happiness. "I had given up hope that at two and thirty years of age I would ever conceive a child. I thought perhaps I had a digestive problem. I was pleasantly surprised when the doctor told me I was with child."

"That is wonderful news, Aunt." Shayla reached over and gave her a hug. "You can count on me to help you. I am so excited."

"Now, not a word to anyone. I plan to surprise your uncle tonight with the news after dinner."

Shayla smiled at her aunt. "I cannot believe it. It is so wonderful. A baby."

## Chapter 17

Henry walked in the door after a very busy day in the shop. "Shayla," he called.

"Evening, Henry. Shayla went skating with Miss Williams after she and her aunt went shopping. She should be along shortly."

He took off his boots and coat and followed Mrs. Lawry to the kitchen. "Did she find a dress?"

"Aye, she did. Margaret helped her pick out a beautiful gown. The seamstress is altering it for Shayla."

"Good."

"I will finish preparing dinner. I am certain Shayla will be along shortly."

"I hope she has the sense to ride home in her friend's carriage. It is getting dark."

"She is a strong sensible girl. I am certain she will be fine."

Henry poured himself a glass of ale and sat down with the evening newspaper. The headline told of another kidnapping in the area. It was the second in the past month. He folded the paper. "I am going out to find her."



Shayla tapped her foot while she and Sarah stood at the edge of the road waiting for the carriage. "If I walked, I could be half-way home by now, Sarah."

"It is dark, Shayla. You cannot walk home in the dark."

"Where is the carriage?" Shayla peered down the road. She saw the lights of the center of town but not an approaching carriage. "Maybe we should walk to the main street. It is not far."

"I have my good boots on," Sarah complained.

Shayla rolled her eyes. Soon a carriage approached slowly from the other direction. "Is that your carriage?"

Sarah peered down the road. "I think so."

"You are not sure?"

The carriage continued rolling toward them. "No, it is not mine, but maybe we know who is in the carriage, and we can get a ride into town. I do not understand why Mr. Jameson is late. I told him to be here before it got dark."

Shayla felt nervous. The carriage moved too slowly. She pulled her umbrella closer to her body. Something was not right.

Suddenly, they heard several men approach them from behind. The two women turned and faced the men. Shayla looked at Sarah who was white as a sheet.

"What have we here? Two lovely young peaches out all alone," one of the grubby men said as they approached.

Shayla kept her eyes on the closest man. He was not that much older than her. He was tall and lanky with black hair shooting out from under the tattered cap he wore. The other two men were shorter. All were shabbily dressed. She slid her reticule up her arm as she slowly reached down into her umbrella and grasped a short pipe hidden there.

"We have money for you if you leave us alone," Sarah told the men in a very high shaky voice. "My coachman is due any minute, and he will give you more."

"Well, that is an interesting proposition, love. But I reckon your father will pay even more to get you back in one piece."

Sarah visibly trembled and looked ready to faint, but Shayla took a deep breath and prepared herself to attack. Memories of her mother filled her head. The maniac who hit her mother's carriage had just kidnapped a young woman. He was fleeing and lost control of the carriage. But he paid. And these men would too. She went over everything her uncle had taught her. She knew what to do. Now she had to do it.

One man lurched and grabbed Sarah. She screamed, but he covered her mouth with his hand. The second man lunged toward Shayla. She jumped back out of his reach and pulled the pipe from her umbrella. She gripped it with both hands, and then she swung it. There was a sickening thud as it connected with the side of the man's head, and he fell heavily to the ground.

The third man snarled at her and moved closer. "You are going to pay for that girlie."

Shayla remained calm and kept her eyes on him as she inched backward. Then she reached into her reticule and pulled out a small pistol. The man froze. Shayla stared at him, and he stared at her finger on the trigger. Her heart hammered in her chest, but her hand was rock steady. The man holding Sarah released her, and the two men took a step back.

Then a shot shattered the night. Shayla turned and gasped. A man fell to the ground only feet from her. She looked up. Adam jumped off his horse and ran toward her. She heard the other men running away, and then a horse neighed. She turned her head. A man on a horse stopped the two from escaping. He pointed a pistol at them, and they dropped to the ground. He dismounted and stood over them.

Adam reached Shayla, and his hand covered her hand holding the small pistol. He pushed her hand down and took it away from her. Adam briefly admired the pearl handle of the small gun and saw the lettering Bulldog on the rim. He would have liked to look it over more carefully, but now was not the time, so he tucked it in his waistband. "Shayla. Shayla, are you hurt?" He looked her up and down. "Are you hurt?"

"N No." She shook her head. She looked at the man on the ground. "You shot him."

"He was about to attack you from behind."

"Thank you." She looked down at her friend on the ground. "Sarah!" Shayla reached down a hand and helped her to stand up.

"Oh, Shayla. Oh, God. Shayla." Sarah swayed on her feet and started to fall. Adam jumped forward and eased her to the ground.

Another carriage approached. A man jumped down and ran toward them. "Miss Sarah," he called. "I was delayed. What happened?"

"The women were attacked," Adam replied as he picked up Sarah. "Get Miss Williams in the carriage and get her home. Alert the Constable on your way. We have four here for them."

"Immediately, Captain." The coachman took Sarah from Adam and put her in the carriage. He climbed in the driver's seat and turned the carriage toward town.

Adam looked at Shayla. She stood very still next to him. Her face was pale. Her eyes were wide, and her breathing was rapid and shallow. He wrapped her in his arms. "You are in shock." He took off his jacket and wrapped it around her, and she clung to him.

In a few minutes, several men rode up fast on horses. Two men took hold of the men on the ground. The Constable looked at Adam. "What happened here, Captain."

"I shot that man before he could attack Miss Toselli, Sir. That man," he pointed to the one sprawled on the ground, "Miss Toselli knocked out."

"She did?" the Constable asked in amazement.

"Yes, I did," Shayla said softly without turning around. She rested her head on Adam's shoulder.

The Constable nodded and bent down to pick up the pipe that lay on the ground. He signaled for one of his men to get the man who was shot. The Constable's eyes passed over Shayla's back. "Miss Toselli, are you hurt?"

Slowly, Shayla turned her head and shook it. "No. I am unharmed."

"I will escort Miss Toselli home," Adam informed the Constable.

"Very good, Captain." He looked at them. "I will need all of you to make a statement," he paused at the angry look from Adam, "in the morning will be fine."

The other man dismounted and walked over to Adam and Shayla. "Miss Toselli this is Major Colin Preston, my brother who is home on leave from the army," he said to Shayla. This was not how Adam intended for Colin to meet Shayla.

"I am honored Miss Toselli." Colin bowed.

"I am pleased to make your acquaintance, Major," Shayla managed to squeak out. She was still shaky.

Adam pulled Shayla closer. "Let me get you home."

Colin looked down at the still unconscious man at their feet. "You did a good job with him, Miss Toselli," he laughed.

Adam glared at his brother. "Do not encourage her behavior."

Shayla raised her head and pushed away from him. "What do you mean by that?" She narrowed her eyes and glared at Adam.

"I mean, you are lucky you were not hurt. Where did you learn to fight like that anyway, and where did you get the Bulldog?" He did not mean to get angry with her after such an ordeal, but his emotions were raw.

Colin opened his mouth to speak but closed it at a look from Adam.

"It is none of your concern where I got it," Shayla snapped. She took off his jacket and handed it to him.

"It most certainly is my concern. Does your father know you have a gun?"

"I am not a damsel in distress, Captain. I can take care of myself." She stepped further away from him and started to walk down the road.

"Where do you think you are going?"

"I am going home."

"You need to stop walking around alone especially at night."

Shayla walked back to him and thrust out her hand. "Give. Me. My. Gun," she demanded emphasizing each word.

"No."

"It is my property. You are stealing."

"I am doing no such thing. Do you even know how to shoot it?"

Shayla barely contained her anger. How dare he talk to her like she was a child incapable of taking care of herself. She straightened up and addressed him. "Despite your low opinion of my abilities, Captain Preston, I know how to use a gun."

He stared at her. "You do?" He could not keep the admiration out of his voice. She was amazing. What am I thinking? She could have been hurt or worse. Instead of arguing, he took her arm.

She pulled her arm from his grip. "Unhand me, Captain."

"I am seeing you home."

"And I told you, I am capable of getting myself home."

Adam picked up his horse's reins. "Up," he said quietly but sternly.

"No." She stared at him defiantly.

He moved closer to her. "You will let me help you up on that horse in a lady like fashion, or I will pick you up and lay you across the saddle."

"You would not dare treat me in such a manner!"

He stepped even closer to her and glared down at her. "Do not. Test. Me. Miss Toselli."

Shayla stared at him for several moments. "Very well. You can assist me and take me home."

She put her foot in the stirrup, and Adam pushed her up into the saddle. He then swung up on the horse behind her.

"Colin, please check on Miss Williams. She lives down the main road. Take the right fork. The home is on Bamberg Lane. I will be at the Toselli home on Maple Road."

Colin contained his amusement. He knew all too well that Adam was very serious, and very upset. There was more to Adam's relationship with Miss Toselli than he had admitted to thus far, but Colin intended to get the whole story from him. When Adam calmed down. "I will meet you at the Toselli home after I check on Miss Williams." Colin tipped his hat, got up on his horse, and rode off.

"I will take you home," Adam said gently. He put his arm around Shayla's waist and realized just how tiny she was. At first, she was tense and sat stiffly, but after a few moments, she relaxed and settled back into him. He closed his eyes for a brief moment. When he saw her standing there with a gun on a man and another coming up silently behind her, his heart stopped. At that moment, he realized how much he loved her. He relaxed his shoulders and dropped his head to her hair. He needed to tell her how he felt about her.

They were not far from her home when Henry came riding down the road. "I have her, Henry."

"Shayla? Adam? What happened?"

"We will explain once Shayla is safe at home."

At the end of the walk, Adam slid off the horse then reached up and helped Shayla down. She looked pale, and he felt her hand shaking when he took it. Undoubtedly, her experience scared her more than she was willing to admit. He admired her courage, but he wanted to protect her. He felt a burning need to protect her. He helped her walk to the front door, and she did not resist him at all.

Mrs. Lawry appeared in the hallway when she heard the door open. "Shayla? Your Papa just went out looking for you." She looked closely. "Shayla what happened?" Fear shook her voice. "Adam? Henry? What happened?"

"Brandy, Mrs. Lawry," Adam said as he took Shayla's arm, led her to the parlor, and helped her into a chair by the hearth.

Henry followed them inside and sat down in front of his daughter. "Shayla, what happened to you?"

"I am fine, Papa," she assured him, but her voice was shaky. "Sarah and I finished skating, and we were waiting for her coachman and carriage when these men tried to abduct us."

Adam saw the color drain from Henry's face. Mrs. Lawry gasped. She stood with her hand to her mouth. The bottle of brandy shook in her other hand. Adam stood. "Here Mrs. Lawry, let me get that." He took the bottle and nudged her into a chair. He turned to the bar and poured four glasses of brandy. He added extra to Shayla's glass. She looked brave, but he felt her body shaking as he helped her up on the horse. He handed out the glasses.

Shayla recounted what happened. Adam added his part. "My brother, Major Colin Preston, and I had left the pub and were very slowly making our way up the road when we heard a woman scream. We rode toward the sound, and we saw Shayla holding a gun on a man."

Henry and Mrs. Lawry gasped. Henry started to speak, but Adam held up his hand to stop him. "Another man was sneaking up behind her, and I shot him."

"You saved her. Shayla, he is your hero," Mrs. Lawry cried.

"Yes, he did save me." She looked at Adam. "Thank you."

"The police are taking care of the ruffians, and my brother is checking on Miss Williams. I asked him to report on her condition to me here."

Henry shook his head in disbelief. "Shayla, where did you learn to fight, and where did you get a gun?" he asked quietly. He could not believe his daughter was capable of harming anyone. Adam took the gun out of his waistband and handed it to Henry.

"I bought the gun on one of our trips to London, about a year after mother died. I carry it in my reticule."

"A dealer in London sold you a gun?" Adam asked.

"They would sell anyone a gun for the right price." Shayla straightened up. "And Uncle Hal taught me to fight years ago. I keep part of a blow pipe in my umbrella for self-defense."

Henry looked at the small gun which fit neatly in his hand. He could not believe his daughter had carried the weapon in her reticule all this time. With a sigh, he placed the gun on the side table then leaned over and took his daughter's hands. He looked into her eyes. "Why, Shayla?"

"Because I do not plan to be a victim without a fight." Her voice was strong and determined.

Henry closed his eyes. "Your mother was not a victim."

"No, but the girl that murderer kidnapped was."

Henry pulled his daughter close. "I am glad you are safe. Adam, I cannot express my gratitude."

"I am happy I was there to help."

Mrs. Lawry stood up. "Come Shayla, you are tired and need to rest."

"Actually, I am starving. I did not eat tonight."

"Nor did your father. He went to look for you. Adam, have you had your supper?"

"I have, thank you."

"Come, I will set out food. Adam, please pour more brandy. We all need it." Mrs. Lawry discreetly dried her eyes as she went to the kitchen to prepare supper. She filled two bowls with hearty lamb stew and brought out bread and butter. Henry and Shayla ate quietly, and Adam sipped brandy. He moved a glass toward Shayla, and she took a sip between bites.

There was a knock on the door. "That must be my brother. May I get the door?"

"Please," Henry replied.

Adam left the kitchen and opened the front door. "Colin, how is Miss Williams?" Adam led him to the dining room where Shayla and Henry were finishing their meal. Mrs. Lawry set out a coffee service and a plate of pastries.

Henry stood up when Colin entered the room and shook his hand. "Thank you for your help this evening, Major Preston." Colin nodded, and Henry indicated he should sit down.

"Miss Williams is scared and shaken, but she will be fine. Her family called a doctor, and he ordered a large brandy, a hot water bottle, and bed for her. He believes she will feel better in the morning."

"Thank god, you girls are unharmed." Mrs. Lawry dabbed her eyes again with her handkerchief.

Two glasses of brandy and hot food made Shayla tired. She closed her eyes and swayed a little. "I am sorry," she said softly, "I think I will retire."

The three men stood up. Henry kissed her. "Sleep well, my daughter." He kissed her cheek again.

"Good night, Papa." She looked at Colin. "My thanks, Major Preston for your help."

He bowed. "My pleasure, Miss Toselli."

Slowly, Shayla looked up at Adam. "Thank you, for saving me from that ruffian."

"I am always at your service," he bowed. They looked into each other's eyes. Adam picked up her hand and kissed it. He felt her fingers tremble, but what did it mean? Was it the events of the evening finally catching up to her, or was it she felt something for him?

"Come, Shayla. Let me get you in bed. It has been a long day." Mrs. Lawry led her upstairs.

When Shayla was in her bedroom and they heard her door close, Henry brought Adam and Colin to the parlor. "Gentlemen, I am indebted to you for helping my daughter and her friend." His hands flexed into fists. "They attacked my daughter."

"There have been other kidnappings. Duke Wellshore is asking for more officers," Adam informed him.

"I stopped and informed Elliot of the attack before coming here. He went to the station to interrogate the men and speak to the Constable."

Henry nodded. "I believe it is time we retain a coachman again."

"I can help you retain one, Henry," Adam offered.

"Thank you." He shook his head. "And this." Henry pointed to Shayla's gun on the side table. "I had no idea she had that gun." His eyes narrowed. "I need to speak to my brother and find out if he knew she owned it."

"May I take the gun, Henry?"

Henry let out a sigh. "Yes. Then I will not have to keep it away from her."

"Shayla is a determined woman. She will try to get another before long. She is of age, Henry, but with your permission, I will make certain she can handle it properly."

Henry thought for a few moments. Adam was right. Shayla would get another one. "You have my permission."

Adam picked up the Bulldog and once again tucked it into the waistband of his trousers. "Good night, Henry." Adam went to the foyer and put on his coat. "We must appear at the police station to make statements tomorrow morning."

"I thought as much." Henry put on his coat as well.

"I will escort Miss Toselli to the station if that is acceptable to you, Henry."

"Thank you. I will inform Mrs. Lawry to ensure Shayla is ready when you arrive." He shook both Adam and Colin's hands again, and they walked to the front door. "I am indebted to you both. Good night, Sirs." Henry walked out the door with them. They mounted their horses, and Henry took his horse around to the stable. He planned to talk to his brother, but first he needed to calm down.

## Chapter 18

Early the next morning, Shayla rose, dressed in a robe, and went downstairs for breakfast.

"Mornin' hun." Mrs. Lawry set a cup of tea and a plate of bread down in front of Shayla. "Your father went to the shop early this morning."

"He did not wait for me?"

"Captain Preston will be here shortly to pick you up."

"I do not need him to pick me up. I can walk myself." She took a bite of bread.

"To the police station?"

Shayla let out a sigh. She forgot she needed to give her statement this morning. This was going to put her behind. Mrs. Lawry set a large piece of pie in front of Shayla. "What is this? You never let me eat dessert for breakfast."

"I thought you could use a little sugar this mornin' to sweeten your disposition." Mrs. Lawry patted her arm and went back to preparing food for the midday meal.

"Thank you." Shayla eagerly ate the pie and drank most of her cup of tea.

"After you finish, you had better get dressed. Wear something pretty," Mrs. Lawry suggested.

"I do not need to wear something pretty. I am going to the police station to give a statement on an attack."

Mrs. Lawry put her hands on her hips and looked sternly at Shayla. "A young woman of your standing must look her best."

"Fine. I will wear something pretty." She finished her tea and went upstairs to get dressed. "Wear something pretty, says she," Shayla mumbled as she looked at the dresses in her wardrobe. "I will wear something pretty. So pretty, Captain Preston will regret the way he talked to me last night. Treating me like a child." Shayla slipped on a light pink dress. It had white lace frill along the modestly low neckline and a satin white sash at the waist. She brushed her hair and put in the combs she received for her birthday to hold her hair back from her face. She added tasteful gold earrings. "There," Shayla nodded as she checked her appearance in the cheval glass. "And I will be a proper lady, batting my eyes and being the poor suffering girl who was attacked last night. Afterall, that is what he wants," she huffed. She picked up her skirts and went downstairs.

Mrs. Lawry approved of Shayla's attire, but she wondered what the girl was up to. She watched Shayla and Adam interact, and she never saw Shayla so flustered in the presence of a man as she was with Adam. There was a knock on the door, so she went to open it. "Captain Preston, my, you look handsome. Adam bowed slightly. He was dressed in his military uniform, and at the end of the walk, stood a large carriage.

"Is Miss Toselli ready? We must make our statements this morning." Then Adam saw Shayla standing behind Mrs. Lawry. He smiled and felt his heart skip a beat. She looked quite demur in that color. It suited her. Then it hit him. Adam always felt like he had seen Shayla before, but he could never remember where. He assumed it must have been on the street in passing when he was in town visiting. However, he now had a clear vision of a young woman at last year's Twelfth Night Celebration.

His mother preferred to come to Canterbury Corner for Christmastide. He could not visit with her for the start of Christmastide last year, but he arrived in time for the end of it. He and Colin attended the Twelfth Night Celebration, and as they passed through the crowds on their way to meet friends, he saw a beautiful woman. She wore a pale pink dress and stood talking with several other young women. She did not notice him, but he noticed her. He asked his brother who she was, but Colin did not know. He planned to ask if any of his friends knew her and could introduce them, but he never saw her again that evening, and he left a day later to return to duty.

"I am ready, Captain," Shayla replied in a soft voice.

He pulled himself back to the present and smiled at her while she put on a long, thick, grey traveling cloak, tied a white fur trimmed matching bonnet beneath her chin, and put on a pair of gloves. Adam extended his hand to help her down the front steps.

"Be good," Mrs. Lawry discreetly muttered to Shayla as she passed. Shayla smiled at her, and Mrs. Lawry distinctly saw the girl's eyebrow arch. Oh boy, she is up to something, Mrs. Lawry thought. She watched from the door as Captain Preston took one of Shayla's arms and helped her into the carriage.

"You look very beautiful this morning," Adam commented as the carriage got underway. He sat on the bench opposite Shayla. "It should not take long to make our statements."

"Good." Shayla's fingers gripped the seat on either side of her.

Adam watched her carefully and noticed that she was taking shallow breaths. "Mr. Lowman is an excellent coachman, I assure you," he said to Shayla.

"I am certain he is."

When they reached the station, Shayla attempted to jump out of the carriage first, but Adam beat her to the door. He held up a hand to help her out.

"I have arranged to take you directly to the Constable's office through a back door," Adam informed her as he hooked her arm in his and propelled her to the side of the building. "I do not want you seeing the prisoner cells."

Major Preston waited by the door. "Good morning, Miss Toselli." He bowed to her.

"Good morning, Major." Shayla inclined her head in greeting.

Colin opened the door, and the three of them stepped inside.

"Shayla," Sarah said her name and burst into tears again. Sarah's mother patted her daughter's back.

Mr. Williams, dressed in his finest, stood up and shook Adam's and Colin's hands. "Thank you both. I shudder when I think what could have happened yesterday."

"Miss Toselli," Duke Wellshore stood up and walked over to her. "It pleases me that you were not hurt yesterday. I assure you, the men responsible will pay for their actions."

"Thank you, Your Grace." She curtsied.

The Constable's office was neat and clean which was different from what Shayla expected. On the wall was a painting of the Queen, but there were few other decorations.

The Constable came in. "Miss Toselli, thank you for coming." He held a chair, and Shayla sat down next to Sarah. He looked at the two young women whose reactions were the exact opposite. "I understand this is difficult ladies, but I need you to recount what happened."

For the next hour, Shayla and Sarah, well mostly Shayla, recounted the attack and answered questions while the attentive Lieutenant took notes and made sketches of what they described. Adam and Colin added their parts in the episode. When the

Constable was satisfied that he had all the information he needed, he stood up, bowed to the ladies, and thanked them for their time.

"Oh, Miss Toselli," the Constable said as he reached for an umbrella, "I believe this is yours."

Shayla nodded. "Thank you."

"I am afraid the pipe is evidence and cannot be returned to you as yet."

"Please keep me informed of any incidents," the Duke said to the Constable. He thanked Shayla and Sarah for making their statements, and he left the building.

Mr. Williams thanked Adam and Colin again and shook their hands. He patted Shayla on the shoulder then he and his wife helped their daughter to their carriage.

Adam watched Shayla. He was not sure what she felt. She presented a calm exterior, but was she calm? He cared about her. He loved her. Yes, he knew she was not looking for a relationship, but he felt her relax in his arms last night. He saw the look in her eyes as she watched him. He knew she felt something for him. He also knew getting her to admit it would be difficult.

Outside, Major Preston said his goodbyes. "Miss Toselli, I hope to see you again."

"And I you, Major." Adam helped Shayla into the carriage.

Colin shook Adam's hand. "The train leaves shortly, and I really must be on it. I have meetings in London, and Mother is expecting me to escort her back here for Christmastide."

"Safe journey, Colin. Give my best to Mother, and I will see you soon."

They had a quick embrace, and then Colin stepped into the other carriage. He closed the door and waved.

Adam stepped into the carriage and seated himself across from Shayla, and Mr. Lowman set off. "My brother must return to London," Adam explained to Shayla. "Yesterday, he was visiting for the day, and we were having a meal in the pub before his departure when the men attacked you."

"I see. I am sorry his departure was delayed."

Now that she took the time to look at it, Shayla saw that it was a beautiful carriage. The interior was painted soft pink, the bench cushions were dark pink, and the windows were etched with a small rose. There were crystal vases on both sides of the door for flowers during the warmer months.

"This carriage is quite beautiful," Shayla commented as she ran her hand along one of the vases.

"I am very pleased you like it."

"Where are we going," Shayla asked when the carriage took the road left instead of going right which would take them to the center of the town and then to the glass shop.

"The Duchess would like to talk to you about another commission. You can lunch with us, and then I will return you home."

Shayla nodded. This was not her plan for today, but if the Duchess wanted another commission, having lunch with her was well worth the time. She watched Adam as he leaned back into the seat and relaxed. She hated to admit it, but she realized his response yesterday was justified. She felt so safe in his arms up on the horse. He was attractive, strong, certainly capable. Life with him would be exciting, but it also would entail many parties and entertaining, and already, she was anxious to get out of the frilly clothes and get back to the workshop.

Adam watched Shayla closely. He knew of her nerves at carriage rides, but she seemed to be more relaxed this trip. On the way to the office, she gripped the seat on both sides of her. This time, while her hands were clutched in her lap, her knuckles were not white.

She looked out the window at the passing landscape. The carriage made its way up the hill to the long driveway. It was picturesque. The three story stone mansion sat at the top of the hill surrounded by fields of white snow. Shayla watched the house come into view as the carriage turned and stopped on the wide circular drive. This time, she waited for Adam to exit the carriage. She extended a hand to him, and he helped her down the steps. Adam offered her his arm, and they walked up to the front door which opened before they reached it.

"Captain. Miss Toselli," the butler addressed them. He took her cloak and bonnet and Adam's coat, and then Adam led her to the front parlor where the Duchess and her guests were listening to a piano recital. As it would be rude to interrupt, they quietly took seats and listened to the music. Most of the others in attendance Shayla did not know, but she recognized the Earl of Huntington and his wife.

After two more songs, the pianist stood up to loud applause. "That was wonderful. Thank you," the Duchess said as she walked over and extended her hand to the young man. He bowed low and kissed her hand. "Come everyone, lunch is served in the dining room." She indicated that everyone should follow the butler. Then the Duchess turned and smiled. "Shayla, I am quite pleased to see you safe after your ordeal. It is a miracle you were not harmed."

"I am fine. Thank you for your concern, Your Grace." Shayla curtsied to the Duchess.

"Come, let us eat. I wish to speak to you."

Adam took Shayla's hand. "I shall join you shortly," he whispered. She felt a tingle when he touched her. His touch was familiar, intimate. Like they were a couple. She nodded and walked with the Duchess.

While the bouillon was served, the Duchess explained her idea for a gift for the Duke. Shayla nodded and assured her that she could make the commission.

When Adam returned, Shayla smiled at him. He took the empty seat next to her, pleased that Amelia seated him there. The maid set a soup bowl in front of him, and he engaged others in conversation while Shayla conversed with the Duchess.

"I will work on your commission immediately, Your Grace."

"As long as I have it for the first night of Christmastide." She patted Shayla's hand and smiled. "Not a word to the Duke."

"Of course not, Your Grace. I shall wrap your items and bring the package to you in your rooms Christmas Eve midday when I arrive to oversee setting out the ornaments for the ball."

"That will be perfect."

The lunch plate was served next. It consisted of Chicken Croquettes, French peas, potatoes, and gravy. Shayla was enjoying the meal when Adam reached for her hand under the table. She gave a small gasp, but she twined her fingers with his. His hand was quite warm. He started to rub his thumb in circles on her palm and was rewarded when a gentle sigh escaped her.

Dessert and coffee were served, and Adam let go of her hand much to Shayla's dismay. "You must try this pudding, Miss Toselli." Adam handed her a spoon and a pudding cup.

She took the spoon and tasted the pudding. "It is delicious, Captain."

The Duchess watched them and smiled her approval. "I am happy you could join us for lunch, Shayla."

"Thank you for the invitation."

The afternoon wore on with more music and conversation. Adam showed Shayla the conservatory which was filled with an assortment of fruit bearing trees, a small herb garden, and many types of flowers. Shayla fanned herself with her hand. "It is wonderfully warm in here," she said as she looked at the tropical plants, "it makes me long for Summer."

Adam picked a red rose and handed it to Shayla. She looked at the delicate flower. Red for love. He was telling her he loved her. She accepted the rose and smiled.

They stayed in the conservancy for a while, and Adam pointed out several varieties of the plants he knew. "My mother spent hours in here repotting, cultivating, and tending to the plants. She did not stay in the house once my father passed, and my brothers took over."

"Did they resent her?" Shayla asked.

"No, but they were bachelors. When father died, mother moved to the Dowager's cottage even though my brothers were rarely here."

Shayla nodded. Adam pointed out the Dowager's cottage on their way to the manor.

He reached up and picked an orange off a tree. "For your breakfast tomorrow."

"Thank you."

They walked back to the parlor. "The carriage is waiting," Adam told her. Shayla thanked the Duchess for lunch, and the butler helped her into her cloak. Adam led her to the carriage, and once she was inside, he told the driver to take them for a ride.

"As you wish, Captain."

Adam stepped inside the carriage and sat opposite Shayla. It would be inappropriate to sit beside her when someone could see inside. The carriage ambled down the driveway, and Adam drew the curtains closed. He reached over, took her hands, and examined

Shayla's elegant fingers that were so talented. They could mold glass into fine exquisite shapes, and he longed to feel them on his skin. They looked into each other's eyes. Her eyes were dark pools that pulled him in, and he wondered what she was thinking.

Shayla saw desire in Adam's eyes. She had already concluded that she loved him. She envisioned life with him, but she was uncertain if she should act on her feelings.

The carriage ambled through the countryside. Adam continued to hold her hands. Then he took off her gloves and kissed each of her palms and trailed tiny kisses up her arm. Since they were on a less traveled road, Adam pulled Shayla to his side of the carriage. She tensed a little as he slowly ran his fingers up her arms and to her hair. He ached to touch her. Slowly, he cupped the back of her head and eased her closer. She did not resist, so he lightly traced the length of her neck with his fingers.

"Shayla," he breathed as he gently brought his lips to hers. She responded by leaning into him, and he took the kiss deeper.

She tasted sweet as he knew she would. His hands gripped her shoulders and pulled her close to his body. She seemed to melt into him. Her hands moved up to his chest, and she grabbed the fabric of his coat and pulled him closer to her.

He ran his fingers around her neck and then gently trailed them up to her ear and back down again. Her skin felt cool. Adam reached under the opposite seat and took out a blanket. He wrapped the blanket around them, and his arms encircled her. Their bodies warmed as they continued to kiss. Their tongues tangled and their hearts raced. Shayla ran her fingers through his hair while Adam ran his hand down the length of her back. It was some time before they pulled back, and Shayla laid her head on his shoulder.

It was late in the afternoon when Adam told the driver to go to the Toselli home.

"I am sorry I kept you from the workshop today."

"I will spend all day there tomorrow. I have a commission from the Duchess."

"She adores your work. You are a talented woman."

"Thank you."

As they approached the house, Shayla moved back to the bench opposite Adam. The carriage stopped, and Adam exited then held up a hand to help Shayla down. "You may put the carriage in the stable, Mr. Lowman."

"In the stable?"

"The carriage and coachman are yours."

"What?"

"Your father asked me to retain a coachman and carriage for your family. Mr. Lowman has worked for my family for nine years. He is honorable and reliable."

"We do not need a coachman and carriage." Her eyes flashed, and she strode purposefully up the walk. Her father opened the door before she reached it. He knew that look and braced himself. "What is this about a coachman and carriage, Papa?"

"I asked Adam to find a man who would be willing to be a butler and coachman for us. It is time we had additional help and a proper carriage."

Shayla looked from her father to Adam. "So, I am to be watched."

"No," the two men nearly shouted at the same time.

Adam took her arm, and Henry stepped back as they entered the house. Adam took off her cloak and laid it over a chair in the foyer then took off his overcoat.

Shayla's eyes were shooting daggers.

"Come, let us have a drink and talk," Henry suggested.

They went in the parlor, and Henry steered her toward the fireplace. "Shayla," Henry eased her down into a chair, "there are more and more kidnappings. I am worried about you. Please use the carriage."

She sat still and stared at her father.

Adam sat down next to her. "Shayla. I was never so scared as I was when I saw that man ready to harm you. The situation is dangerous right now. The Duke asked for more policemen to patrol, but it may take time for them to arrive." He took her hands. "The men who attacked you are not the men who have been kidnapping women. The group from yesterday were copycats. You may not have survived the real kidnappers."

Shayla looked at him. "Copycats? They were not the men doing the kidnapping?"

Adam shook his head no. "The men yesterday were amateurs. They were just trying to make some quick money. They were not professionals. Please. I am asking you to listen to your father and take the carriage from now on."

She glared at them for a few long moments. "Fine."

"Good." Henry smiled and went to pour drinks. He was a little disappointed that he could not convince her to use the carriage, but Adam could. Still, it did not matter as long as she used it. "Adam, stay for dinner?"

"I would be delighted."

## Chapter 19

Shayla stretched and then got out of bed. Adam said to be ready early and to wear her work clothing. She wondered what he planned. She washed and dressed and practically bounced down the stairs. "Good morning," she said happily as she picked up a toasted English muffin from the plate on the counter.

"Good morning. Would you like jam with your muffin?"

"Yes, thank you."

"I am cooking eggs as well."

"Captain Preston will be arriving shortly. He said he wants to show me something before we work this morning."

"You are going out dressed like that?!"

"Adam said to wear my work clothes."

"Hum," Mrs. Lawry grunted as she put eggs on a plate and set them before Shayla. She poured her a cup of tea and then poured another for herself.

There was a knock on the door, and Mr. Lowman answered it. "Captain."

"Good morning, Mr. Lowman."

Mr. Lowman led Adam to the kitchen as he was instructed to do. Shayla smiled at Adam as he came in.

"A cup of coffee for you, Captain?"

"No thank you, Mrs. Lawry." He looked at Shayla. "Are you ready?"

She nodded, finished drinking her tea, and stood up. Mr. Lowman helped her put on her overcoat and they went outside to Adam's waiting carriage.

"Where are we going?" Shayla asked as the carriage went down the street.

"You will see."

The carriage rolled out of town and down the main road toward the next town of Glastonbury. It was a four mile trip, so Shayla settled in for the ride, but then the carriage pulled over and stopped.

Shayla sat up straight. "Why are we stopping?"

Adam stood up and opened the carriage door. "Come. I want to show you something." He reached out, and Shayla took his hand. They walked down a small path to a clearing. Adam took Shayla's Bulldog out of his coat pocket. "I want to teach you to properly shoot the gun."

Shayla smirked. "That implies that I do not already know how, Captain."

Adam raised his eyebrows. "Then show me." Adam reached into a bag he carried, brought out an empty bottle, and set it on a stump, He walked back to Shayla. He reached into his coat pocket then pulled out the gun and handed it to her. He then held out his other hand and opened it.

Shayla knew this was a test. She took one bullet from his open hand and put it in the gun then did the same with the other four.

"Try to hit the bottle," Adam said smugly.

Shayla nodded. She faced the bottle, took aim, and fired. She missed. She narrowed her eyes and took a deep breath. She knew she could hit the bottle. She was nervous with Adam watching her. She just had to concentrate. She carefully aimed again and fired. The bullet shattered the bottle. Shayla gave a triumphant little cheer.

Adam stared in disbelief. Not only did she handle the gun correctly, but she hit the bottle on her second try.

Adam set up another, and again Shayla hit it.

"You are quite good at shooting," Adam said as he set up another bottle. How did you get so good?"

"Practice."

"Practice? When and where do you practice?" He imagined Shayla riding her bicycle out this way and shuddered. Being alone on this stretch of road was dangerous for anyone let alone a woman.

"I have been practicing almost every week since I bought the gun."

"Really?"

She nodded.

"First, tell me how and where you were able to purchase it."

"As I said, if you offer enough money, you can buy anything in London. When we went to see that murderer hang, I looked around London and saw several dealers. I saved my money, and when my father and I went back later that year, a maid who worked at the inn where we stayed, and I went shopping. We went to a gun dealer, and I bought it. The dealer assumed I was buying it as a gift for my fiancé, and I did not correct him. I asked him to show me how to load it and fire it. He had me fire it in the shop without bullets, and then he showed me how to load the gun. When I returned home, I rode my bicycle out along the railroad tracks and shot it when the train went by to cover the noise. I have been practicing every week since."

"I did hear shots that morning!" Adam exclaimed. "You told me you did not hear shots."

"No. I said I was not certain if I heard anything unusual," Shayla replied smugly.

"You were out picking greens for the windows and practicing. Am I correct?"

She shrugged. "I know a place to practice that is a lot easier to get to than here."

Adam took the gun from her and picked up his bag. "Show me where you practice."

They got back in the carriage and drove back to town. They rode past the shop, and Shayla directed the driver. There was a narrow path along the railroad tracks that became too narrow for the carriage to pass.

"I guess we will have to walk from here." Shayla stood up, and Adam opened the door, and they stepped down.

"Mr. Cooper, please wait for us here," Adam said to the driver.

Shayla and Adam walked along the path and then veered to the left. They passed through a small clump of trees to a clearing. "I do not have any problem getting here on my bicycle," Shayla told him.

Adam kicked a small pile of spent cartridges that littered the ground.

"I always come here when the train is passing by. It muffles the sound of the shots." Adam looked at her, and she gave him a nervous smile. She picked up a piece of wood that was lying on the ground. She threw the rope that was attached to it over a low hanging tree branch.

"That is your target?" Adam asked. The target was swaying in the light breeze.

Shayla nodded. She held out her hand, and Adam set the gun and several bullets in it. She competently loaded the gun, took aim, and fired, hitting the target. She did it two more times. "I told you I knew how to shoot," she told Adam smugly.

He took the gun from her and looked at it. "I should never have doubted you. You are amazing." Adam pulled her close to him and kissed her. She responded to him, and he continued kissing her. It felt good to have her in his arms.

After several minutes, Shayla pulled away and looked him in the eye. "Can I have my gun back, now?" Adam nodded. "Good," she said as she flung her arms around his neck and kissed him.

It was just after nine o'clock when Adam and Shayla walked into the shop. Henry noticed that his daughter was smiling, and her cheeks were rosy. He also noticed the gleam in her eyes when she looked at Adam.

"I am going out back to see if Hal needs me. I will meet you later for lunch," Adam said as he walked to the back of the shop.

"Hi, Papa." Shayla kissed her father's cheek. "Hello, Mrs. Bell. How are you this fine day?"

"I am well, thank you," Mrs. Bell replied. She watched as Shayla practically danced through the store and out the back door to the workshop.

Shayla went right to work on the Duchess' commission. First, she sketched out the set of three pens and holder the Duchess wanted for the Duke. The Duchess said she wanted an eagle on one of the pens, but the rest was up to Shayla to design. Shayla included a great many flourishes accented with gold since they were for the Duke's London office. When she was satisfied with the design, Shayla got right to work.

"How is the Duchess' commission coming along?" Henry asked when he went out back for a late lunch. He looked over at the pen Shayla was working on. "That white pen with the golden eagle on top is impressive." He walked over and peeked carefully in the annealing oven at the other pens she made. They were all beautiful. A brown pen featured a falcon and a midnight blue one had an owl on top. Shayla walked over and added the white pen.

She stretched. She had been hunched over the flame for quite some time. "I was thinking, in London, other Noblemen will see these pens. It could lead to more commissions."

"Yes, that is a possibility."

"Papa, what do you think about opening a second shop? I was thinking that we should open a shop in London."

"You want to expand?"

"Why not? We have plenty of blowers and inventory."

Henry nodded and thought about the proposition. London would provide more customers. Shayla's creations would fetch a higher price in London where people had the inclination to spend money on something that was largely decorative. "We will have to discuss it with your uncle, but I think we should seriously consider it in the new year."

"Good. Are you ready for lunch? I am starving."

"I am. Let us see what Mrs. Lawry packed for us today?"

Adam and Hal walked in and washed up while Henry set a stack of sandwiches on the table. Henry and Hal sat down and began eating. Shayla set a pitcher of cider down on the table, and then Adam held the chair for her.

"Thank you."

"You are most welcome."

The two brothers exchanged looks and watched as Adam and Shayla smiled at one another and began eating their sandwiches.

Henry left the table first. The shop was very busy, and he was needed to help with customers. Hal and Adam left for the commercial factory a few minutes later, and Shayla went into the office to put the finishing touches on her sketch for the holder for the pens.

As she walked out of the office, she saw Jacob's young daughter sitting at the table reading. "Hello, Tara. How are you today?"

"Good," the young girl replied. There was a touch of sadness in her tone that had Shayla turning around to look at the girl.

"Whatever is the matter?"

Tara shrugged.

Shayla took a bag of crisps off the countertop. "How old are you, Tara?"

"Twelve." She looked up as Shayla sat down next to her. Shayla opened the bag of crisps and offered her some. Tara took a crisp. "Your work is so beautiful, Miss Shayla."

"Thank you."

"Are you going to work today?"

"I am. I have a new commission from the Duchess of Wellshore. I will be making the pen holder this afternoon." She slid several sketches over so Tara could see them.

"They are beautiful. When did you learn to make glass pieces?"

"I was about your age." Shayla looked at the girl. "Do you have an interest?"

"Tis fascinating to watch," Tara replied eagerly.

Shayla handed the girl the bag of crisps then she excused herself and went into the main workshop. She located Jacob and beckoned him to her. "Jacob, I was talking to Tara."

"I hope she is not bothering you."

"Not at all." Shayla waved her hand dismissively. "She said she had an interest in glass."

"Aye, she asks me about my work all the time, and I am sure you noticed she comes to watch me work often."

"Would you allow Tara to be my helper?"

Jacob's mouth opened, and then he closed it. "Help you?"

"Why not? She is certainly old enough to learn the trade. I can show her how to work the glass, and she can hand me tools and stock the oven. Young Joseph can come work here in the shop when Tara works with me. It will give him more experience too.

"Yes," Jacob replied happily, "if she is willing to work with you then you have my permission."

"Good."

"Thank you, Shayla. You know her mother has been away often caring for her sick aunt."

Shala nodded. It brought back painful memories of her own mother attending her sick aunt and never returning. She closed her eyes to stop the sting of tears. "Tara can work with me most afternoons. I will send Joseph to you on those days once she has learned what to do." She went back to the preparation room where Tara was once again reading a book. "Tara," the girl looked up, "would you like to assist me in the workshop?"

"You mean it?"

"I do."

"Yes!" the girl exclaimed.

"First, we need to tie up that dress. Can you get a pair of your brother's old britches for tomorrow?"

"I can."

"Good. For today, I want you to mostly watch Joseph and learn what he does. Tomorrow, you can work alone with me. I will of course pay you the same rate as Joseph."

"The same as a boy?"

"Of course. You do the work; you get the pay." The young girl beamed with happiness. If only that were true in the real world, Shayla thought to herself. Well, in her world, it would be the truth. "We will gather up that skirt and tie your hair up with a ribbon." They went back into the office and got ready to work.

Chapter 20

Although Shayla was not always thrilled to go out with a coachman and carriage, when the weather was snowy and the roads were icy as they were today, she welcomed them.

"Let me get those packages for you, Miss Toselli."

"Thank you, Mr. Lowman." She handed over the shopping bags and pulled her cloak tight to her body. Her bonnet was already covered in snow, but she had more shopping to do. "I wish to make one more stop, and then I will have finished my shopping."

"Very well, Miss."

Shayla carefully walked down the icy sidewalk. She stopped and admired a beautiful white cloak with white fur trim and a matching muff in a shop window. After looking at it for several minutes, she walked to the bakery. Inside, the shop was warm, and the air was filled with the scent of gingerbread and cinnamon. Shayla selected several marzipan Santa Claus figures for Mrs. Lawry to use to decorate the cake for the Christmas celebration in the shop tomorrow evening. She also picked up a bag of ginger almond biscuits, which were one of her father's favorite treats.

She was looking at a stack of thin waffle cookies when Adam walked in the bakery. Several women turned and smiled at him, and she was happy to see he did take notice of any of them.

"Good afternoon, Miss Toselli. It is lovely to see you today." He bowed low, then picked up her hand, and kissed it.

"Good afternoon to you, Captain," she curtsied and smiled.

"Have you finished your shopping?"

"Yes. My packages are in the carriage."

"I am glad to hear you have taken the carriage today. The weather is frightful."

"It is, and I am grateful for the carriage."

Adam smiled at her. She complained about having a coachman and carriage at first, but now she seemed to take it more often.

Shayla decided to get the waffle cookies. She then moved to her place in the cue. "I will be wrapping presents this evening for the Christmas celebration for our families at the workshop tomorrow night," she informed him in a very formal tone of voice.

"I am looking forward to the party, and I would be happy to help you wrap the presents. I have grown quite fond of everyone in the shop," he replied. Shayla saw the slight wink he gave her, and she hid her smile behind the items she carried.

"Thank you, Captain. That is most kind." Shayla was next, so she placed her order. "Three chocolate croissants, *s'il vous plait*."

"Croissants?" Adam asked.

"*Mais oui*." She put the items she was purchasing on the counter. When she paid for her items, Adam took the packages from the clerk and escorted Shayla from the shop. He walked her to the carriage. He handed the packages to Mr. Lowman who stored them inside then took his place on the seat above. Adam opened the carriage door.

"Thank you, Captain. I will see you this evening. Six o'clock for dinner before we work?"

"I look forward to it, Miss Toselli." He took her hand and lingered over it while he smiled up at her. Shayla saw the playfulness in his eyes, and she blushed. Finally, Adam kissed her hand. "I will see you at six."

"Good afternoon to you, Captain Preston."

Adam held Shayla's hand and helped her inside the carriage. He closed the door and nodded to Mr. Lowman. Shayla looked out the carriage window and saw several of the ladies staring at them from inside the shop. She was fully aware of the jealousy of those ladies, and she smiled.

She was in a very good mood when they arrived at her home, and Mr. Lowman opened the carriage door for her.

Mrs. Lawry met Shayla at the door. "My, you did shop."

Mr. Lowman brought in all her packages.

"We have gifts to wrap tonight, Mrs. Lawry." Shayla opened several packages to show her what she purchased.

"These are lovely," Mrs. Lawry commented as she looked through the assortment of small tin toys that Shayla spread out on the table. "You have more than enough of these for the boys."

"Most of the boys have younger siblings. I want to give toys to all the children in the family. I also have these small dolls, ribbons, and hair combs for the girls, and checkers, balls, jump ropes, and dominos for the older children."

Mrs. Lawry laughed out loud. "My oh my, we are like Father Christmas."

"Yes, this is the best time of the year. Oh, Adam will be joining us for dinner, and he will help us wrap the presents for the children tonight."

Mrs. Lawry nodded and smiled. She was thrilled to see Shayla so happy.

Henry walked into the kitchen. He picked up one of the tin toys, a Santa Clause figure pulling a sled piled high with packages. "It is amazing what can be made now."

"Oh, I forgot the marbles I made at the shop. Adam and I can go get them later."

"Adam is visiting tonight?" Henry asked.

"Is that ok, Papa?"

"Yes. I like him very much. He is a good man, and I am happy to see you two spending time together."

"We are just enjoying one another's company."

"Are you sure that is all there is to it?"

"Of course. His family is noble, and we are commoners."

"We are not that common."

"I cannot see myself being content going to tea with the ladies and spending my day in leisure."

"Who says you must live that way? Adam knows you are a glass blower and business owner. He will not expect you to stay at home and lie around the house."

"He might if all his friends' wives do."

"Then again, he might not," Henry pointed out.

That gave Shayla something to consider. "Well," she let out a deep breath, "I am going to get dressed for dinner." She turned and went upstairs.

Henry looked at Mrs. Lawry. "Did she say she was getting dressed for dinner? She is already in a fancier dress than she wears to church on Sunday."

Mrs. Lawry smiled and nodded.

After dinner, Shayla, Adam, Henry, and Mrs. Lawry gathered around the large dining room table and wrapped the toys. Despite her reservations about marriage, Shayla thought it would be nice to be with Adam in the evening. They would talk about their day and maybe listen to music. She looked over at what he was doing. "You are meant to cover that toy with the paper, Adam," she said as she took the toy and adjusted the paper to completely cover it. She tied it up with a length of ribbon.

"I have not had much practice wrapping toys," he replied.

"Put the bows on then." Shayla smiled at him.

"I can do that."

"More tea," Mrs. Lawry asked as she finished wrapping the last toy in her pile and placed it in the basket.

"Yes, please," Shayla replied.

Henry wrapped the last toy in his pile and let out a deep sigh of relief. "Adam, would you care for a drink"?"

"A big one. I never knew wrapping presents was so difficult." Shayla put a wrapped gift in front of him, and he slapped on a ribbon bow. "Done," he said with satisfaction.

"We still have to get the marbles and wrap them," she reminded him.

"We can go to the shop for the marbles after you have a cup of tea, and I have a well-deserved drink."

"Let us adjourn to the parlor for that drink," Henry suggested.

"Go," Shayla pushed Adam after her father. "I will join you shortly."

Adam followed Henry to the parlor. Henry walked to the bar and poured two glasses of brandy. "Thank you, Henry." Adam took the glass from him and settled himself in a chair in front of the hearth. He was very comfortable in the Toselli home, and he enjoyed their company. He heard Shayla and Mrs. Lawry singing holiday carols as they cleaned up in the kitchen.

Henry sat in a chair opposite Adam and took a sip of his drink. "Tis nice to see Shayla so happy. You are a good influence on her, Adam."

"As she is on me. You know, I have not had a nightmare in weeks. And this morning, I caught myself singing carols while I shaved."

Henry took another sip. "I imagine you would have nightmares after your experiences. Might I inquire how you were injured?"

Adam held the glass in his hand. "We were pinned down and had to hold until reinforcements arrived. One of my men was shot, and I saw him moving out in the open area. I could not let the man stay out there bleeding, so I left the cover of the trees and ran to him. I managed to lift him up, and then I hunched over and started back to safety." He took a swallow of brandy. "I almost made it. I stepped up over a fallen tree when the first bullet grazed my left leg. I was not so fortunate with the second bullet."

"Did the man live?"

"He did, and I was sent home. My injuries allowed me to resign. I never want to go to war again." He drank down the remaining contents of his glass in one gulp.

"It is snowing," Shayla called happily as she walked into the parlor. Adam and Henry stood up and looked out the window. Snow was indeed falling. "Shall we walk to the shop and get the marbles, Adam. It is a perfect night for a walk."

"I am your servant, Miss Toselli," Adam said with a flourish of his hand as he bowed. "I will get our over coats."

Shayla put on a hat and gloves, and Adam helped her into her coat. He put on his coat, hat, and gloves and opened the front door. Snow was falling heavily now. Adam offered her his arm, and they walked out into the snow.

"Thank you for helping with the gift wrapping tonight."

"It was my pleasure. You and your family are so welcoming. I feel very much at ease when I am in your company."

"I am at ease with you as well."

They snow dampened their footsteps as they walked arm in arm to the shop. Shayla unlocked the door, and they went inside. It was dark, so Shayla lit a lamp. The marbles were near the cash register where she left them. It was so quiet they could hear the dull roar of the furnaces. As Shayla turned off the lamp, Adam wrapped his arms around her waist. Shayla leaned back and Adam moved her hair aside and kissed her neck.

A shudder of pleasure rippled through Shayla. Adam turned her in his arms and slowly brought his lips to hers. Shayla held the marbles in one hand and brought her other hand up and touched Adam's face. "You make me feel…wonderful," she sighed breathlessly, and he deepened the kiss.

"You are wonderful, Shayla," Adam whispered against her lips. "I better get you home, now." Adam took Shayla's hand, and they left the shop. The snow had dwindled to a flurry, but everything had a clean layer of white. At her door, Adam pressed a kiss to

Shayla's hand. "Good night, Miss Toselli. Thank you for a wonderful evening."

"Good night, Captain Preston. You are always welcome here."

## Chapter 21

The morning after the Christmas party, Shayla went to the shop with her father. "Shayla, you do not need to come in this morning. It is Saturday and you have the Earl's party today."

"I have plenty of time to get ready, Papa. I want to see the pieces I made yesterday." She was too eager to wait for the boys to finish unloading the oven, so she helped them.

"That is the boys' job, Shayla," Hal feigned a growl when he saw his niece.

"I am anxious."

Hal shook his head. Finally, Shayla walked away from the oven holding a glass stein. Hal walked over to take a look. "The brown glass is quite unique."

"I like it." Shayla turned the stein back and forth. The brown glass had red undertones which were set off by the black accents.

"Tis for Adam, is it not?"

"Perhaps it is," she replied.

"Do not be coy with me, girl," Hal laughed. "I see the pony. Adam's unit had a light brown pony as a mascot." He watched his niece's cheeks flush with color, and he smiled.

Henry walked over and examined the stein more closely. "I like this color. We need to mix more of it. It is quite unique. How did you make it, Shayla?"

"I have the formula written down with my sketches. I will start mixing the glass."

"Jimmy," Henry called, and the young man walked over. "Watch as Shayla mixes this brown glass and make notes."

Jimmy nodded and looked closely at the glass Shayla still held. "Are there gold flecks in the glass?"

"Yes," Shayla nodded. She took the stein and wrapped it in thick cotton material. She planned to take it home, wrap it in festive paper, and present it to Adam on Christmas day. Shayla placed the stein in a box and set it on the table then began mixing the colored glass.

She stayed at the workshop longer than she planned, but they now had an ample supply of the brown glass with the gold flecks. Before leaving, Shayla blew two goblets with the glass, and when she left, her uncle was busy making more.

"The carriage is waiting to take you home," Henry said as he kissed his daughter's cheek. "Enjoy the party."

"Thank you, Papa." She hurried out the door to the waiting carriage.

Fortunately, it did not take Shayla long to get ready. Mrs. Lawry looked her over and said she would do. Mr. Lowman waited for her, and when she came out of the house in her party dress, he helped her into the carriage.

"We are picking up Miss Williams."

"Very good, Miss."

Mr. Lowman drove to the Williams' home, and Shayla waited in the carriage while he knocked on the door and then helped Sarah into the carriage.

"I am very happy to be going to the party with you, Shayla," Sarah said as she sat on the opposite bench.

Sarah's mother could not attend this party, so Shayla suggested they attend together. She was relieved to see Sarah smiling. She worried about her friend after their near abduction.

"This is the only event I normally attend. The first social engagement I attended with my mother was at the Earl's home." She drifted off thinking about her mother who told her that attending social engagements when invited was not only good for business, but it enabled her to meet people of a higher social class. That season, Shayla attended several parties including two hosted by the Earl and his wife. That was just before her mother went to care for her sick aunt.

"Shayla?" Sarah called softly.

She shook her head. "Sorry. The Earl of Huntington is such a nice man. And he is a great customer."

"I hope there are many single men at the party."

"I thought you favored Joseph Grant?"

Sarah shook her head. "He's not what I am looking for in a man." Sarah smoothed down the front of her sunny yellow dress. "I saw him having tea with Caroline Warren yesterday in the tea shop."

"Oh, Sarah, I am sorry, but I think it is better to find out now that he is a rake than to be surprised later."

"The exact words of my mother."

"She is a wise woman."

"Will Adam be at the party?" Sarah asked.

Shayla shrugged her shoulders. "I do not know. Now you mention it, perhaps."

They arrived at the Earl's mansion, a three story white home with black shutters and a columned entry. The two women exited the carriage and walked up to the front door. "Good day ladies, please come in." the butler bowed, and another man took their coats.

They waited smothered their dresses as they waited by the parlor entrance.

"Announcing Miss Shayla Toselli and Miss Sarah Williams," the butler called to the other guests.

The Earl's wife came forward. "I am so happy you both could make it today."

"Thank you for inviting us, Lady Huntington." Shayla replied, and she and Sarah curtsied.

They walked over to the Earl and curtsied. "Such fine and beautiful ladies you both are." He kissed their hands. "Let me introduce you to some of the other guests." He held up his arms, and Sarah and Shayla each took one as he led them around the room. The Earl introduced them to several men and women then went to greet more guests.

A waiter came to offer a glass of wassail. They each took a glass, and then they saw several women they knew, so they walked over to talk to the other ladies. Another waiter passed a tray of canapes. As Shayla took a bite, she heard, "announcing Captain Adam Preston," and she looked up. Adam stood tall and looked commanding in his uniform, and Shayla took a steadying breath. Sarah watched Shayla's reaction and knew her friend fancied Captain Preston.

Adam entered the room, and Shayla watched him discreetly as he moved to greet the Earl and his wife. She knew the instant he spotted her. Their eyes met, and he smiled and nodded his head. She did the same. He engaged in conversation with several people before he finally made it to her side. "Miss Toselli, I am delighted to see you today." He bowed low. She was dressed in a soft blue colored chiffon dress. Her hair was arranged and held up with the pearl combs from her aunt and uncle, and she wore the pearl necklace and earrings that her father and uncle gifted her on her birthday.

"Captain Preston, A pleasure as always." She curtsied and looked up at him and smiled.

Adam escorted Shayla to the dining room, but they were not seated near each other. However, throughout the midafternoon meal, they glanced at one another and made eye contact. The gentleman to

Shayla's right did his best to keep her engaged in conversation. Mr. Brown, a Mathematics professor at the nearby university, was a likeable man. He had short brown hair and wore glasses. He was particularly interested in Shayla's glass blowing abilities.

"Would it be possible to see you work the glass, Miss Toselli?"

"Of course. I am in the shop most days."

"I will stop by one afternoon while I am on break from the university."

"I will inform my father that you will be stopping by. Simply give him your name, and he will bring you to the workshop in back."

"Thank you. My mother has a birthday coming up. What would you suggest?"

"Perhaps a vase or a perfume bottle."

"Both would be appropriate."

Adam watched Shayla and Brown talking. He knew Brown from other social engagements and never knew him to talk to a woman as much as he was conversing with Shayla. What were they discussing? He certainly was smiling at her a great deal. And she smiled at him quite often as well. Adam's blood began to boil. He took a drink. Why did it bother him that Shayla was talking to someone? He was not courting her. Not officially. Although in his mind, he was courting her. He just had not officially sought permission yet.

"Captain?" the young woman next to him said to get his attention.

He turned to her. "Forgive me, Miss Charlotte, I was lost in my thoughts."

After the main meal, a band played soft music in the parlor, and several people danced while waiters served dessert and tea.

Shayla stood near the hearth and talked with a small group of women. They dipped pieces of fruit in the chocolate fountain and ate them. Adam was engaged in conversation with several men including Professor Brown when he saw a man he did not know approach Shayla.

"May I have this dance, Miss Toselli?"

Shayla nodded. "Yes, you may, Lord Bard." She had been introduced to the Lord earlier that afternoon. He took her hand and placed his other hand lightly at her waist. They danced around the room, keeping a wide distance between them. They smiled and moved gracefully to the music.

Adam narrowed his eyes. Who was that man dancing with his Shayla? His Shayla. When did she become his, he wondered, but there was no denying that he thought of her as his. He wanted her to be his, so why had he not asked her?

"They look good together," the Earl of Huntington commented next to him as he watched Shayla and Lord Bard dance.

"You think so? Who is he?" Adam scrutinized the man. He looked to be in his early thirties. He had golden hair that came just to his collar. He was not much taller than Shayla, but he had a rugged build.

"Lord Marcus Bard, Winifred Bard's nephew. You have not met him? He is friendly with your brother, the Duke."

"He was not at the Duchess' charity party, and he has not been to any of the dinner parties I have attended at the estate."

"I am certain you will see him at the Christmastide Ball. Bard purchased the Marlow estate, and he and his aunt only just arrived in Canterbury Corner two days ago. They are staying for the holiday. His aunt Winifred grew up here. Her husband passed away suddenly this Spring, and Marcus was his heir. He lived with his aunt and uncle for years. Rumor has it, Bard is looking for a wife."

The color drained from Adam's face. He watched as after the dance Lord Bard returned Shayla to her friends. He bowed deeply and kissed her hand. Did she blush? Adam turned to reenter the conversation with the Earl and the other gentlemen. He did not notice that Professor Brown had moved away. Several minutes later, a waiter appeared with brandy. As Adam reached for a glass, he spotted Shayla dancing with the professor. He stared at them as they danced. The man said something to Shayla, and she laughed as they moved around the room. First Lord Bard danced with Shayla, and now the professor was eyeing his girl. It was too much, and at that moment, jealousy consumed him. He did not take the brandy but walked purposefully toward the dancing couple. He did not wait for the dance to end but tapped the professor on the shoulder. "I would like the hand of my fiancé," he said without looking at the man.

"Fiancé?" Shayla and Brown said at the same time.

Adam roughly pushed the man aside and grabbed Shayla's hand. She did not move, and their actions and voices drew the attention of the other guests.

"I am not your fiancé. You never asked me to marry you. We are not even officially courting."

"I am asking you now."

"Have you spoken to my father?"

"You are mine."

"I am no man's property, Captain Preston." Shayla pulled her hand out of his and walked away from him.

Adam grabbed her hand, and she turned back to him. There was fire in her eyes. "Unhand me this instant," Shayla demanded. Adam released her hand.

The Earl appeared beside them. "Is there a problem?"

"There is no problem, My Lord, but I am afraid I must be going." Shayla walked toward Sarah.

"What is he talking about? You are not engaged." Sarah glared back over her shoulder at Adam.

"We are leaving," Shayla stated firmly, and she walked to the entry hall.

The butler called for their carriage while he helped them into their coats then Shayla and Sarah left the party.

After dropping off Sarah, Shayla instructed Mr. Lowman to bring her to the workshop. She jumped out of the carriage and stormed into the shop.

"Shayla, you are back early." Henry looked at her and realized she was upset. "What happened? Are you alright?" He was terrified something had happened to her again.

"I am fine, but Captain Preston is not going to be fine when next I see him."

"What happened?"

"He had the gall to call me his fiancé in public without my or your consent?"

Henry shook his head. "What? Why would Adam do that?"

"He said I was his. Well, I informed him that I am no man's property. How dare him." She picked up her skirts and stormed to the workshop. She went into the office and slammed the door. She changed into the britches and shirt she kept at the shop. She took off her jewelry, pulled the fancy combs from her hair, and stuffed it under a cap. As she stomped into the furnace room, she tied on an apron and pulled on gloves. She slammed open the furnace door a bit too hard and then took a deep breath and settled down to work.

## Chapter 22

Adam could not stay at the party any longer. He bid a quick goodbye to the Earl and his wife and left. The carriage pulled up to Wellshore Manor, and Adam jumped down and walked inside. He knew he would have to talk to Elliot, and it became clear to him that it was time he had his own home.

"Oh Adam, you are back early. How was the Earl's party? You know he has it every year. I guess he prefers an afternoon party to evening parties as he is getting up in years." The Duchess stopped talking abruptly. She looked at Adam's face and knew he was upset. "What is wrong, brother?"

Elliot walked out of the parlor when he heard his wife. He stepped up to her side and looked at his brother. "Adam, what is bothering you?"

"Nothing is wrong," Adam snapped. He took off his overcoat and handed it to the butler.

"Come have a drink," Elliot steered Adam to the parlor and poured him a large glass of brandy. He handed the glass to Adam then he sat next to his wife on the settee.

Adam remained standing. He started to pace. "Fine. I will tell you what is wrong." He drank down half the glass of brandy. "Miss Toselli was at the Earl's party. She danced with two men, someone named Bard whom I do not know and that Professor Brown."

"So?" Amelia replied. "That is normal. She did nothing wrong."

"Well, I cut in and told Brown I wanted my fiancé back."

"Your fiancé?" Elliot asked.

"That is wonderful, but Adam, even if she is your fiancé, she can still dance with other men at a party. When did you speak to her father?" Amelia asked.

Adam drank down the rest of the brandy. "I did not speak to him."

"You did not?" Elliot and Amelia questioned together.

Elliot shook his head. "Look Adam, I know she is past the age of majority and an independent woman, but still, it is proper to ask the father for her hand in marriage."

"A fact that she loudly pointed out before abruptly leaving the party," Adam informed them.

"Shayla left the party?" Amelia was confused.

"Yes. She did not agree."

"Adam you are not making sense," Amelia sighed. "She did not agree with what?"

"To be my fiancé."

Elliot jumped up. "What do you mean she did not agree to be your fiancée?!" Elliot roared. "You made a public announcement of an engagement without asking the father or getting the woman's consent?" He glared at his younger brother. "How can you be so crude?"

Amelia touched her husband's arm and gave him a look that asked to let her handle this. "Adam," she began quietly, "that is not like you. Why would you do such a thing?"

Adam shrugged. His anger was abating, and he was beginning to feel like an ass. "I saw her talking to Brown at dinner, and then I saw her dancing with the two men, and I snapped."

"And did you explain yourself to Shayla?"

"No, I said she was mine. Then she informed me, in a loud and clear voice, that she is no man's property and left the party." Adam walked over and refilled his glass. He drank it straight down then left the room without another word.

Amelia looked at her husband. "Perhaps you should go after him, Elliot," she suggested. "Talk to him."

Elliot watched his brother walk away. "No, Amelia. He has to handle this himself."

## Chapter 23

Shayla's mood was sour. She worked furiously. She formed the glass and added bold red color. She added more glass and drew the sculptural piece higher. She called for tools, and the boy immediately jumped to get them for her.

Henry wanted to check on Shayla more often, but the shop was busy this close to Christmastide, and he, Aaron, and Jason rarely had a break between customers.

"Thank you, Mrs. Hennessey," he bowed to the woman, opened the door for her, and handed her footman the heavy package of candle sticks she purchased. "Happy Christmas."

Henry saw the glow of the streetlamps in town. Normally, the shop would have closed hours ago, but many people were still out shopping. This year was going to be their best year ever.

When the shop finally closed, Henry went out back. Now maybe he could find out everything that happened between Shayla and Adam. He thought she would be in the office, but he saw she was still working. Hal stood by the window drinking a cup of coffee as he watched Shayla in the furnace room. Henry poured himself coffee and went to join his brother. "Have the workers gone home for the day?"

"Aye. Long ago." Hal took a drink. "She is upset about something," he observed.

Henry took a drink of coffee. "Apparently, Adam announced their engagement at the Earl's party this afternoon."

"He asked for her hand in marriage? Why did you keep it a secret?"

"He did not ask me. Apparently, he did not ask Shayla either."

"It must be the green eyed monster got him," Hal laughed.

"That is my guess as well."

"Her response was not favorable I surmise." Hal looked at his niece. She still looked angry.

"She told him she is no man's property."

Hal winced. "In front of everyone at the party?" Henry nodded. "Poor Adam."

They stood and watched Shayla work. "She really does nice work when she is angry. So expressive. So vibrant," Hal commented. Shayla's latest piece was a vase with streaks of color resembling fire. It was tall and elegant, and it flared out at the top like a starburst.

"She is using a great deal of red." Henry frowned and shook his head. "No one but the Queen will be able to afford it." The clock chimed seven times. "Are you going to supper?" Henry asked.

"I think I will stay here and see what happens. Do you think Adam will show up?"

Henry shrugged. He walked to the icebox. "There are sandwiches here. Want one?"

"Yes. I am hungry." Hal took a sandwich, and the two men sat down to eat and wait.

Nearly two hours later, Shayla wiped her brow. She inspected the piece she made and decided it was finished. She told the boy helping her to go home some time ago, so she carefully loaded the last piece into the oven. Several shelves were filled with pieces she made. All in shades of red she noted as she closed the door. She checked the oven temperature and sat down heavily in the blowing chair that she sometimes used in front of the furnace. She was exhausted. Her anger burned up in the molten glass. She pulled off her hat, leaned back, and closed her eyes.

"Perhaps we should send for Adam," Henry said to Hal as they stood at the window and looked at Shayla.

"No need, Henry. I am here."

The two men were startled and turned to see Adam coming down the dark hallway. He walked to where they stood and looked at Shayla. He loved her so much. Seeing her exhausted and sad broke his heart. How could he let this happen? Why did he not tell her he was in love with her and wanted her to be his? Why did he act like a cad? She did not dance with him, but then, he did not ask her to dance.

Adam took a deep breath and turned to Henry. "I apologize Henry. I overstepped my bounds as you have undoubtedly heard. You are within your right to order me to leave." He bowed to Henry.

"What happened?" Henry asked. He did not hold any hard feelings against Adam. He liked him and thought he was the right man for his precious daughter. He knew if Corrine were here, she would know exactly what to say.

"I was consumed by a jealous rage. I saw her innocently dancing with another man, and I could not stand it." He ran his fingers through his damp and tangled hair. His clothes were dirty and disheveled. His eyes were puffy, and his face was flush.

Adam let out a breath. "Henry, I announced to the room that she was my fiancé which is disrespectful to her and to you. You have my most sincere apology."

"Do you love her?" Henry asked. He needed to hear the answer to that question from Adam's mouth.

"I have more love for her than I ever thought I was capable of having for another. I acted like a crazed possessive man. I assure you, Henry, I do not wish to possess her. I love her, and her independence is one of the qualities I love most about her. I should have asked to officially court her weeks ago. I should have told her I love her weeks ago."

Henry saw in Adam's eyes that he was telling him the truth. "Love is all that matters. You should tell her you love her, Adam. It is time you two talked honestly about your feelings for one another."

Adam nodded. "I know we have not officially courted, but with your permission, I would like to ask Shayla to be my wife."

"You have my permission." They shook hands. "But I am not the one you have to convince."

"She is exhausted." Adam looked at Shayla slumped in the chair her face wet with tears. "May I talk with her and then take her home?"

Henry and Hal looked at one another. Henry put his hand on Adam's shoulder. "Go to her," he said, "make up to her, and tell her how you feel. You must assure her that you love her and will not smother her. She may or may not believe you."

Adam took a deep breath. He too was exhausted. "I have been riding hard for hours. Thinking." He straightened up. "Do not worry. Regardless of her answer, I will get her home safely. Thank you, Henry."

Henry and Hal put on their coats. "Be honest with her, Adam," Henry said, and he and Hal left the workshop.

Adam waited until he heard the front door close and lock. It was time to bare his heart to the woman he loved. He just hoped she would not cut it to pieces and throw him out. Adam opened the door to the furnace room and stepped inside.

Shayla lifted her head when she saw him. "Adam." She reached for him. She knew she should still be angry with him, but her anger was gone. He was here, looking a bit ragged. He looked as tired as she felt.

He knelt in front of her. "Shayla, I beg your forgiveness. I acted the fool. I would never try to possess you. Please, you must believe me."

She saw sincerity in his eyes, but she had to be certain. "I was shocked that you would behave in such a manner."

"Jealousy is a poor excuse, but it is the honest truth. I love you, Shayla. I love you so much, and I could not stand to see another man hold you in his arms with hope in his eyes that you would return his affections. I realized at that moment that I want to be the only man to hold you and have your affections."

He picked up her hands and kissed them. "Shayla, will you do me the honor of being my wife?" She stared at him. "I have asked your father, and he gives his consent if you want to marry me."

She framed his face with her hands. "You want to marry me?"

"I do."

"What do you expect from me?"

"Your love is all I require. I love you. We will be equal partners in marriage. I will help you in any way you require with your business, with our home, with our children." He pulled her hand to his chest. "I will purchase a home here near your family, and I will purchase a town home in London for when I must be there for business, and you wish to accompany me."

"London?"

"Yes, I told you that my brother was arranging a position for me in our family business."

Shayla nodded her head. "You did say working in the glass shop was only temporary."

"I am to begin managing the railway investments for my family in the new year. The work will require me to be in London several times a year." She did not respond right away, and he worried that she was going to refuse him. He knew family was very important to Shayla, and perhaps she did not want to be away from them at all. "I could speak to my brother if that does not suit you. I am certain he can find me a different position."

She smiled. This was too good to be true. Adam loved her and wanted a home here and in London. "It suits me, Adam. I spoke to my father recently regarding opening a shop in London. I wish to expand our market."

Adam let out the breath he did not realize he was holding. "Thank you." He looked into her eyes. "We are well matched, Shayla. Please tell me you will be my wife. You are the only woman I have ever loved. The only one I have ever wanted to spend the rest of my life loving. I will do my best to be a good husband."

Shayla nodded her head. "I will be honored to be your wife, Adam."

Adam stretched up and kissed her passionately. "Thank you. Thank you," he said between kisses. "Shayla, you have made me a happy man."

"You make me happy, Adam. I never thought I wanted marriage, but I want it with you. Only you." She grabbed his lapels, pulled him closer, and kissed him with a fire she never knew before. She wanted this man in every way.

They continued to kiss, and their passion grew. Adam slid his hands inside her shirt. There was too much material. He needed his hands on her.

"Shayla, I need you." His voice was rough as he continued to ravage her mouth with his.

"Adam," she breathed.

His hands quickly unbuttoned her shirt. She did not protest, so he pushed the shirt open. Finally, he felt skin and the glory of it nearly undid him. Her body was hot, her breathing was ragged, and all Adam could do was steep himself in her. She wore only a plain white cotton camisole under the shirt, and he lowered his head and tasted her. She was divine, and he feasted on her.

Shayla's delicate hands fumbled with the buttons of his shirt. She had to feel him. When she finally had the shirt undone, she slid her hands up his back over his taunt muscles.

His mouth returned to hers. He lowered the back of the chair and eased her down. He kissed her as he lay on top of her. Their skin seemed to fuse together while their tongues explored one another.

"Shayla," Adam whispered as he nipped her lower lip. "Be mine, Shayla."

"I want you, Adam."

"And I want you so desperately I can barely breathe, but not here."

She let out a sigh. "I did not think we would make love here," she replied softly.

"Not tonight."

"Why not? I agreed to marry you."

"I want our first time to be special, in a comfortable bed with soft light. You deserve no less, my love."

She took a steadying breath. "I can wait."

Adam kissed her sweetly. "Come. Let me take you home. You are exhausted."

Shayla shook her head and held him still. "Not yet. I want to be with you a while longer."

"I promise you, Shayla, I will always respect you and love you."

"And I will love and respect you, Adam."

They laid together on the chair. It started to cool down in the furnace room, so Adam wrapped Shayla in his arms, and she rested her head on his chest. Holding Shayla like this felt so right. Adam knew he could not wait long to make her his wife.

Shayla yawned. "I could stay like this all night."

"You would not be happy if you slept here all night. You would be quite stiff in the morning."

Shayla laughed. "You are right, but I still want to stay with you."

"And I you."

Reluctantly, Adam buttoned her shirt and then his own. He stood up and reached out a hand to help Shayla to her feet. Before leaving, Shayla checked the annealing oven and put her tools away. They locked up the door and went outside. Adam's horse was tethered in front of the shop. He helped Shayla up on the horse's back and then swung up behind her. He wrapped his arm around her waist, and she relaxed back into the warmth of his body. Adam started the horse toward Shayla's home at a very slow and even pace. He was not in a hurry to get her home.

## Chapter 24

The next morning, Adam arrived at the Toselli home in time for breakfast. Mrs. Lawry outdid herself making omelets with shallots and mushrooms and biscuits.

Once they were seated at the table, Shayla took Adam's hand. "Papa, Mrs. Lawry, we have an announcement." She nodded to Adam.

"Last night, I asked Shayla to marry me, and she accepted."

"Congratulations!" Henry stood up as did Adam. They shook hands then Henry kissed his daughter.

"I am so happy for you both," Mrs. Lawry kissed them and dried her eyes on her apron.

"We must toast." Henry left the kitchen to get a bottle of brandy and glasses. "Mr. Lowman," he called out the front door on his way into the parlor.

Mr. Lowman dropped what he was doing and ran inside. "Sir, is something the matter?"

"No. Yes. We must toast." Henry poured a generous amount of brandy into each glass and put them on a tray. A confused Mr. Lowman took the tray from Henry and followed him into the kitchen. He handed out glasses, and Henry cleared his throat. "To my beautiful daughter, Shayla, on her engagement to Captain Preston, a good and honorable man. A long and happy life for you both."

"Here. Here," Mrs. Lawry and Mr. Lowman cheered.

"Thank you," Shayla and Adam responded, and they lifted their glasses and drank.

"Now, let us sit and eat this wonderful breakfast Mrs. Lawry has prepared."

After breakfast, Mr. Lowman and Mrs. Lawry left to go to the market, and Henry went in his office to finish up end of the year paperwork before he and Shayla left for the shop.

"What are your plans today, my love," Adam asked as he kissed her cheek and over to her ear."

Shayla sighed. When he did that, she could not think. "What? Oh, I must get to the shop this morning. I have glass to unload, and there are always last minute commissions."

"I am sorry, but I have business matters that I must attend today, and I must leave for London in the morning. There is an urgent matter that requires my attention in London." He took her hands. "I will be back on the first train on Christmas Eve morning."

"I do not plan to work in the shop on Christmas Eve. I need ample time to set the ornaments on display, bring the Duchess her commission, and then get home to dress myself for the ball."

Adam ran his hands over her hair. "I will arrange a maid and a room for you in the house. I will help you set up the ornaments, and then you can rest and get ready." He kissed her. "I must leave. I have an early appointment." He kissed her again.

"Papa and I will be leaving for the shop soon anyway. I expect business to be very busy today this close to Christmastide."

Adam wrapped one arm around Shayla's waist and put the other behind her head as he kissed her. He took his time savoring her lips. He wanted the taste of her to last until he returned. When he released her, Shayla touched her hand to his cheek and smiled at him. "I am very happy."

"As am I." Adam kissed her again. "I will come to the shop when my business is concluded today." He kissed her. He just could not get enough of her. "The next time I must go to London, you will accompany me."

Shayla sighed as he kissed her neck. "Will you have dinner here tonight?" she asked in a breathless voice.

"Yes. Thank you. I want to spend every minute I can with you." He leaned back. "You better get ready for work, and I must get to my first appointment."

Shayla nodded and started to walk upstairs, but she turned around and threw herself into his arms and kissed him. "I will miss you."

"And I you."

Reluctantly, Adam watched as Shayla went upstairs. He did not have much time before his appointment. He turned and went to Henry's office. "Henry, there is an important matter I wish to discuss with you. May I have a word?"

"Of course. Come in."

"Thank you," Adam replied as he closed the door.

Chapter 25

On the train to London, Adam found his compartment and took off his overcoat. The compartment was warm as this train was heated by the steam from the engines. It was one of the newer innovations in train travel. His brother Elliot decided to invest in the expanding railways for himself and his brothers, and it had proved a wise investment.

He had a very early breakfast with Shayla and her family. Mrs. Lawry's food was filling and more delicious than anything available on the train, so he did not need to go to the dining car. Therefore, he settled back in his comfortable seat and was lulled by the movement of the train as it got underway. The other man in his compartment sat quietly and sipped a cup of tea. The men exchanged greetings upon their arrival but then picked up their papers and did not converse anymore. Adam read the headlines, but he was not particularly interested in any of the articles. Mentally, he made a list of the stops he wanted to make before going to his mother's London townhouse. He planned to complete his tasks quickly, so he could take the first train back to Canterbury Corner on Christmas Eve morning.

Adam let out a sigh of relief. Shayla said yes. He wanted to marry her soon, so before leaving, he wrote to the vicar to have the banns announced in church on Sunday. Typically, the banns needed to be announced three times over a period of three months. Three months. Adam shook his head. Three months was unacceptable. He knew traditionally the bride selected the wedding date, but he hoped she would be agreeable to his idea. If she agreed, he needed to obtain a special license, and for that he needed Elliot's help. He took a notepad out of his jacket pocket, made a few notes, and then closed his eyes and rested for the ride to London.

When the train pulled into Paddington station, Adam promptly made his way off the train and out of the station. He turned at the end of the ramp and walked by the Great Western Railway Hotel which was bustling with guests coming in and going out the front entrance. This was the perfect place to take Shayla when they returned to London, he thought.

Adam was meeting with a manager at the railway office. His brother wanted to expand the service to Canterbury Corner, and Adam was to make the appeal in person. Adam never believed he would have any role in the family businesses. Their father had set up trust funds for all his sons, but the main businesses went to his two eldest sons. Elliot was now the head of the family, and unlike James and Jonathan, he not only wanted his brothers' help, but he made certain that all three were equal partners in everything that was not titled property.

The door opened as he approached the railway office. "Captain Adam Preston to see Mr. Sabastian."

"Very good, Sir. I will announce you. May I take your coat?"

Adam let the doorman help him out of his overcoat. He took Adam's valise and then led him down the hallway. Adam glanced in the other offices as he was led through to Mr. Sabastian's office.

"Captain Adam Preston to see you, Sir."

Sabastian jumped to his feet. "Captain Preston," he bowed, "come in. Please sit down. I expect you had a good trip to London?"

"Yes, thank you, Sir." Adam sat in a very comfortable leather wing back chair in front of the desk.

"Good. I have everything ready for you. May I offer you coffee or tea?"

"Yes, coffee, thank you."

Sebastian nodded to his secretary, and the young man left the room. "We can begin now if you are ready."

Adam nodded. "That would be ideal."

"If you would come this way, I will bring you to your office."

Adam rose and followed the man down the hall.

It was late in the afternoon when Adam dispatched a telegram to his brother appraising him of the progress that was made during the meetings. Adam realized that the business world was much like the military: take charge, show no fear, and you can survive. Logistics were Adam's specialty, and he knew Elliot's choice of work for him was going to be something he was going to enjoy. He left the telegraph office and got in a carriage to make his way to his next stop.

At Covent Garden, Adam took a leisurely walk and looked in the shops. A cluster of perfume bottles in a window brought up thoughts of Shayla. She would love the shops, he thought, and he planned to bring her here when they came to London on business soon after the new year.

He was looking for a special gift for Shayla. He saw her looking at the clothing in a shop window the day he saw her in the bakery. He wanted something special as a Christmastide present for her. When he spotted a beautiful white cloak and muff in a shop window, he knew they were perfect. They were quite fashionable, and he pictured her wearing them. He sighed at the thought. He missed her.

After he made his purchases, he walked to the main street corner. A for sale sign in one of the shop windows caught his eye. He took his notebook out of his pocket and wrote down the landlord's name. This might be the shop for Shayla. He could not believe his luck. Adam was feeling very good when he took a carriage across town to his mother's townhouse.

"Hello, Franklin," he said as he took off his hat and coat.

"Good evening, Captain. Your mother is in the parlor awaiting your arrival." He took Adam's coat and hat, and Adam made his way to the formal sitting parlor. The room had a thick Oriental carpet in the center around which were placed several cream colored velvet upholstered wing backed chairs and a settee covered in silk with a peacock design. Along one wall was a Davenport desk and a leather armchair.

"Mother." Adam kissed her cheek. Grace Preston, the Dowager Duchess of Wellshore was still beautiful. Her long blonde hair was pulled up on top of her head in an intricate arrangement. Soft tendrils of hair curled and framed her face making her look younger than her actual years.

"Adam, this is Mr. Guthrey from the bank. He has kindly brought over the jewels so you may select a ring for your bride to be."

Adam turned to face the man, and they shook hands. Mr. Guthrey was a rather tall and thin man with hair that was grey at the temples but otherwise was dark and thick. With a wave of his hand, he directed Adam's attention to a chest that sat on a small cherry side table. Adam walked over and opened the chest. Inside was a tray of rings.

His mother stood and went to his side. "Do any of these appeal to you?"

Adam nodded his head. "Perhaps."

"There are two other trays in the chest," she replied. "What color does she like?"

"She wears mostly tan pants and a white shirt in the shop."

"Colin said she was a glass blower, but really you must see her outside the shop," his mother said.

"I first saw her in pink, but she wears teal and blue often, and mostly pearls for jewelry." Adam looked at the rings on the second tray. "I am certain one of these will speak to me." He pulled out two rings that he liked then looked at the third tray. He knew instantly when he picked up the ring that it was the one. "This one," he said to his mother. "This is the ring for Shayla."

"It is beautiful," she assured him.

Adam walked away from the chest and held the ring up to the light. "I can picture it on her hand."

"Thank you, Mr. Guthrey, I think my son has what he needs."

"Very well, Madam. Shall I return the others to the vault at the bank?"

"Yes. Thank you for bringing them here." She called for the butler while Mr. Guthrey packed the rings back in the chest. When he finished, he bowed to the Dowager Duchess and left the parlor.

"Adam, your telegram saying you wanted a ring for your fiancé took me by surprise."

"Yes. Thank you for saving me a trip to the bank." Adam was about to ask when Colin would be returning from his meetings when he heard Colin's booming voice in the foyer off the parlor.

"Adam," Colin called as he entered the parlor and strode to his brother and embraced him. "How are you faring?"

"I am well. You look well."

"Thank you." Colin went to his mother who sat near the fire in one of the wing backed chairs that she loved so much she took them with her when she traveled between houses. Colin seated himself in a chair next to her, and Adam sat back down in the second wing backed chair.

The maid walked in with a tea service. "I will pour Madeline. Thank you," the Dowager Duchess said dismissing the maid who curtsied and left the room. Adam watched as his mother expertly poured tea into three teacups. She added a cube of sugar to her cup and passed cups to her sons. She sat back in her chair and smiled at them then sipped her tea.

Adam appraised his brother. Colin's hair was very short, he obviously had a haircut when he returned to London. He wore his uniform since he had just returned from a meeting. There was only thirteen months between them, and they looked very much like brothers. He sipped his tea. "How was the meeting?" Adam asked.

"It was long and boring. You know the type." Colin took a sip of tea and looked at Adam. He wore a black waist coat and dark charcoal grey trousers. His hair was longer than Colin had seen it since they were boys, and it skimmed the collar of his white linen shirt. "Civilian life suits you," he said to his brother. "I was not sure you were up to it."

Adam laughed loudly. "Believe me, civilian life is a lot better than military life."

Colin nodded. "Your injury and our older brothers' deaths have brought me to a decision." He took a long drink to draw out the suspense. "I am resigning my commission effective in March."

Adam looked at his brother. "You are resigning?"

"I made it official today. I will be working with you by April."

"I am surprised, but I am pleased because Elliot has big plans for our futures," Adam commented as he took a swallow of his tea.

"That is your brother's job," their mother commented as she set her teacup down on a side table. "As Duke, it is his responsibility to see to his younger brothers' livelihoods."

Colin scoffed. "He's just bossy because he's the oldest."

Adam laughed. "It will be good to have you around." He finished his tea. "And Amelia can set her sights on finding you a wife."

Colin's eyes widened. "I do not need a wife."

Adam laughed. "That's what I thought, but I am getting married."

"Speaking of getting married," his mother broke into the conversation, "I was not even aware that you were officially courting the young woman. Tell me about the girl you plan to marry."

Adam turned and smiled at his mother. "You will love her," Adam said as he began telling her about Shayla. He recounted their first meeting up until the disaster at the Earl's party.

"Oh, Elliot must have been furious," Colin laughed.

"It is not funny," the Dowager Duchess said firmly to her son.

"Well, after I apologized, I asked Shayla's father for her hand, and Shayla agreed to be my wife, so it is all fixed now."

"Well, I cannot wait to meet her."

"Are you all packed, Mother?" Adam asked.

"Nearly."

"I promised Shayla I would be on the first train back Christmas Eve morning."

"Do not worry. I will be ready."

The butler appeared in the doorway. "Excuse me, Madam. Dinner is ready," he announced.

"Thank you, Franklin." She stood up and Adam and Colin rose and stood on either side of their mother. She hooked one arm with Adam and one arm with Colin. "It is going to be so good for all of us to be together at Christmastide," she remarked in a light and happy voice as they walked to the dining room.

Chapter 26

Christmas Eve morning, Shayla dressed in a pretty, red day dress. It was fancier than was normal for day wear, but it was Christmas Eve, and she was going to Wellshore Manor soon. She pinned up her hair and added a festive sprig of holly. She wanted to look pretty for when Adam visited this morning. He had not been gone long, but she missed him terribly.

She bounded down the steps into the kitchen and saw Mrs. Lawry cooking bacon.

"Why are you cooking so much bacon?" she asked.

"Oh, we want to be certain we have enough," Mrs. Lawry replied with a smile that Shayla found odd.

"Is Uncle Henry and Aunt Margaret, and Uncle James coming over too because you have enough bacon, biscuits, and eggs to feed a small army," Shayla laughed.

"Yes, they are in the parlor awaiting breakfast. I am glad to see you looking pretty this morning."

"Well, Adam has been away, and I want to remind him of what he missed while he was gone," Shayla chuckled. She walked into the parlor and bid her family good morning. She knew she should not appear so anxious to see Adam, but she did not care. She missed him.

There was a knock at the door, and Shayla waited as patiently as she could for Mr. Lowman to walk down the hall to answer it. She was about to go to the door herself when her father walked out of his office. She stared at him. He wore a day jacket which he rarely did at home. She was about to ask what was going on when Mr. Lowman, whom she noticed also had on a fine jacket today, announced, "The Duke and Duchess of Wellshore and the Dowager Duchess of Wellshore, Major Preston, and Captain Preston."

Shayla stared at the guests walking into the parlor and dropped into a low curtsy. Henry bowed. "Welcome to our home," he said.

"Thank you for receiving us," Elliot offered his hand.

Shayla bid them good morning as Henry indicated they should go further into the parlor.

Shayla grabbed Adam's hand and pulled him back into the foyer. "What is going on? You did not tell me you were bring the Duke and Duchess, the Dowager Duchess, and your brother." she whispered.

"It is tradition for the groom's family to visit the bride's family after an engagement," Adam explained. "Your father did not mention it?"

"No," she said in an exasperated tone.

"Oh well. Come, I will introduce you." Adam tucked Shayla's hand in his arm and walked back into the parlor. "Mother may I present my fiancé, Miss Shayla Toselli."

"Your Grace." Shayla dipped into another low curtsy.

The Dowager Duchess smiled at Shayla and took her hands. "Oh, my dear, you are lovely. I was so happy when Adam told me he planned to marry, and now I can see why he is anxious to marry you."

Shayla smiled and bowed her head.

"You remember my brother, Major Preston," Adam said to Shayla.

"Miss Toselli, a pleasure to see you again." He bowed and kissed her hand.

Henry introduced Hal, James, and Margaret. Shayla saw that Aunt Margaret was flush and looking excited. She looked over at Shayla and smiled. Henry then handed out glasses of champagne. "To the merging of our families."

"Well said," the Duke concurred.

They drank, and Henry refilled the glasses.

"Mr. Toselli," Mrs. Lawry said in a most formal manner as she curtsied, "breakfast is ready, Sir."

Shayla stared at her, and then her father offered his arm to the Dowager Duchess, and they led the way to the dining room. The Duke and Duchess followed, then Uncle James and Uncle Hal escorted Aunt Margaret. Shayla looked stunned and did not move. Adam and Colin walked up on either side of her and held out an arm. She looked wide eyed at them, then took their arms, and they escorted her to breakfast.

In the afternoon, Adam watched as Shayla arranged the boxes on a table draped in gold material. She opened the boxes, so the globes, nestled in soft velvet, were visible. Light from the small chandelier above the table reflected down on them highlighting the gold and silver accents.

"They are magnificent," Adam commented as he looked over her shoulder. "You are beautiful." He kissed her neck, and she turned in his arms. "Would you go to tea with me before resting for the ball."

"Of course."

"And it is beginning to snow."

"Christmas Eve snow is magical." Shayla hugged him.

He kissed her forehead. "Get you things. I will wait here."

Shayla walked up the grand staircase to the room she had been assigned. She picked up her reticule and her gloves.

When she descended the stairs, Adam waited at the bottom dressed in a black overcoat and top hat. He helped her into her grey cloak. She tied on her matching bonnet then he took her hand, and they went outside to the waiting carriage. Warming bricks had been placed in the carriage's foot warmer, to heat it for them. Shayla stepped inside, and Adam closed the door behind them and drew the curtain part way. He then lifted the cushion of the opposite bench and took out a heavy fur blanket which he placed over Shayla to keep her warm. Since they were engaged, Adam sat next to her, and Shayla pulled the blanket over to cover him as well.

"It is a lovely afternoon." She laid her head on his shoulder and gazed out the window as the carriage went down the driveway and out onto the street. Soon they drove down the main street. People bustled from store to store. The lamps were lit already because the clouds were heavy and dark. Then the carriage stopped in front of the tea shop. Adam opened the door and extended his hand and helped Shayla down.

"I thought we would take our tea here."

"A wonderful idea."

Adam led Shayla to the table by the roaring fire in the hearth. He slid off her cloak and took off his coat, and a woman took them and hung them up. A waitress came to the table and set down a pot of tea and two cups. She poured the tea and left. Right behind her, another woman appeared and set down a plate of petite fours. Shayla looked at Adam. "My favorite. How did you know?"

"It is a groom's job to know what his bride likes," Adam replied happily.

"Is that so?"

"And I plan to learn everything you like," he whispered as he leaned close to her and picked up a small cake.

Shayla smiled and blushed. She could not wait to discover what he liked.

They talked and laughed as they sat cozily in front of the fire. People came and went, and finally they departed the shop and returned to Wellshore Manor. The snow was falling very hard covering everything in a blanket of white.

Adam walked Shayla to her room. She looked up and down the hallway to make certain they were alone, then she pulled him to her and kissed him quickly before anyone came down the corridor.

He stroked her arm. Adam wanted nothing more than to take her in his arms, but now was not the time. He opened the door to her chamber, and she stepped inside. "Rest for a while before the ball." He kissed her forehead. "I am two doors down the hall."

Shayla watched Adam walk toward his room and wished he stayed with her. She stepped back and closed the door. She looked at herself in the cheval glass. In a few short weeks her life had changed. She smiled. It was a good change. Bridget, her maid, came in and turned down the bed then helped Shayla undress. She helped Shayla into bed, and when she left the room, Shayla slid down between the soft silky sheets, and soon she was asleep.

Shayla dreamt she was standing in front of a sparkling Christmas tree when Bridget gently aroused her. "Time to get ready for the ball, Miss."

Shayla opened her eyes. "Is it time already?"

The maid nodded, and Shayla sat up and slid off the bed. Her toes curled in the thick carpet, and she padded over to the wash basin. The maid helped style her hair and get into her ball gown. Again, Shayla looked at her reflection in the cheval glass. She hardly recognized herself in the elegant gown. She was an engaged woman and about to attend a ball.

"You look beautiful, Miss."

"Thank you, Bridget."

Adam waited for Shayla at the bottom of the steps. He paced the floor until Henry and Hal came in. He shook their hands.

"Good evening, Adam." Henry looked at this strong capable man who was going to marry his little girl and let out a heavy sigh. Hal sensed what Henry was thinking and clasped his hand on Henry's shoulder. They exchanged a nod of understanding.

Adam looked up. Shayla stood at the top of the stairs. Henry and Hal followed his gaze, and they both beamed with pride. Shayla was dressed in a lavender velvet gown that was trimmed with white fur. There was a silver fabric flower at the waist, and she wore silver dancing slippers on her feet. Adam stared at her as she descended the stairs. He reached for her hand, and she came down the last few steps and stood beside him.

"You are a vision," he said.

"Thank you."

Henry walked up to Shayla. He had no words. There were tears in his eyes. He kissed his daughter. Finally, he found his voice. "I love you."

"I love you too, Papa."

"You are beautiful." Hal kissed her cheek. "So, grown up." He too had tears in his eyes.

"Thank you, Uncle."

"Shall we make our entrance, Miss Toselli?" Adam asked.

Shayla curtsied. "Yes, Captain. I would be delighted." Adam bowed, Shayla placed her hand on his arm, and they walked down the hall and entered the ballroom together.

"This is amazing," Shayla gasped as they walked through the doors. All day, the doors into the room were locked. The decorators outdid themselves. The walls were lined with gold fabric that shimmered in the light of the many chandeliers. The small orchestra sat on a platform at one end of the ballroom. There were large urns filled with fresh flowers placed about the room, and their fragrance filled the air.

The first notes of the waltz began, and Adam and Shayla took to the dance floor with many other couples. The women's gowns twirled around their bodies as their partners spun them around. The couples bobbed and swayed then circled back. Shayla never had more fun than she was having right now. Each time she turned back to Adam, he embraced her, and she felt desire flare.

Adam watched her face as he held her for a moment before turning her again. His body felt on fire, and it was not only due to the speed of the dance. His heart raced for Shayla, and he intended to go to her tonight if she would allow him. Adoration shone in Adam's eyes when he looked at her. Shayla knew that for him, she was the only woman in the room, and she liked how that made her feel.

Shayla danced with Colin, and then she danced with Duke Wellshore. He was taller than Adam but so well coordinated. Elliot spun his sister-in-law to be around the dance floor. He could see why his brother fell in love with her. She was beautiful and witty, and she was genuine. She did not pretend to be someone she was not, and that was refreshing. At the end of the dance, he returned her to his brother and bowed.

Adam and Shayla took their places on the dance floor when the supper dance began. "Are you ready to be Mrs. Preston?" Adam asked while they moved gracefully across the dance floor.

"I am ready. We will be Captain and Mrs. Preston of Canterbury Corner and London," Shayla replied. She turned her head for a moment and smiled at him.

As the song ended, Adam pulled her close. "I cannot wait to be Captain and Mrs. Preston and have you forever in my life." Adam paused and grinned. "And in my bed," he whispered quietly in her ear causing Shayla to blush scarlet. He bowed to her. "Would you like to go to super?"

Shayla nodded, took Adam's arm, and they walked together to the dining room.

The evening sped by in a swirl of dances and conversations. There was an abundance of food and drinks. Mistletoe had been strategically placed throughout the rooms, and people stopped and indulged in tradition when caught under it. And when the bells chimed midnight, fireworks erupted out on the lawn. The guests gathered on the terraces and at the windows to watch the fireworks display. Adam placed Shayla's wrap around her shoulders and stood close to her on the terrace. He breathed in the lovely scent of the lavender water she used on her hair.

Red, green, and gold fireworks lit up the night sky to usher in the festive season. This began the days of celebration which ended with a large party on Twelfth Night.

After the fireworks display, people returned to the dining room and took refreshments of hot chocolate and cakes. When they were ready to leave, the guests walked to the table where the ornaments were displayed and made their selection. Shayla stood nearby alongside Henry and Hal and watched as the guests contemplated the choices. Several people had difficulty deciding which one to take, and everyone raved about their beauty.

"The ornaments are a great success," the Duke of Wellshore said to them. A waiter stood by his side with a tray of glasses, and he handed each of them a glass. "Thank you for your hard work, and Happy Christmas," he toasted. They nodded and drank.

"My first Christmastide ball was a magnificent success," the Duke said with a broad smile.

"That it was, Your Grace," Henry agreed. "You are a gracious host."

"You may call me Wellshore as all my friends do. Afterall, we are going to be family."

As the last of the guests left, Shayla said good night to her father and uncle. "Are you certain you do not want to stay here tonight?" she asked them. "Adam says there is plenty of room."

Henry took his daughter's hands. "You stay. We will return for the Christmas breakfast tomorrow morning. They are also your family now, and you should spend time with them."

"Happy Christmas, Papa." Shayla hugged him tight.

"Happy Christmas, my daughter." He held back the tears he felt coming on.

"Happy Christmas, Shayla." Hal kissed his niece. "Your Aunt Margaret is beside herself with excitement about having Christmas breakfast with the Duke and Duchess tomorrow morning."

"I am glad she is excited."

"Good night," they said as they put on their coats and went outside to their waiting carriage.

The Duchess walked over to Shayla. "I never had a sister, three brothers, and I am so happy that you will be my new sister." Amelia hugged her.

"I am an only child, and I am happy you will be my sister."

They walked to the front parlor. "I never thought when I married Elliot that I would be a Duchess." Amelia took a cup of hot chocolate from a waiter and handed it to Shayla, and then she took one for herself. "I have to admit, I was nervous at first, but now, I love it."

"As you should. You are a thoughtful and gracious duchess. Most are not as concerned with those who are less fortunate."

Amelia laughed. "Thank you for your kind thoughts. It is true many women are not concerned about the poor. I believe being a duchess is more than giving parties and looking good on her husband's arm."

Shayla nodded. "I agree."

"I would like your help with several charity projects I am planning in the new year if you are willing."

"I am very willing, and I look forward to helping you, Your Grace."

"Please, I am Amelia. We are soon to be family."

Shayla nodded. They sipped their hot chocolates and moved close to the parlor's fireplace. Christmas greens, holly, and candles decorated the hearth. The scent of pine filled the air. Logs crackled in the grate.

Amelia smiled at Shayla as she stared into the fire. "And as your new sister, I feel it is my duty to tell you something." She grinned and sipped her chocolate. Shayla glanced at her and then back at the fire. Amelia continued, "I stayed in the room you are in when I came to meet the Duke and Duchess when I became engaged to Elliot."

"That is interesting," Shayla replied. She was unsure where the conversation was headed.

"You know, Shayla, there is a passageway behind the rooms on that side of the building." Amelia hid a smile behind her cup.

"There is?" Shayla turned her full attention to the Duchess.

Amelia nodded. "You just might have a visitor tonight," she smiled and took another sip. "I know I did when I stayed in that room, and the brothers think alike in many ways."

Amelia smiled and patted Shayla's arm, and Shayla felt the heat rise in her body as she thought about Adam coming to her during the night.

"The lock is on your side of the door," Amelia explained now in a serious tone of voice.

Shayla nodded she understood. The choice to admit Adam would be hers. She laughed to herself. There was no choice. She was in love with Adam, and if he came to her in the night, she would admit him to her chamber.

Amelia watched Shayla's face as she made the decision. She leaned closer to Shayla and whispered, "I instructed my maid to place two silk chemises in the vanity drawer in your chamber."

"Two chemises?"

"The start of your wedding trousseau. A gift to my new sister."

Shayla stared at Amelia. "Thank you, it is most generous of you," she finally managed to say. She was overwhelmed by the Duchess' generosity.

"You are welcome. I am going to like having a sister."

"I am going to like it too," Shayla replied, and the two women hugged.

"Ladies," Elliot called as he and Adam entered the parlor. "It is snowing outside again. Would you be interested in a midnight walk in the snow?"

"Shayla?" Amelia asked.

"I would love a walk in the snow."

The two couples, all bundled up against the cold, walked arm in arm out the front door a few minutes later. The men carried lanterns to light the way. The air was crisp, and the snowflakes were large. Shayla leaned her head back and stuck out her tongue to catch a snowflake. "Christmas snow is magical snow."

Adam caught a snowflake on his tongue. "I agree, but I can think of something more magical," he whispered so only she could hear. They walked down the paths that had been cleared through the snow covered gardens. Adam and Shayla took one path right while the Duke and Duchess went left. When they were obscured from the view of others, Adam lowered his head and captured Shayla's mouth with his in a searing kiss. "You are delicious."

Shayla sighed. "As are you." She grabbed his coat, pulled him to her, and kissed him.

They walked a little further, and Adam stopped again. "May I come to you tonight, Shayla?" he whispered in her ear.

She smiled and kissed him again. "You may." Adam sealed it with a kiss that held the promise of the passion that was to come.

Reluctantly, they continued down the path that went back around. They joined Elliot and Amelia once again, and the two couples meandered back toward the house.

Chapter 27

Adam walked Shayla to her room. He bid her good night, kissed her hand, and then went two doors down to his own room. He took off his shoes, untied his cravat, and took off his jacket. He opened the panel on the back wall. He and his brothers used this passageway often when they were children. They 'raided' one another's rooms and used the passages to move around unseen. Shayla was in the chamber reserved for the governess that was now used for guests.

He was nervous and wondered why. It was not as if he never laid with a woman before. This was different, he thought, He loved Shayla and love changed the act. He stepped into the narrow passageway and made his way in the dark to Shayla's room. He gave a knock and heard her walk toward the sound.

"Adam?" Shayla's voice was shaky.

"Lift the latch, so I can open the panel," he instructed her.

Shayla looked around and found the latch which was hidden behind a loose section of wallpaper. She lifted it, and then she stood back as Adam opened the panel.

He stepped into the room and closed the panel behind him. He stood and looked in wonder at his Christmas present. The maid had helped Shayla out of her gown, and she stood in front of him in a frilly pale pink lace chemise that hugged her subtle curves. The light from a single sconce illuminated the room softly. He wanted to savor this moment, and he took her in his arms and gently kissed her.

"Adam," she whispered. She was nervous. She knew sex was natural between a man and woman, and she knew basically what to do, but she had no experience, and she wanted to please him. She unbuttoned his shirt and slid it off his shoulders. His muscles tensed, and she felt him shudder as she kissed her way down his neck.

"I want you so badly. I want to unwrap you and watch your face as I pleasure you." Adam whispered softly. He untied the garment and lifted it over her head. He felt her tremble in anticipation. "Do not be afraid. I will be gentle, and you will feel amazing. I promise."

She nodded. "I know you will be gentle. I trust you, Adam." She reached for his pants, but he stilled her hands.

"Let me show you how much I love you. Let me show you how love can be," he whispered. He picked her up and laid her down on the bed. He took a moment to look over her body, so strong and thin. She was perfect. Her body shivered. "Are you cold?"

"No."

He kept eye contact with her as he untied his pants and took them off. Shayla's eyes widened at the sight of him. She reached up, but he caught her hands in his and brought them to his lips. He laid on the bed by her side and began kissing her. He placed her hands at her side. "Let me do everything. Just relax and feel," he breathed in her ear.

He kissed her softly on her lips, on her cheeks, down her throat, and up to her ears. His hands roamed down her arms and up her stomach. His touch was light and left her skin tingling everywhere he touched. Shayla closed her eyes and soft sounds escaped her as his hand cupped her breast. Adam kissed his way down to take it in his mouth. She gasped and then moaned and arched against him. His name came out on a sigh, and he smiled. While he sucked at her breast, his hand slowly inched down over her hip and thigh, and then up until it was between her legs. He found her moist and hot already, but he felt her tense at his touch. He needed to make certain she was ready for him since it was her first time.

Shayla wanted to feel Adam inside her, but he was moving so slowly. While one hand gently probed her most intimate part, his mouth moved back up to her mouth. "Adam, now," she breathed.

"Patience, my love." He began to kiss his way down her body until his mouth replaced his hand. Shayla sucked in a breath as his tongue lapped at her core, and his finger gently entered her. This was so intimate, so intense. She squirmed beneath him, but he held her in place while his tongue did the most wonderful things to her body.

Her breath was ragged, and she tangled her fingers in his hair and drew him in closer. He increased the pace and the pressure just a little, and she felt the tension build and build until she reached the top and her body climaxed. Light flashed behind her eyes. Shayla never felt anything so wonderful. Her body shuddered in pleasure, and Adam placed himself at her opening while she still rode those waves of pleasure. Very slowly he entered her.

Shayla realized what was happening and opened her eyes.

"Are you ok, love?" Adam asked in her ear.

"Yes. It does not hurt as much as I thought it would." She brought her legs up and wrapped her arms around his back as he pushed in a little deeper.

"Good." Adam closed his eyes and concentrated on moving slowly as he waited for her body to adjust to him. He kissed her, and he felt her body relax and open. He slid all the way in and waited. His muscles ached as he held still. Desire threatened to rage uncontrolled, but he refused to give in to the temptation to move too quickly. He felt her body accept him. He kissed her and desire flared again as she responded and whispered his name. Finally, he began to slowly move.

He pushed her hair back from her face as he increased the pace. He brought one hand down, circled her nub, and Shayla's body responded. "Adam. Oh, Adam." Her fingers dug into his back as she climbed higher and higher.

Adam knew he could not hold on much longer. "Open your eyes, Shayla. I want to see your eyes as we reach our climax."

It took effort, but her eyes fluttered open. They were hazy and heavy with passion. His were dark. His hair was damp. His mouth was partly open, and his hands gripped the sheets on both sides of her head. The look of pleasure on his face encouraged her, and she linked her legs around his back. He moved in and out faster, and she felt herself rising and rising.

"Let go, Shayla," he moaned. His name was on her lips as they reached their peak and fell over the edge together.

Adam collapsed on top of Shayla, and she clung to him. As her breathing returned to normal, she smiled that she was able to please him too. She rubbed her hands over his back, and he lifted his head and looked into her eyes. "You gave me the best present I have ever received. Happy Christmas, my love."

"Happy Christmas."


Adam woke. It was his habit to wake before dawn each day. He watched Shayla as she slept beside him. She was so lovely. She seemed to smile as she slept. Perhaps she was having a good dream. He hoped he could make her happy, forever. He leaned over and kissed her. She lazily opened her eyes. "Good morning, my love." Adam kissed her again and smoothed back her hair.

"Good morning. What time is it?"

"It is early. Take a ride with me this morning. I wish to show you something."

Shayla framed his face in her hands. "Of course." She stretched up and kissed him.

"I will dress and call for a carriage." He kissed her a long time, and he heard her sigh when he leaned away. "Dress warm. It is cold outside." He got out of bed. Shayla watched him as he slipped on his clothes. "I shall wait downstairs." He opened the panel and slipped into the passageway.

Shayla laid in bed and thought about the amazing night she spent in Adam's arms. She could not wait to be his wife and spend every night with him. She rose from the bed and slipped on her chemise and dressing gown. She was brushing her hair when there was a small knock on the door. "Enter."

"Good morning, Miss. Happy Christmas."

"Happy Christmas to you too, Bridget. Captain Preston asked me to go for a carriage ride this morning."

"Tis a beautiful day for a ride. We had several inches of fresh snow during the night, but not so much as to hinder the carriages."

Shayla put on her dress for the Christmas breakfast later, and Bridget helped her fix her hair. "How do I look."

"Very pretty." Bridget took a spring of holly and attached it to her hair with pins.

"Thank you," Shayla smiled at her reflection. The holly was a festive touch. "Bridget, I know tomorrow is boxing day, but as I do not know if I will see you then, I wish to give you a present." Shayla held out a box.

Bridget took it. "For me?"

"I want to thank you for your help and kindness."

The girl smiled and opened the box. Inside was a Christmas ornament decorated with white poinsettias and a tiny red bird. Bridget's name was written on one of the glass ribbons that adorned it. "Thank you, Miss. I will cherish this always."

Shayla placed another box in her bag. "I will see you later, Bridget. Thank you." Shayla opened the door and walked down the hallway to the staircase.

Adam watched her come down the stairs toward him in a dark red velvet dress with white trim. He imagined her walking down the aisle to become his wife. It was something he never thought he wanted, but he ached to see Shayla walking down the aisle toward him. He reached up and took her hand.

The butler held her cloak and she slipped into it. She tied on her bonnet and put her hands into thick white gloves.

"Please tell the Duke and Duchess we will return in time for breakfast," Adam told the butler.

"Very good, Captain."

Adam led Shayla outside. "A sleighride!" Shayla exclaimed excitedly when she saw the sleigh.

"I thought why waste all this beautiful snow." Adam settled Shayla in the sleigh with a thick warm blanket over her lap and then got in. He picked up the reins and started the horses. Bells jingled as the sleigh glided smoothly over the freshly fallen snow.

Shayla hooked her arm in his and leaned close. Adam took the sleigh through the town, and they waved to people who stopped to watch the sleigh go by.

"Are we going to my home?" Shayla asked as Adam approached the road that led toward the shop and her home.

"You will see." Adam leaned over and kissed her cheek. Soon, he stopped the sleigh in front of a magnificent home several blocks from the home she shared with her father. "Why are we stopping here?" Shayla thought perhaps it was the home of someone he knew, but Adam just hopped out and reached up for Shayla's hand. "Let us look around."

Shayla stepped down, and they walked up to the front door. It opened, and the butler bowed. Adam discreetly put his finger to his lips. The butler nodded and simply said, "welcome. Please come in."

Shayla stepped into the large foyer. An ornate mirror hung on the wall to the right. Under it was a skinny table that held a large flower arrangement. The butler took her cloak and Adam's coat and led them into the spacious parlor. A fire blazed in the hearth. The room was furnished, but not as fully as one would expect.

"Whose home is this?"

"If you are agreeable, ours."

"O o ours?" Shayla stuttered.

"Let us look through the house before you decide."

Adam led her through two more parlors, the dining room, the library, and the small conservatory on the first floor. He took her upstairs to see the five bedrooms, two of which had sitting areas, a crying room, and an upstairs parlor. Every room was beautiful. The walls were covered in silks, rugs were scattered on the highly polished wood floors, and heavy brocade draperies framed the windows.

"What do think?"

Shayla smiled. "I love it."

"It is a short distance to your shop and your father's home. Out back there are two greenhouses, a stable, several outbuildings, and plenty of areas for gardens." He took her hand. "Come, let us look at the kitchens and the lower level." They walked down the stairs. Several servants came to attention when they stepped into the kitchen. "Mrs. Haversham the cook, Mr. Haversham the butler, Floyd the second butler."

"How do you do," Shayla nodded. The men bowed.

Mrs. Haversham curtsied. "Pleased to make your acquaintance, Miss."

Shayla looked around then Adam took her back to the front parlor on the main floor.

"What a pretty tree," Shayla commented when they walked in the room.

"I know you like Christmas trees. We can decorate it later if you like," Adam suggested. On a side table was a present. Adam picked it up and handed it to Shayla.

"For me?"

"Happy Christmas."

Shayla took off the white wrapping paper and then opened the box. She gasped. Inside was a white cloak with delicate gold embroidery and white fur trim. There was a matching bonnet and muff. She smiled at Adam and threw her arms around him. "It is so beautiful. Thank you." She kissed him and held him close.

"I have something for you as well." Shayla took the box out of her bag. "Happy Christmas, Adam." She held out a red and green box adorned with an iridescent glass ornament crowned with white and gold glass ribbons that circled around the globe and highlighted two elegant white swans.

"Swans. We pulled two swans from the prize basket." Adam leaned over and kissed her.

"Open the box," Shayla smiled.

Adam lifted the lid. He pulled out the brown stein with a pony on it that Shayla made for him. He looked at her. He never saw anything like it. "This is spectacular." He held the stein up to the light, and the gold flecks glittered.

"I created the color of the glass for you."

"It is wonderful." He held up the mug and the ornament. "Shayla, your work is beyond compare. It can be delicate and intricate and strong all at the same time. I will cherish these pieces, forever." Adam set them down and then reached inside his jacket. "I have something else for you." He pulled out a small box and handed it to her.

Shayla took the gold and white box and lifted the lid. She pulled out a small round clear glass ornament. At the top of the ornament was a bow of fabric ribbons and attached to one of the ribbons was a ring. Shayla gasped. The ring had a sapphire center stone surrounded by diamonds. She put her hand to her mouth. The ring sparkled in front of her.

Adam pulled one of the ribbons and released the ring. "Please wear my ring, Shayla." He gently took her left hand and slid the ring on her finger.

"Adam," Shayla breathed, "it is beautiful." There were tears in her eyes as she leaned toward him and kissed him. He brought his arms around her and deepened the kiss.

"Do you love the house?" he asked in her ear.

"I do, Adam."

He leaned back. "Good. I will make the final arrangements. Is the staff to your liking? Mr. Lowman will come here, and we will add additional staff as needed."

"Everyone is fine."

"Am I correct that you still do not want a personal maid?"

"You are correct." She paused and looked at him. "Perhaps Bridget would be willing to come here and be my maid if the Duchess can spare her."

Adam kissed Shayla gently. "I am certain something can be arranged." He took the box from her and set it and the ornament on the table. He took her hands. "Shayla, I know it is traditional for the bride to select the wedding date, but I want to get married right away. I want to begin our lives together. How do you feel about a Twelfth Night wedding?"

Shayla's mouth fell open. "That is in eleven days."

"Too soon?"

Shayla smiled. "No. It is not too soon. I am anxious to begin life with you too." Adam raised her hand and kissed it. "Can we plan a wedding in so short a time?" Shayla asked.

"My mother and the Duchess believe it is possible." He kissed her hand again. "I hope you are agreeable to a fancy, not too small wedding."

Shayla tensed. "By not too small, you mean large and fancy? In eleven days?" Adam nodded. Shayla took a deep breath. She could tell this meant a great deal to him. "Adam, tell me, why Twelfth Night?"

Adam took Shayla's hand and led her to the chairs by the hearth. They sat down, and he leaned over and took both her hands in his. "Last year, I came home in time for Twelfth Night. I went to the town's celebration with my brother, Colin."

"I was there."

He nodded. "Yes, I saw you."

"You did?"

"I saw a beautiful young woman in a lovely pink dress talking with her friends. Of course, I could not approach the young woman without first being introduced. I hoped to find someone who knew her, but later, I could not find her again. I was left with only a memory."

"You looked for me?"

"I did."

"My aunt took ill, and we left early."

"The vision of that beautiful woman kept me going when I was shot. I kept thinking I would come back this year and find out who she was. When I met you, Shayla, you were so familiar to me, yet I knew I never met you before. Then the day we went,"

"To give our statement to the police," Shayla finished for him. "I wore that dress."

"Yes, and I knew it was you I had been dreaming of."

Shayla looked into Adam's eyes. "I will be honored to become your wife on Twelfth Night." Shayla kissed him delicately on the lips.

"Thank you." He kissed her.

"Come, let us hang our ornaments on the tree." Shayla picked up the ornament Adam gave her, walked over to the tree, and hung it on a sturdy branch.

Adam walked to her side and did the same with the ornament she gave him. "The tree could use more ornaments."

Shayla looked at the little tree decorated with only two very special ornaments. "It is perfect as it is. Our first Christmas tree."

"Everything is perfect." Adam lowered his head and captured Shayla's mouth in a kiss that sent sparks through her entire body. The clock in the foyer chimed out nine times. "We need to return for Christmas breakfast with our families," he said between kisses.

Shayla nodded and kissed him again.

Chapter 28

Epilogue

Adam and Shayla did not get an opportunity to be alone after the first day of Christmas because of the wedding preparations. When Adam said his mother and sister-in-law were planning a large and fancy wedding, he was not kidding. Amelia showed up at the workshop two mornings after Christmas with a notebook and several magazines. She sat in the furnace room while Shayla worked.

"What do you think about these dresses?" Amelia shoved several Harper's magazine clippings under Shayla's nose.

"Oh, I like that one," Shayla pointed to a dress. She turned her attention back to the globe she was blowing. When she was satisfied, she took a gather of glass and added a hanger to the top. Tara handed her a pointed tool which Shayla used to make a hole in the center of the hanger. She looked at the globe again and handed it off to Tara.

Amelia checked her notebook. "Good, because I have dresses arriving on the train tomorrow morning, and that is one of them." Amelia fanned herself.

"What?" Shayla began another globe.

"You have an appointment tomorrow afternoon to try dresses on. I already informed your aunt, and she will be there too." Amelia watched as Shayla shaped the glass, added blue color, and detached another globe. She was amazed at Shayla's skill. She watched her make another globe. They were roughly the same size and color. "Those globes are beautiful," she said.

"Thank you. I am making them for wedding favors," Shayla informed the Duchess. Tara handed Shayla another pipe, and she gathered more glass. "I plan to make one for each family."

Amelia smiled. They were perfect for Shayla and Adam's wedding. They symbolized what brought the two of them together. "Ok. I can cross favors off the list," Amelia said as she turned her attention back to her notebook. She read down her list, and then she fanned herself. "How do you stand it in here all day?"

Shayla laughed. "You cannot wear a heavy gown and skirts in a furnace room."

"I will wear something cooler tomorrow." Tara handed the Duchess a towel. "Thank you, dear." She patted her face. "Now menus," Amelia said as she opened her notebook again. "Do you like pheasant, Shayla?"

"I do."

"Halibut?"

"Oh yes. It is my favorite."

Amelia shook her head. Her brother-in-law certainly knew what his bride to be liked. "Main menu solved. I will let the chef decide on the rest of the dishes. This is going much easier than I imagined," she said happily. "You are an easy bride to please, Shayla." She checked menu off the list.

Amelia watched as Shayla continued to blow globes. Tara took the finished pieces and stacked them in the oven. The two women worked well together. "The men will be back by teatime. Will you be stopping work by then?"

"Yes, once the annealing oven is full, I am finished for the day," Shayla informed her.

"I hope they do not have any problems," Amelia muttered as she looked over her lists again.

Meanwhile, the Duke of Wellshore wrote to the Archbishop requesting a special license so Adam and Shayla could be married so quickly. Adam, Elliot, and Colin took the train early in the morning to meet with the Archbishop, pay the required fee, and secure the license.

They sat in a private car and sipped brandy. "We are going to be very wealthy," Elliot said to his brothers. "With all the new stations, the railways will be quite profitable.

Adam and Colin agreed that Elliot's decision to invest in the railways was a sound one.

The three men exited the train and made their way to the Cathedral. The meeting was very quick, and soon, they left having secured the license.

"Thirty guineas! I believe that is how the church raises money," Elliot stated sternly as he and his brothers walked down the path back to their waiting carriage. They got in and the coachman took them to their next stop.

"Maybe Shayla and I should have eloped to Scotland instead," Adam suggested.

Elliot shook his head. "Mother and Amelia would have been very upset, as would Henry and Margaret. Eloping is not allowed, and there is no turning back now." Elliot slapped his brother on the shoulder.

"Believe me. I do not want to turn back. I am only looking forward."

"Looks like I will be the only bachelor left," Colin remarked. "I will think about you married men when I am playing cards and staying out until whenever I please."

"I would rather be home with Amelia than out alone," Elliot replied.

The carriage stopped, and the three brothers stepped out. They went inside one of the pubs near the railway station to have lunch and wait for the return train to Canterbury Corner.

The morning of the wedding, Shayla woke up early. She went downstairs where Mrs. Lawry was flipping pancakes.

"Morning, Shayla."

"Morning." She looked around. "Where is Papa?"

"Getting his tailcoat." Mrs. Lawry set a cup of tea on the table, and Shayla sat down. "Afternoon weddings were not allowed when I married. We were at the chapel by this time of the morning."

Shayla yawned.

"Drink your tea, hon."

Shayla nodded and took a sip. The day before had been busy with last minute wedding preparations before an elaborate dinner at Wellshore Manor that was given by Adam's mother. The Dowager Duchess invited everyone she knew to the dinner, and Shayla had never curtsied that much in her life. After dinner, there was dancing which did not end until well past midnight. She was very tired, and she leaned against Adam and started to fall asleep in the carriage on the way home. She could have stayed at the Manor, but she wanted to spend the night before her wedding at home. Besides, she did not want Adam to see her on their wedding day until she walked down the aisle to marry him.

After breakfast, Shayla took a bath. She looked around her room. Most of her belongings were packed and ready to be moved to her new home while she and Adam were away on their honeymoon. She picked up her mother's perfume bottle. She held it in her hand and tears came to her eyes. "I wish you were here, Mama," she whispered.

"She is."

Shayla jumped. "Papa."

He went to his daughter and hugged her. "She is always with us."

"I know." Shayla wiped her eyes.

Henry took the perfume bottle. "I remember when she made this." He took off the top and breathed in the scent. "Wear this perfume today, Shayla. It will bring your mother close to you."

Shayla nodded and rested her head on his shoulder.

"Time to get ready." Henry kissed her. He left the room, and she finished packing her bags.

Shayla and her Aunt Margaret arrived at Wellshore Manor in a white carriage. They walked up to the front doors that were decorated with garlands of greens interspersed with white and pink roses. When the butler opened the door and Shayla stepped inside, she could not believe her eyes. Everywhere she looked there were flowers. The Duchess and the Dowager Duchess had the expansive mansion decorated with a profusion of white and pink floral arrangements accented with long tendrils of ivy. Several large arrangements lined the foyer and garlands of flowers adorned the doorways, balustrades, windows, and fireplaces making the rooms smell fragrant.

"Shayla," Amelia called as she came down the staircase to greet her. "You look radiant as a bride should." She turned to the footmen, "please bring Miss Toselli's bags to her chamber on the third floor. Mr. Ferguson will show you the way."

The butler helped Shayla and Aunt Margaret out of their cloaks.

"Everything is so beautiful. Thank you." Shayla looked around and was overwhelmed with the beauty and extravagance that surrounded her. In just a few days, all the Christmas tide greens and flowers had been replaced with pink and white arrangements.

"Wait until you see the ballroom," the Duchess replied.

"Where are the men?" Shayla asked.

"They are in the east wing, and that is where they will stay until it is time for the ceremony." The Duchess hooked her arm in Shayla's, and they walked in the parlor. "We do not want the groom to see the bride before the wedding. It is bad luck."

"Shayla," Sarah called as they entered the parlor.

"Sarah, thank you for being my bridesmaid."

"I am honored."

"Tara, thank you for being my flower girl."

"I am so honored, Miss Shayla," she replied with a curtsy.

"Since we are all here, let us go upstairs to get ready for the ceremony." The Duchess led the women to the main hallway and then up the wide staircase.

Shayla stood in her underthings and looked at herself in the cheval glass. Her dark hair was curled and twisted in an intricate design on top of her head. Tendrils of hair framed her face and the rest fell in waves down her back.

Aunt Margaret had tears in her eyes. "You are so beautiful."

"Here is your something blue." Sarah held up two blue garters.

Shayla sat down and put on her stockings, then slid on the garters. Sarah put six pence in Shayla's shoe for future wealth before she put them on. Shayla stood up, and the women helped her into her wedding gown. Shayla smoothed the front while Amelia fluffed up the large sleeves. "Something new is my beautiful gown," Shayla said as she looked at her reflection.

"What about something old?" Amelia asked.

Shayla lifted the perfume bottle from her train case. She removed the top and dabbed her pulse points with the perfume. "Something old." She handed the bottle to her aunt.

Margaret's eyes filled with tears again when she saw the perfume bottle. "Thank you. I miss her so much." Margaret tipped the bottle and dabbed on perfume then hugged Shayla. Amelia, Sarah, and Tara also dabbed on the perfume.

Sarah helped Shayla clasp a necklace of sapphires and diamonds behind her neck. The jewelry had also been her mother's. They all stood quietly for a moment, and Shayla felt her mother was with her in spirit.

"Time to put on the veil," Aunt Margaret announced. Shayla sat down on the vanity chair.

"Your something borrowed is a tiara loaned to you by the Dowager Duchess," Amelia said as she placed the diamond tiara on Shayla's head. "She also loaned it to me for my wedding, so we have a tradition going."

Sarah brought over the long veil, and Amelia attached it behind the tiara. Then Amelia tucked in several orange blossoms for tradition and pulled the short veil over Shayla's head covering her face. "Are you ready?"

Shayla took a deep breath. "I am ready." She was going to be married in a matter of minutes. She put on white gloves, and Amelia handed her a large bouquet of white roses and ivy. Amelia then handed Sarah and Tara their flowers, and together they all went downstairs.

At the bottom of the staircase, Henry, in full dress black tailcoat, white waistcoat, white shirt and cravat, and white gloves watched as his daughter came down the stairs. "Shayla you are a vision." He held out his hand for her. He kissed her cheek and stood quietly for a few moments.

"Papa, are you alright?" Shayla asked.

Henry took a handkerchief out of his pocket and dabbed his eyes. "You are so beautiful and grown up, but you will always be my little girl."

"I love you, Papa." Shayla leaned over and kissed him.

"I love you too."

Amelia and Aunt Margaret hurried off to take their seats while Sarah and Tara stood by the entrance to the conservatory until it was time for the ceremony.

Henry put his handkerchief away and stood up straight and tall. "Are you ready?"

Shayla hooked her arm in Henry's and took a deep breath. "I am ready."

Henry placed his hand over hers and led her to the conservatory and her groom.

Adam waited nervously at the end of the aisle in the conservatory. There were large floral arrangements interspersed among the plants. Chairs were arranged for guests, and a runner led the way to the podium where the vicar would perform the ceremony. The conservancy smelled heavenly from all the fragrant blooms. It was warm, and Adam pulled down the jacket of his full dress uniform that was adorned with medals he was awarded. He took a deep breath and let it out slowly then looked at his brother Colin who stood beside him. Colin also wore his military uniform adorned with medals. The two brothers were quite the sight, which many women in attendance noticed as evidenced by the frantic fan waving.

Several musicians dressed in formal wear were seated off to the side, and they played soft music while the guests took their seats. Finally, everyone was seated, and the vicar came out to the podium. It was time. Adam and Colin came to attention as the music changed.

Sarah appeared at the back of the conservatory. Slowly, she walked down the aisle dressed in a pale pink silk bridesmaid gown that had white silk flowers all around the waist.

Next, Tara walked down the aisle. She wore a white chiffon gown and carried a basket decorated with white flowers. As she walked, she carefully scattered white rose pedals. She took her place next to Sarah beside the podium.

All the guests stood for the bride's entrance. Henry escorted Shayla down the aisle. She walked over the rose pedals which released a lovely fragrance as she made her way toward Adam. He thought no woman ever looked as lovely as his bride. Shayla wore a gown of pure white organza. The bodice had an open neckline and was covered in white lace and trimmed with tiny silk flowers. The skirt of the gown had an overskirt of white velvet that was gathered at points to reveal the white organza dress below. At each pick up point there was a white silk bow. A long, sheer, white lace veil trailed behind her, and a smaller sheer veil covered her face.

Henry and Shayla stopped when they reached Adam. Henry shook Adam's hand and then placed Shayla's hand in Adam's hand. Henry took his place next to Hal and Mrs. Lawry in the front row. Everyone was seated as Shayla and Adam turned toward the vicar who began the ceremony.

"We are here today to witness the joining of Shayla Ana Toselli and Adam Nicholas Preston." The vicar talked about love and finally, Adam repeated the vows, placed a simple gold band on Shayla's finger, and said, 'I Will'. Shayla repeated the vows and said, 'I Will'. While not always part of the wedding ceremony, Adam spoke with the vicar beforehand, and finally he heard the words he longed to hear, "you may kiss the bride." Adam carefully lifted the veil from Shayla's face. He looked into her eyes and smiled at her. She was radiant and smiled back at him, and then he leaned close and kissed her softly. They were now united. The musicians struck up Mendelssohn's Wedding March, and with their heads held high, Adam and Shayla turned and walked back down the aisle, past the guests, and down the hallway to the dining room for the reception.

They received their guests while soft music played, and then the waiters passed out champagne for the toast. The Duke made the first toast. "Thank you one and all. Today, we celebrate the union of Adam and Shayla. May your lives be long, your love never faulter, and your children be many." Adam and Shayla nodded as everyone drank then sat down to a magnificent dinner that began with consume and included halibut and pheasant for the main course which were favorites of the bride and the groom.

After the lavish meal, the guests gathered and waited for the bride and groom to make their entrance into the ballroom. The orchestra played a special waltz, and Adam and Shayla stepped onto the dance floor to open the ball.

The ballroom was lavishly decorated in purple, pink, white, and gold. Flowers were everywhere. All the chandeliers were lit, and silk white banners hung from the ceiling and fluttered as people moved around.

"This has been the most wonderful of holiday seasons, my wife," Adam said to Shayla as they twisted and turned to the music.

"Truly, it has been, my husband."

Shayla's gown shimmered in the light of the chandeliers as Adam twirled her around the dance floor. Duke Wellshore and the Duchess joined the bride and groom on the dancefloor, and the two couples crisscrossed back and forth. Henry bowed and escorted the Dowager Duchess to the dance floor, and Major Preston escorted Sarah. Shayla felt like a princess.

At the end of the dance, they bowed, and everyone clapped. Then the music started again, and other couples started to dance.

Later in the evening, Shayla looked over and watched Sarah dancing with Major Preston again. The two women caught one another's eye as they danced. Shayla thought Sarah and Colin were well matched. Sarah's delicate features and blonde hair complimented Colin's very short brown hair and rugged good looks. Amelia also watched Sarah and Colin dancing. She and Shayla smiled and nodded as they passed by one another.

"Why are you and Amelia smiling like that?" Adam asked Shayla as they danced.

"We are just so very happy," she replied with a wide smile.

Adam glanced down at his beautiful wife. "You two are going to play match maker with Miss Williams and Colin."

"Adam," Shayla replied with a tilt of her head, "do they not deserve the same happiness we have?"

Adam shook his head and sighed. "Of course, my love." Adam laughed to himself. He told Colin this would happen, but he was a happy man, and he wanted his brother to be just as happy. When the song ended, Adam pulled Shayla close and kissed her cheek.

The evening was full of laughter and dancing. Shayla never danced so much. She danced mostly with Adam, but she had a dance with the Duke, Colin, her father, and both her uncles as well. Aunt Margaret danced several times, but she was tired and chose to sit and watch. Uncle James stayed close to her.

After they danced another waltz, Adam led Shayla off the dance floor. "Would you like some refreshments?" he asked.

"Yes, thank you." Shayla took Adam's arm, and they went to the dining room for a cold drink. The table was covered in a white cloth that went to the floor, and over it was a shiny gold cloth. The assortment of cookies and pastries were placed on gold platters, and a champagne fountain stood next to the long table.

Adam picked up a cream puff in the shape of a swan. He and Shayla each took a bite of it. "Swans represent our relationship, Shayla. They are a symbol of loyalty and strength." Adam picked up her hand and kissed it. "And you will have my loyalty and strength, forever." He delicately kissed both her cheeks.

"You have my loyalty and strength as well, Adam." She kissed him sweetly on the cheek. They ate another swan cream puff before returning to the dance floor.

Traditionally, there are three cakes at a wedding, the white bride's cake, the dark groom's cake, and then an elaborate cake decorated with white frosting for the guests. However, because tonight was Twelfth Night, the guest cake was a traditional Twelfth Night cake. The tall confection was frosted in gold and had delicate white sugar lace around the bottom of each layer with white sugar crowns and stars above. The guests were awed by the splendor of the cake as it was wheeled into the dining room. People gathered around as it was sliced and handed out to guests. Of course, everyone hoped to find the bean hidden in the dense fruit cake, so he or she could be the 'Lord of Misrule'.

"I found it," young Tara called excitedly. She took the bean out of her mouth and raised it in her hand high over her head.

"You are the queen of the party, now," the Duke told her. "How may I be of service, Miss?" he asked with a bow and a flourish. Twelfth Night was a time when royals acted like commoners and commoners acted like royals.

Later in the evening, Shayla and Sara returned to her room. "Thank you for being my bridesmaid, Sarah." Following tradition, Shayla took a rose out of her bouquet and handed it to her. Sarah added it to her own flowers, and then she helped Shayla out of her wedding gown.

"I saw you dancing with Major Preston," Shayla casually mentioned as she slipped into her dark blue traveling dress. "He is a fine man."

Sarah blushed. "He is, but he said he will be returning to London in a few days."

"True. However, he is leaving military service in a few months."

Sarah smiled but quickly looked down so as not to appear eager. She helped Shayla put on her boots. "Do you have any idea where Adam is taking you for the honeymoon?"

Shayla finished packing her necessities and closed the small valise that she planned to carry with her on the train. "He is very secretive. His only comments were to bring several fancy evening gowns which the Duchess kindly helped me secure." She stopped and looked at Sarah. "When we were girls, I never imagined I would get married at Wellshore Manor, or anywhere for that matter. I never thought I would like shopping for fancy evening gowns, but I like it. I am so happy and in love with Adam."

Sarah hugged Shayla. "You deserve to be happy."

"As do you, Sarah."

"You will have to tell me everything about your trip when you return."

"And you will have to tell me all about Major Preston."

The two women hugged again, and they went back downstairs where Adam waited patiently.

"Colin has gone ahead to the train station to load our luggage," Adam told Shayla as he helped her into the white cloak that he gave her at the start of Christmastide. She tied on the matching bonnet and slipped one hand into the muff. The footman brought down Shayla's valise and put it in the carriage.

Both families came to see the bride and groom off and bid them good-bye. Adam and Shayla talked to each of them, and lastly, Shayla hugged her father. "Have a good time," he said.

Shayla nodded. There were tears of happiness in both of their eyes. "Thank you, Papa."

Henry shook Adam's hand. "I will guard her with my life, Sir," Adam told him.

"I know you will, Adam. Be well."

Shayla felt like a princess as Adam helped her into the white carriage pulled by four beautiful white horses. They settled in on one side of the carriage together, and they waved as the carriage pulled away from the mansion.

Now that they were finally alone, Adam leaned over and took Shayla's lips in a long sensual kiss. He waited all evening to hold her in his arms again. She sighed and seemed to melt into him. "Are you ready for our honeymoon, Mrs. Preston?"

Shayla purred and kissed him back. "I am. Will you not give me a hint where we are going?"

"Soon, my love."

It was a short ride to the train station, and Adam kept close to Shayla as they boarded the night train to London. Colin spoke with Adam and then left the train and the newlyweds settled into their private compartment as the train got underway.

"We are spending the night in London?" Shayla asked.

"The Great Western Hotel at Paddington Station in London awaits, and tomorrow the adventure begins." Adam pulled the shades down on the window. He sat down next to Shayla and pulled her onto his lap. He held her tight and kissed her. She moaned and slid her hands inside his coat. She kissed down his neck, and it was his turn to groan. After some time, Shayla laid her head on Adam's shoulder. The train bounced along the tracks, and then there was a knock on the door. Shayla moved to the chair next to Adam.

"Enter," he called.

The waiter came in carrying a tray and set it on the table between them then without a word left the compartment. On the tray was a pot of hot chocolate and biscuits. Shayla poured two cups and handed one to Adam. They sipped the chocolate and nibbled on biscuits. They talked about their wedding and their joy at being married.

"Will you give me a hint as to where we are going on our honeymoon?" Shayla pleaded. She was excited and wanted to know what Adam had secretly planned.

Adam knew she would be curious. Her curiosity was something Adam admired and cherished. He did not want to keep her in suspense any longer. He reached into his waist coat pocket, took out a small package, and handed it to her. "This is the only hint I will give you."

Shayla took the box and studied it for a moment. She opened it and gasped. Her eyes were wide in anticipation as she slowly held up a necklace with a small gold Eiffel tower charm. With it still in her hand, Shayla jumped into Adam's lap and kissed him. "How did you know I wanted to see Paris?"

"I told you, love. It is a husband's job to know his wife's every desire."

Shayla kissed him. "I love you."

"And I love you." Adam cupped Shayla's face with his hands, looked into her eyes, and kissed her.


The End

Thank you for reading *Glass Ornament Christmas.*

If you enjoyed the story, please leave a favorable review on Amazon or Goodreads. Posting a review is the best way to thank an author for a story that you enjoyed.

Read on for recipes, holiday tips and tricks, and suggestions for making this a great holiday. Hopefully, you will find the ideas helpful and the recipe delicious.

**Bonus Christmas Ideas and Planning**

If you are like me, Christmas is not just a day with gifts, a ham, and a tree; it is a season. Christmas is a season that I delight in and plan for throughout the year. There are many faucets to Christmas: traditions, entertaining, cooking, shopping, and crafting to name a few. Giving of oneself, of one's time and energy, and the thought that goes into making a gift are the things that are important at this special time of year.

With so many things to do to get ready for the holiday, it is no wonder people's holiday spirit plummets and stress levels soar. Spend a little time making lists and adding everything to a calendar. During the holiday season, more than any other time of year, a person must be organized to handle the unexpected when it happens, and it always will. Do not feel guilty if you do not get everything done. Do what is truly important first and the rest will take care of itself. Take shortcuts. There is a reason why the grocery stores are full of prepared foods and treats at this time of year. Get family members to help with cooking dinner, wrapping presents, and shopping, or hire a teenager to lend a hand.

Take care of yourself. It is important for you to take time to rejuvenate. Spend the day with a friend or at the hair salon. Shop for an outfit or have a quiet lunch. Mostly importantly, remember that this is a special and joyous time of the year. To coin an old phrase "Stop and smell the roses". Take time to be thankful for all you have and all you have accomplished. The rest is just details. I hope you find the information contained within these pages helpful in planning for this year's most wonderful and festive season.

*Happy Holidays!*

## Organization

Organization and planning are the keys to a smooth holiday. Obviously, the earlier one starts planning the holiday celebration the more a person will be able to accomplish. Since most of us cannot devote November and December to Christmas preparations, our projects and celebration needs to have some boundaries and direction. A complicated Christmas project is best started during the summer when time is abundant, and there is less stress.

Sit down at your computer (or take out a sheet of paper). List what you would like to accomplish this year. Yikes. Do not get scared, the list will be large, but it will be whittled down to a manageable size. The list will probably include: write out holiday cards, mail cards, mail packages, shop for gifts, bake, make decorations, get the tree, decorate the tree, put up outdoor lights, wrap. Do not forget to make time for lunch with friends. It is just a wish list.

Once the list is completed, look at each item and ask yourself if you Have To, Need To, or Hope To do the task.

Have To are things that if not accomplished the holiday will be a disaster.

Need To are those things that should be done in order for the holiday to be complete.

Hope To are those things that you would like to accomplish but the day would not be ruined if they were not completed.

Remember you don't have to do everything you've always done in the past. The object is to have a holiday that you and your family enjoy. If no one eats fruitcake don't make it. Cross off those things that you Can't Do or Do not Want To Do.

 **Gifts**

Although gifts are a large part of the holiday, they are not what makes the holiday memorable. Years from now, people will not remember the gifts, but they will remember the special times spent together.

Gift giving is the aspect of Christmas that can bring the most joy and the greatest stress. Think about the spending habits of past Christmases. Were you paying for last Christmas in July? Did you delay bill paying in order to purchase presents? Overspending to give extravagant gifts may bring momentary gratification but cause a great deal of stress in the months to come. This year set aside money each month for gift purchases and resolve to set up a gift budget and stick to it.

Wrapping all the presents can be a daunting task. Presents can be wrapped as they are purchased or wrapped after the shopping is finished. To make wrapping easier, set up a wrapping center. My husband rolls his eyes and teases me about my wrapping center, but it really does work. Cover a card table with a holiday cloth, and store ribbon, bows, scissors, tape, gift tags and decorations in a box under the table. Stand rolls of wrapping paper in a container next to the table. If space allows, set up a wrapping center in a spare room or a room where it can be left up for a while. With everything handy and convenient, wrapping is easier, and stress is reduced.

Try to be creative when wrapping up gifts for family and friends. Select an ornament to tie on the present that reflects the person's interests. Little touches make the gift extra special, and they need not be purchased. A pretty bookmark made from last year's Christmas cards and covered in clear vinyl is useful and adds a nice touch to any gift.

**Some examples of inexpensive but always well-received gifts.**

• **Baked Goods:** A quick bread mix will make three small loaves. Wrap each in foil and then in colored cellophane tied with a ribbon. Top with an ornament or other small trinket.

• **Kid's basket:** Select a bright colored crate, add bubbles, coloring books, crayons, books, barrettes, whistles, jacks, or other small toys. Gear the contents to the age and interest of the child.

• **For Coffee Lovers:** Line a basket with an interesting towel or napkin. Add a mug to suit the person's personality, some gourmet coffee, a pastry, bread or box of crackers, and jam.

• **For Gardeners:** Select a terra cotta pot and fill it with seeds, a trowel, garden gloves, and some plant food.

• **Pasta Lover:** Fill a basket with pastas in assorted shapes and flavors. Add several jars of sauce: marinara, alfredo, pesto, a loaf of fresh Italian garlic bread, and some parmesan cheese.

• **Chocolate Lovers:** Fill a basket with gourmet chocolates, fudge sauce, chocolate baked goods, and hot chocolate mix.

• **Teacher:** Fill an apple basket with assorted craft supplies, pens, pencils, and a sign personalized with the teacher's name for the classroom door.

## Traditions

Traditions are the heart of the Christmas celebration. Traditions are a source of comfort and joy, and they are eagerly anticipated each year because many traditions remind us of our heritage and our childhood. For example, putting up a tree, hanging stockings, visiting Santa, going to midnight mass, even making a ham for Christmas dinner are all traditions that help make the holiday special. Traditions are a way for family and friends to create memories and spend time together.

Although most traditions are enjoyable, when something becomes a burden or a dreaded activity then the tradition needs to be re-evaluated. A tradition should be followed only if it brings you and your family joy and not simply because it has always been part of the celebration. If the tradition causes emotional or financial distress, then it should be modified or discontinued.

Do not be afraid of change. If you modify or eliminate a tradition and do not like the change, you can always go back to the old way next year. Traditions should not govern the celebration, instead they should enhance the celebration.

An advent calendar will help count the days until Christmas. Many beautiful calendars are available at card and gift shops or craft one at home. One easy way to make a calendar is to purchase one of the many cardboard holiday decorations available for under a dollar at the grocery or department store or draw and paint a holiday scene on paper. Make a calendar grid on the computer or by hand. Cut a piece of lightweight cardboard the length of the picture and the calendar grid. Cover the cardboard with colored paper. Glue the picture to the top of the cardboard, glue the calendar grid to the bottom, and place stars or stickers on each day to count the days until Christmas.

**Traditions can be simple, some require planning, but all are a lot of fun.**

- Use an advent calendar to count the days until Christmas.

- See a local production of The Nutcracker or other holiday play.

- Take a drive to look at the Christmas lights.

- Organize a neighborhood caroling night.

- Make gingerbread houses.

- Bring a food basket to a needy family in your town.

- Set aside a day or an evening to watch holiday movies.

- Attend a choral concert.

- Put up a bird feeder for winter birds.

## Decorations

To make room for holiday decorations, take down some of the everyday decorations and pack them in the holiday decorations boxes. While unpacking boxes, go through the decorations and discard those that are broken, old and tattered, and those that do not fit the decorating scheme. Look at all decorations before putting anything out and decide which decorations to use this year. Nowhere is it written that every decoration must be used every year. Get the entire family involved in decorating the house by planning a decorating night. Serve cookies, listen to music, and make some decorations. Crafting is a great way to get everyone in the Christmas spirit, and everyone will have fun making paper chains, stringing popcorn, and making glitter ornaments.

Almost every home has a decorated tree for the holidays. The tree is usually the largest decoration in the home, and therefore, it becomes the centerpiece of the holiday decorating. The evergreen tree is a symbol of life and decorating an evergreen at Christmas time is a tradition that dates back to 16th century Germany.

## Decorating Ideas to Try:

- Purchase a special tree ornament each year so the tree is full of memories.
- Staple Christmas cards to a long ribbon and hang somewhere prominent.
- Put an electric (or battery operated) candle in each window.
- Line the walk with luminaries.
- Cluster poinsettias on a small table in an entry.
- Hang real candy canes on the tree as treats for friends and family.
- Set up a Christmas village and add to it each year.
- Set up a nativity scene under the tree.
- Use silk poinsettias as tiebacks for curtains.
- Place candles on a mirror for soft shimmery illumination.
- Place fresh flowers and greens around the house.

## Wreaths

Hanging an evergreen wreath on the front door is almost as popular as having a Christmas tree. Wreaths are a beautiful way to decorate the inside as well as the outside of the home. A preserved pinecone wreath is a beautiful decoration that will last for years, and the ever-popular evergreen wreath on the entry door is a nice way to welcome visiting friends and family.

Wreaths can be decorated simply with a red velvet bow or quite elaborately. To achieve beautiful results, stick to a theme and be sure the elements are in the same color range because pastels and bright colors generally don't work well together. Decide on the focal point of the wreath. The focal point is often a bow, but it can be anything, and then work around the wreath from the focal point.

Specialty wreaths also make great gifts.

**Wreath suggestions. The possibilities are endless, just use your imagination.**

- **Fishing Wreath:** Wrap a straw wreath with a fishing ribbon and add a loopy bow. Glue on tied flies or lures, and add small novelties like a fish, small creel, net, and a bobber. Make a "Gone Fishing" sign out of a small chalkboard, foam, or wood.

- **Santa Wreath:** Choose an evergreen wreath and add a Santa print bow with long tails. Add a few sprigs of holy, a couple of candy canes and a Santa ornament or two.

- **Teacher Wreath:** Loosely wrap ABC ribbon around a grapevine wreath. Add a loopy bow of the same ribbon to the top right side of the wreath. At the bottom of the wreath, add a small chalkboard with the teacher's name written on it. Glue on some plastic apples, a small eraser, a piece of chalk and a small ruler.

- **Coastal Wreath:** Begin with a natural colored grape-vine wreath. Gather seashells, starfish, and sand dollars then spray them with gloss spray, let dry. Select artificial grass or other greens that can be cut up to fill in around seashells. Arrange the items and glue them on. A large star fish can take the place of a ribbon and bow.

## Baking

Baked goods are a lovely way to show friends and family how much they mean to you. Choose a container for the cookies that reflects the recipient's interests or personality. For example, put cookies for a teacher in an apple basket or fudge brownies for the fisherman in a creel. Most people love a home baked gift.

Look at the calendar and set up a baking schedule. Try to bake early in the season or even in the fall and freeze the goodies. Consider baking during the late summer. Turn on the air conditioner and the Christmas music and have fun. Schedule a day or so for more difficult baked goods such as a gingerbread house which is a fun and festive activity for the entire family.

## Cookie and Holiday Baking Tips:

- Mix a variety of doughs one day and store them in the refrigerator to bake another day for fresh baked cookies without the fuss and mess. Most dough can be mixed ahead and baked later, just check the recipe to see if dough can be baked right from the refrigerator or if it should first be brought to room temperature.
- Bake a batch of chocolate chip or gingerbread cookies from premixed dough before guests arrive and the house will smell heavenly.

- Spend a little extra time making the baked goods look good. Now is the time to really decorate cookies, cakes, and other confections.

- Don't package soft and crisp cookies together or the crisp ones will become soft. A slice of bread in the bag will help keep cookies soft.

- Strong cookies such as peanut butter cookies should be packaged separately, or all the cookies will have a peanut butter taste.

### Some Cookie Favorites to try:

- Chocolate chip cookies, the classic cookie
- Peanut butter cookies
- Sugar cookies, cut in holiday shapes, decorate with royal icing.
- Spritz, buttery and in holiday shapes are a Christmas favorite.
- Thumbprint cookies filled with a chocolate kiss or jelly.

**Bonus cookie recipe.**

My grandmother made these cookies every holiday.

### Italian Brown Cookies

Preheat oven to 375 degrees

Ingredients:

4 eggs

1 cup oil (canola or vegetable)

1 cup brown sugar lightly packed

1 cup white sugar

1 cup finely chopped pecans

1 bag of semi-sweet chocolate chips

1 tsp baking soda

1 ½ tsp cinnamon

3 1/2 (plus) cups of flour

Beat together eggs, oil, and the two sugars. Add cinnamon and baking soda and mix. Gradually add the flour. More flour may be needed. The dough should be thick and sticky. Mix in pecans and chocolate chips.

Form the dough into loaves. Pat the top to slightly flatten. Place the loaves on a baking sheet 3 inches apart. Bake 20 mins. Remove from oven and cook on a wire rack. When cool, dust the loaves with powdered sugar. Slice diagonally into approximately ½ inch slices.

## Children

Children love Christmas. They are excited and cannot wait for Santa to come down the chimney. As children, we anxiously awaited the arrival of Christmas Eve and Santa Claus. We marveled at the colorful lights and the splendid decorations. As adults, we want to try to recapture the magic of our childhood celebrations, and we want to make Christmas enjoyable and memorable for the children in our lives.

As soon as the decorations begin to appear in the stores, children begin to ask when Christmas is coming. With the stores putting out Christmas decorations early, some stores in July, the wait can be a long one. Once Thanksgiving is over, it becomes harder and harder to control the excitement.

Letting children handle some of the preparations gives children a sense of accomplishment and makes them feel that they are truly part of the celebration. Let the children decorate the tree as high as they can reach and let them help bake cookies. Even little ones can stamp, seal, and put return address labels on cards, and they can decorate their bedroom.

Crafts are a fun way to occupy the children when you are really busy, and they are bored. Children love to cut, paste, and craft, and there are a variety of projects children can make without a lot of supervision. When doing crafts, have an old tablecloth, smocks, and paper towels close at hand.

## Some craft suggestions to try:

- Paper Chains. Cut strips of paper, (construction paper, wrapping paper or foil paper), make a loop and fasten with staples, tape, or glue. Put the next strip through the loop and fasten.

- Mosaic. Glue seeds, beans, macaroni, buttons, fabric, almost anything to white or colored cardboard to create pictures.

- Pencil Cups. Cover a clean, dry juice or other tall can with contact paper, wallpaper, or construction paper. Use stickers, drawings, cut up cards, foam shapes or Popsicle sticks to decorate the can.

- Garlands. Thread macaroni, O cereal, or popcorn to make garlands. Popcorn should be popped the day before or it will crumble when stringing it.

- Gold tipped seashell ornaments. Use gold paint and add sparkle to seashells picked in the summer.

- Reindeer Puppets. Place an unopened paper bag upside down with the bottom facing you on the table. Add antlers cut from brown construction paper to the part of the bag at the top. Add black paper eyes and a red circle nose. Put your hand inside the bag and play.

**The best memories of the holidays will be the**

**ones you make with your family and friends!**

*Merry Christmas!*

Cheryl A. Hunter writes in several genres including Contemporary Fiction, Historical Fiction, and Paranormal Fiction. Visit her Amazon Author's Page for a list of books available and to read excerpts. https://www.amazon.com/Cheryl-A-Hunter/e/B07K657RKJ/ref=aufs_dp_fta_dsk

Visit her website to sign up for Cheryl's newsletter and receive a Holiday Planner download with additional tips, recipes, and planning pages, as well as chapters from her other books. When you sign up, you will also be the first to learn about new releases, bonus chapters, and special promotions.

Visit Cheryl's website: http://www.cherylahunter.com/

Follow Cheryl on social media

Facebook: https://www.facebook.com/CherylAHunter101

Twitter: @CherylAHunter4

9 781732 835184